The LEGEND of PEDESTRIO

ABNER SERD

BISAC Subject Codes:
FIC016000   FICTION / Humorous / General
FIC077000   FICTION / Nature & the Environment
FIC009080   FICTION / Fantasy / Humorous

Library of Congress Subject Headings:
Walking—Fiction
Storytelling—Fiction
Travelers—Fiction

Library of Congress Control Number: 2022901584

Paperback ISBN: 979-8-9853926-0-9
Ebook ISBN: 979-8-9853926-1-6
Audiobook ISBN: 979-8-9853926-2-3

Contact email: info@abnerserd.com
Quincy, MA

Book and cover design: MC Writing Services

A Note on Style

When it is simply a matter of identifying a speaker, a comma is used after said*... to introduce a quotation. Such usage is more traditional than logical...*

THE CHICAGO MANUAL OF STYLE (17TH ED), 13.14

The Legend of Pedestrio is a story told out loud, then written down in the form of a book. In general, the usual bookish style rules are followed — except when those rules change the way a line is supposed to sound.

In oral storytelling, *I said* isn't just a stage direction — it's a part of the narration. The spoken line: *I said "stop breaking the rules!"* is meant to flow naturally, without a break or pause. A comma would interrupt that flow. And since the quotation is not syntactically independent, there is no need to capitalize the first letter of the quote.

Every line in this book has a sound to it, and I've tried to punctuate each line accordingly. Sometimes that means removing a comma. Other times it means inserting one to suggest a pause. Some readers may find these style choices distracting, but here's the good news: the audiobook contains no unusual punctuation whatsoever. If you close your eyes and listen, you can almost see the commas falling into place...

PROLOGUE:
The Truth of the World

THERE are those who believe the world and everything in it grew from a single seed. This seed originated in the core of a distant planet (let's call that planet the Cosmic Apple). When the Cosmic Apple ripened, the seed was scooped out and cast into space, where it began to germinate. Meanwhile, the Apple — having served her purpose — soon withered and decayed.

Now, like all planet seeds, the Earth was self-watering and self-fertilizing. For a million years, the tiny grain of a planet drifted through the cosmos, acquiring girth, and gravity, and atmosphere.

Then it blossomed!

Rivers and mountains formed. Plants and animals appeared. Life begat life all over the place! And slowly, ever so slowly, the Earth developed into a mature, fully-grown planet with seeds of her own.

Some believe the cycle is nearly complete. The Earth is ripe, they say. The time of the Great Scooping is at hand. Now, the Scooping… well, I won't trouble you with the details, on account of that might spark panic, but I'll tell you this: the Scooping will involve massive earthquakes and devastating atmospheric conditions. It'll be a cataclysm powerful enough to roil the stomach of every living being on the planet, including oak trees — and you know how hard it is to roil *their* stomachs. If you believe the single-seed theory, you'd best eat nothing but unbuttered toast from here on out.

'Course, not everyone does believe it. Many wise and learned scholars insist that the Earth is not a fruit. Nor is it a vegetable. It is, in point of fact, an egg.

The truth is this: the world and everything in it did indeed sprout from a single seed. That's true — and this is also true: the world was hatched by an interstellar dopplerix (you know what a dopplerix is, don't you? It's a very large, elongated space bird with a blue beak and a red tail). And while we're at it, you know what else is true? The world was conjured into being by a powerful magician known as the Great Whizbang. The world was blasted out of a black hole like pumice from a volcano. The world was folded into existence when the universe — by accident or design — creased itself in space and time. Yes indeed, and you can tell your friends: we live on an origami planet.

The truth is this: the world has always been here. The world *will* always be here. The world was never here at all.

The world only exists as long as you and I believe in it. You and I exist because the world believes in us. The world has pockets containing many other worlds. Somewhere in this world is an ancient tree whose roots are the only things holding the world together.

The world is a dream, given form and substance by a confederation of supernatural Beings. These Beings are all around us — They just don't like to show Themselves. The world as we know it, in whole or in part, can be undreamed at any time.

The truth is this: the world is far larger than any of us could ever possibly imagine. It contains many layers of meaning, and many equally valid stories. Within those stories are an infinite number of whole truths and half-truths and metatruths and quasi-truths, and only six outright lies.

Do you know what the six lies are? No? Me neither — I mean… not all of them. They change, you know, from time to time. Some of them are pretty closely guarded secrets. Some are too big to tell, and some are too small to be heard. I don't believe there's a soul on this planet at any given moment who knows all six of them. Apart from The Cozener, of course.

I could tell you one, though. Would you like to hear one of the six outright lies?

All right, here goes: you won't find a single one of the other five lies anywhere in this book. You won't find a single one of them even mentioned. Not even in passing. Not even in the footnotes.

Especially not in the footnotes.

CHAPTER 1:
So There I Was...

So there I was: running for my life from a pack of vicious wild chooks, dodging and diving through the trees, leading them on a wild, frenetic chase halfway across the Wandering Hills, when somebody stole my hat.

I figured it was a low-reaching jack pine, larking about at my expense. I nearly stopped. I did take a moment to marvel at this atypical behavior — it's rare to catch a pine tree in a playful mood. When I find one with a sense of humor, I like to give it a pat on the bark and few words of encouragement — followed by a polite request for the return of my hat. But seeing as how I was only a slip and a stumble away from being shredded into jerky, I thought it best not to tarry.

I broke left. The chooks flew after me, squawking like the hinges on a boxful of bitter ends. I leaped across a swollen stream and zigzagged through the wood. The birds couldn't keep up. Chooks don't fly that well, and these ones had no end of trouble changing direction. They kept crashing into trees, which only got more of their feathers up.

But wild chooks are a lot smarter than any ordinary, domesticated variety of chook. I suspected they were herding me.

One of them flanked me from the left. I zagged right, and durn near ran into another one. The second one raked the air with angry talons. I ducked just in time.

Two more chooks dove at me, beak first. I dodged between a pair of pines. The pines just stood there, looking mournful. I slid down a needle-covered slope, rolled under a fallen log — and accidentally flushed a sharp-tongued grouse out of hiding.

All four chooks flew off, screeching, in pursuit of the startled grouse. The grouse gave back as good as it got, decibel-wise. It fussed and squabbled until the whole ruction flew out of earshot. As for me, I climbed back up the slope and hightailed it to town just as fast as my feet could go.

In all the excitement, I sort of forgot about my hat. It wasn't until the next morning, when I walked in the door at Elmer's Café, that I remembered it.

CHAPTER 2:
A Gentleman of Undiscovered Talent

Now, before I get too far along in this narrative, it might be best if I explain the difference between your world and my world.

There is no difference.

It's the same world, and it's no surprise if the particulars vary. After all, you and I are following different paths. Of *course* the scenery doesn't match.

And who am I? Well, you might call me a Gentleman of Undiscovered Talent. A spinner of yarns. A presenter of tales. A raconteur. A fabulist. A storyteller. Until now, my efforts may have escaped your notice, but I will not remain undiscovered for long. Someday I'll find a story with legs, and when I do, I mean to ride that beast all the way to Glory. Till then, I find ways to make myself useful.

On mornings when I get up early enough, I supervise the sunrise. In the spring, I perform quality control on the budding trees, ensuring that each individual specimen has been assigned the correct form of leaf. It's embarrassing to see an oak tree sprouting maple leaves. You'd be surprised how often I catch them doing it. And of course, every fall, I stand guard against the devious machinations of the Guy in Charge of Winter, who always endeavors to shake loose the first flurry of snowflakes well before the rest of us are ready.

Because of these duties, I spend a lot of my time out on Wild Side — those uncivilized regions out beyond the edge of town.

I keep no house. I prefer to sleep on the ground, under an open sky, where I can see the stars. Such arrangements are few and far between, here on Town Side — but you can still find such a camp, if you know where to look.

For instance, the night after the wild chook attack, I stayed atop a little one-story gift shop where my friend Bill O'Sale sells made-ins.[1] The building is conveniently located and has a flat roof. As long as you stay low, you can't be seen from down below — and on a clear night, you can see the handful of stars that poke through the glare of the city lights.

A retail establishment rooftop is one of the few places in town where you can be reasonably sure nobody's gonna stumble across your slumbering bones in the middle of the night. But you can't sleep in at a camp like that; you've got to get up early enough to stow your gear and climb down without being spotted. All of which is to say that I didn't have a chance to get myself all spruced up before I walked into Elmer's Café that morning.

Elmer was shaving a potato onto the grill to make hash browns. He took one look at me and said "what happened to you?"

"What do you mean?"

"You look like you just crawled out from under a log."

I glanced at my reflection in the left-hand wall. That's the south wall. The mirrored surface is pasted all over with cartoons and comic strips and pictures of incongruous congroos, and the glass is stained and spotted from Elmer's occasional habit of throwing food at his customers. It took some head-bobbing, but eventually I caught a glimpse of myself through the various layers of dirt and decoration.

Sure enough, I still had twigs in my hair and a bit of moss sprouting out of my collar. I said "yeah, well, there's a reason for that. It so happens I was inspecting them."

---

1 A made-in is a local souvenir manufactured somewhere else, usually stamped on the bottom so you know where it really comes from. For example, a knickknack with your city crest on it might say Made In Schmaydin, even though Schmaydin is a million miles away.

Doc said "inspecting what? Rotten logs?"

Doc usually sits up at the north end of the counter. There are no booths nor tables at Elmer's Café — just nine swivel stools and a countertop. The north end is warmer in the wintertime, seeing as how it's closer to the grill and further away from the door. But you have to be a trifle more careful if you choose to sit at that end, on account of the way Elmer likes to flail about with the spatula.

I said "technically, I'm supposed to inspect them before they become logs. It's just easier when they're lying on the ground."

Stanley Oliver Terrick occupied the number four stool, just to the right of the cutout — a removable piece of countertop that provides access to Elmer's side of the counter. He said "if a tree is already lying on the ground, isn't that a sign it's probably going to fail the inspection?"

"You're probly right," I said. "But we still have to go through the motions, anyway. May I have a dumpster, please?"[2]

Right about then, the café door opened and Rosetta Stone walked in. She said "hi Abner! Where's your hat?"

"It's in the shop," I said. "They're checking it for leaks."

"Leaks?" Rosetta took a seat between Stanley and Doc.

"Yes, I keep running out of ideas. Hat must have sprung a leak, somehow."

Doc said "maybe it's your head."

I said "my hat is easier to fix."

Stanley laughed. I don't know why.

I suppose I could have just told Rosetta about the jack pine with the sense of humor. But then I would have had to tell everybody why I was in such a scurry that I left my hat behind, and frankly, I didn't think they'd understand.

Most folks only know about the relatively tame varieties of chook. They don't know about the wild ones — the marauders — the

---

2 A dumpster is a kind of an omelet made of everything Elmer can find in the refrigerator, except meat. They're not as bad as they sound — and they're a lot cheaper than a landfill, which is everything plus the meat.

chooks who hunt in packs. Wild chooks are closely related to the cockatrice, and some of them even breathe fire! But if I tried to explain all that to the folks down at Elmer's… well, I reckon they just wouldn't be able to move past the part where I got chased halfway across the territory by an angry chicken.

I'd never hear the end of that. Doc still calls me "whale snot" from the time I got stuck in a whale's blowhole. But that's another story.

Elmer filled the tea kettle and put it on the front burner. He did that without being asked. He knows Rosetta doesn't drink coffee.

He said "what's going on, Ro?"

She said "I think I've found another signal."

Rosetta is a translator of global communications — and when I say global, I don't mean communications from *around* the world; I mean communications *from* the world.

She finds messages written into the landscape. She studies weather patterns as if they were handwritten documents. Rosetta believes something Out There is trying to talk to us, and if we want to talk back, we need to learn to read the signals.

Elmer said "what does it say?"

"I don't know yet. I'm still working on the translation."

I said "what's the signal?"

Rosetta took the sugar bowl, the salt and pepper shakers, the napkin dispenser, and Stanley's coffee mug, and arranged them on the countertop. She said "it's a pattern that looks like this:"

She said "this pattern was made using five bits of a stone called milky quartz. I found them stuck in a bed of gypsum out by Nothing Flat. Must have been there for a million years."

Elmer said "I didn't do it."

Rosetta gave him one of those looks. You know, the kind you could use to pry the lid off a can of won't. Elmer turned around and busied himself scraping the grill.

I said "so you reckon that pattern is supposed to mean something?"

"Of course it means something," Rosetta said. "All signals mean something. The trick is figuring out what."

Stanley gazed at the pattern thoughtfully. "Well, it's obviously a shopping list. Somebody's neolithic reminder to pick up five quarts of milk and some… what do they make out of gypsum?"

Elmer said "drywall, I think."

I said "did they even have drywall a million years ago?"

Perhaps I should have told you about the sign up on the wall, above the cash register. It says "Beware of Sharp Turns." It's not a road sign; it's a dialogue warning.

Discussions down at Elmer's Café have been known to veer off in unexpected directions so suddenly, your head feels like it's been spun around in a maelstrom, then dropped off a cliff. If you commence to feeling dizzy, it's best to step back.

Doc stepped back by hiding himself behind a wall of newspaper.

Rosetta said "the type of rock doesn't matter. What matters is the arrangement. I've seen this particular pattern before — "

Elmer said "it looks kind of like a snake wearing a party hat."

Stanley said "maybe it's his birthday."

Doc couldn't help himself. He put the paper down and scowled. "It's just a random scatter plot, that's all."

Rosetta said "it's not random. Those rocks were placed in that precise pattern."

"A million years ago?"

"Well, I've got an alibi," said Elmer. "Want to hear it?"

"No," said Rosetta. "Is that tea water hot yet?"

I said "if Elmer didn't do it, then who did?"

Elmer said "my money is on the snake."

S. O. Terrick said "if it *was* his birthday, then maybe this is some kind of prehistoric birthday card."

Rosetta leaned forward and set her elbows on the countertop. "I'm pretty sure that's not a snake."

"Could be a worm," said Elmer.

Stanley shook his head. "Worms don't wear party hats."

"You're right," said Elmer. "That settles it, then. It's gotta be a snake."

INTERLOGUE:
A Signature, of Sorts

ON the remote, rocky shore of Lake Vastwater, a solitary figure sits just beyond reach of the lapping waves, facing west. The setting sun touches the horizon; the surface of the lake glows red, like a pool of magma.

The figure leans back, propping himself up on one elbow. He watches quietly as the sun disappears, dragging its colors behind it. He watches as the sky turns purple and shadows creep out from behind every rock and boulder. Idly, he picks up a fragment of greenstone. He places it just so. Then he reaches for another fragment.

As the last light of day melts away, the figure stands and stretches. He takes one last look at his surroundings, then turns and disappears into the shadows. Behind him, he leaves a signature, of sorts — an obscure pattern of stones, just at the water's edge:

CHAPTER 3:

Vern Acular

WELL, I didn't want to get into any more chook fights, but I did need to get my hat back. A good hat is hard to find. A good hat does so much more than keep the rain and sun from getting in your eyes. A good hat's got a wide brim that keeps your ears and the back of your neck from getting sunburned. It stays on your head in blustery weather. It's got ventilation, so as not to cook your brain on hot days. And it's rugged enough to handle just about any adventure. A hat like that is a treasure worth fighting for — so as soon as I finished my breakfast, I headed out the Yonder Track in the direction of the Wandering Hills.

According to local legend, the Wandering Hills aren't from around here. The way I heard it, they wandered into the territory about a million years ago,[3] and finding no native hills between Jagged Creek and the coast, they settled down on what used to be level ground and raised a few bumps of their own. I don't give the story a whole lot of credence — although, come to think on it, that could explain the presence of some rather unusual plant and animal species. The mocking tree, for instance, is a species of woody plant that isn't found anywhere else west of the Great Empty Desert. Its leaves mimic the appearance of other trees' leaves, only the shapes and colors are wildly distorted. It's almost as if mocking trees are deliberately satirizing their neighbors. There is no apparent evolutionary reason for such behavior. Some folks say, if we only knew where the Wandering Hills came from,

---

3 Not the first time I've told you something happened a million years ago. Won't be the last, either. You gotta understand, I'm a storyteller — not a paleontologist. Point is, it happened a really long time ago.

we might learn a lot more about the environmental conditions that drove mocking trees to become so mean.

I had just about reached the grove where my hat disappeared when I spotted my friend Vern Acular moving carefully through the woods with his eyes fixed on the ground.

I said "hey, Vern. Whatcha doing?"

"Tracking."

Vern is the best tracker I know. He once found a set of dinosaur footprints and followed them all the way to the meteor crater. I've seen him track a deer so close, the deer thought it had two shadows. "I can see that. You're not tracking chooks, are you?"

"No."

"Good. I didn't want to find them again, anyway."

Vern didn't have anything more to say, so I hung back and watched him work.

I wasn't surprised to run into Vern. He pretty much grew up in the outback. His family lived in the last house on the far edge of town. His backyard had no fence around it, and Vern would just walk out the back door and sometimes not come home again for days. As he got older, days turned into weeks, then a month or more, and finally one day he simply never came back a-tall. He's wandered the length and breadth of Wild Side, and I've crossed paths with him in any number of unlikely places. But tell you true, I'd probly never catch a glimpse of him if he didn't know me from back when. Vern's a mite shy around folks he doesn't know.

He wasn't wearing a jacket — although I'll wager he had one stashed somewhere. The seed moon wouldn't be full for another week. Some north-facing patches of ground hadn't even thawed out yet. The early spring weather may have lost some of its bite, but it still had a few teeth left.

He wore a pair of moccasins that he made himself and a boiled-wool overshirt that looked homespun. Probly traded for it, somewhere out in the Wild. His only visible store-bought possessions were his belt knife and his plenty-pocketed cargo shorts. The shorts were threadbare and thorn-snagged. I guessed he was about due for a trip to the outfitters — but knowing Vern, he'd put it off as long as he could. I can't imagine where he gets the money to buy anything ready-made.

'Course, it's none of my business.

I said to Vern, I said "what are you tracking?"

"The wind."

"Why? What did it do?"

Seconds ticked by. I shifted my stance. Vern's eyes stayed on the ground. "Hmm?"

Vern suffers from a terrible affliction called Undivided Attention Syndrome. When he focuses on something, it's hard to tear him away. I've been trying to help him through it. Problem is, I keep getting distracted.

I tried again. "What are you going to do with it when you catch it?"

He looked up. "What?"

"You're not trophy hunting, are you?"

"No..."

Vern sounded like he was having trouble catching up with the conversation. He doesn't get much practice talking to people. I decided to be blunt.

"You're not gonna cut off the headwinds and mount them on your wall, are you?"

"No," he said, "of course not. I'm just practicing. I don't want my skills to get rusty."

I said "how do you track the wind? Does it leave footprints?"

Vern looked relieved to be getting back to level ground. "No, but you can see telltales, if you know what you're looking for. Like over there, for instance."

I looked where he was pointing. "Vern, that's a leaf."

"I know that."

"It's probly been lying there since last fall."

"Not in that particular spot," he said. "Last week it was over there, next to that rock."

I marveled out loud at Vern's power of recollection.

"Not recollection, observation. The rock would have blocked any breeze coming from that direction, not to mention most of the sunlight. You see how that leaf shows less sign of deterioration than all the others?"

Vern could have been a schoolteacher, if you could ever get him inside a classroom. He'll wax pedantic when the mood takes him.

"So you're tracking the wind that blew through these parts about a week ago?"

"Oh no," he said. "I'm tracking the cross-breeze that blew through just yesterday."

"What cross-breeze?"

"The one that knocked a week's worth of dust off that leaf."

He got down on all fours, with his nose an inch away from an old, brown sourbark leaf. "Looks like a light gust — not strong enough to pick up the leaf itself, but it sure did leave an obvious trail of dust particles. You see? They've all been scattered off in that direction."

Vern took off again, scanning the ground for motes of dust as if they were bread crumbs. I tagged along. "Say, you haven't seen my hat by any chance, have you?"

"No. Where did you leave it?"

"I didn't leave it anywhere. I was running from a pack of chooks, and a jack pine snatched it off my head."

Vern said "good for Jack!"

Vern shares my opinion that the entire arboreal community would be better off if pine trees would just lighten up a bit. So you're a pine tree. No point in brooding about it. World's gonna turn, so you might as well cut loose every once and again.

"Yes, good for Jack," I said. "It was a merry prank, but now I need my hat back. Geez, I hope the chooks didn't run off with it."

"Why would the chooks run off with your hat?"

"I don't know," I said. "Bait for a trap?"

Vern allowed as how that could be a possibility. "If you see it lying around somewhere, don't just rush over and grab it," he advised.

It didn't take long to find the spot where I'd slid down the bank. From there, I backtracked all the way to the grove where my hat got snatched.

Only it wasn't there. I examined every inch of ground. I glared at the trees. For a brief moment, I thought about chopping off limbs until somebody talked.

I know. It's a vile thought. I can't believe I thought it. For a moment, I considered scolding myself. I thought of long, heavy words to describe my perfidy. Then a soft, ominous clucking filtered down through the treetops and landed in my ears.

That's when it suddenly occurred to me that I'd neglected to tell Vern how much I admired his tracking abilities.

It further occurred to me that I should go and find him, and tell him, and that I should do it right now.

And so, without further deliberation, I departed from the grove at best possible speed and set off in search of Vern.

CHAPTER 4:

How to Spook a Chook

"They won't attack us if we stick together," I said. "Right?"

"They might. If they think they can overpower us. Are you sure you want to walk behind me like that?"

I had been letting Vern take the lead as we hiked back to the chookery. "Well, I figured you should go first, since you know so much more than I do about these things."

"Oh, I don't know about that," he said. "But I do know they like to pick off the stragglers."

"On second thought, maybe I'd better show you the way."

"Too late. We're here."

The clucking had grown louder. The chooks were getting restless. I scanned the treetops, but couldn't spot any roosts. "What do we do?"

Vern said "can you fly?"

I thought about it. "Not very well."

"That's too bad. If you could fly, we could pretend we're flying foxes, and go up there and chase them away."

"Can *you* fly?"

"No, but one flying fox always has to stay on the ground, in case the chooks try to escape on foot."

"Nice of you to volunteer."

A staccato burst of clucks rained down from the treetops. The sound made my scalp itch. I rubbed the back of my neck as the other chooks joined the chorus. Vern said "quick, kneel down and pull your jacket up over your head."

He dropped to his knees. His head and hands disappeared inside his overshirt, like a turtle vanishing into his shell. I followed suit, just as the first chook came flapping down to earth.

Vern made ghost sounds. So did I, waving my arms around for good measure. "WoooOOOooohhh! WooOOOOOOOooohhh!!!"

The chook chucked in surprise.

Still on our knees, we shambled and lurched in her direction. "WoooOOOOOOOooo!!!"

The chook gobbled frantically and flew out of there so fast, half her feathers couldn't keep up. Squawks of alarm and frantic wingbeats resounded through the canopy as the other chooks hied after her. In seconds, the forest was quiet again.

I peeked out through the neck of my jacket. Vern was calmly stuffing chook feathers into a gunnysack. "What just happened?"

"Chooks are afraid of ghosts," he said. "Especially short, headless ones. Must trigger some sort of genetic memory."

"How long till they come back?"

"Hard to say," he said, tying the gunnysack to his belt. "Too bad we didn't have a chopping block in the background. That would have really spooked them."

"Maybe next time. Do we need to get out of here, or can I look around for my hat?"

"Oh, the lead chook won't be back for at least an hour, is my guess. But I doubt she'll be leader much longer."

"Why is that?"

"Chooks don't respect a warhawk who turns chicken all the time. They think it's a negative stereotype. First one back wins the pack — that's the general rule."

"Well, I'd best get busy, then." I started shinnying up the nearest pine tree.

Vern said "where are you going?"

"I figure they must have stashed my hat in one of the roosts."

He watched me grab a branch and hoist myself up. "I admire your determination."

"I like that hat," I said, reaching for the next branch.

"Obviously. But it's not up there."

I peered down at him. "How do you know?"

"Come down and look over here."

Vern directed my attention to a tiny tuft of brown fur that was caught on a low-hanging pine bough. I said "what's that?"

"I reckon it's hornswoggle hair."

"Hmm." I examined the tuft of hair with interest. I've never seen a slick-fingered hornswoggle, though Vern swears they're pretty common. Also, they're very good at blending in.

Vern's eyes swept the ground. "Looks like you ran right under him. I bet he grabbed your hat while you were distracted."

"That sneak! Where did he go?"

"Took off that way."

"Can you track him?"

"Oh, sure," said Vern. "That part's easy. The hard part is getting your hat back."

CHAPTER 5:
Tracking the Slick-Fingered Hornswoggle

HORNSWOGGLES aren't especially dangerous, per se. I mean to tell you, nobody ever lost a fight with a slick-fingered hornswoggle. But very few people ever walk away from a hornswoggle encounter without losing *something*.

You see, hornswoggles have mastered the art of deception. They can masquerade as virtually any other kind of beast you can imagine. My friend Buford Colic once thought he'd caught one — stuffed it into an old seed sack, tied off the end, and called all his neighbors together for the Great Unveiling. Everybody gathered 'round the sack, but when Buford opened it, the only thing they found inside was a sleeping possum.

Well, they poked and prodded that critter, but it just went right on snoozing away. So they yelled and screamed and banged pots together, but no matter what they did, they couldn't wake it up. Then they all fell to bickering with each other about what to do next, until Buford finally looked around and noticed the possum was gone.

All of Buford's neighbors had a good laugh at Buford's expense. They rode him pretty hard about mistaking a possum for a slick-fingered hornswoggle. Until they noticed their wallets were gone, too.

Anyway, Vern followed the trail while I kept an eye out for chooks. I said "if a hornswoggle can disguise itself as any other animal, how do we know it when we see it?"

"We've got a trail. Whatever's at the end of this trail is a horn-swoggle, no matter what it looks like."

"But the tracks keep changing." Back at the chookery, Vern had picked up the trail of a feather-tailed tree skunk. We'd followed it for a mile or so, but the trail had taken us into a swampy area where the footprints had morphed into big-toed toad prints. Then, on the other side of the swamp, they'd morphed again. At the moment, we seemed to be following a medium-nosed bandiscoot as it scooted up the side of a ridge. "I mean, how do you know the skunk and the toad and the bandiscoot didn't just cross paths?"

Vern looked at me like I had an expiration date tattooed on my forehead, and it was long past. "You ever seen a bandiscoot around these parts?"

"Nope. Heard they're pretty fast, though."

"It's the hornswoggle," he said. "Traveling no faster than a hornswoggle can go."

"Well, I wish he'd turn himself into a snail. Then we might catch him before nightfall."

Vern waxed pedantic again. He said "it's important to remember that hornswoggles don't actually turn into other species. They're just very good at camouflage. This one probably threw on the tree skunk disguise to discourage the chooks from eating him.[4] That was a smart move — but if they'd attacked him anyway, he couldn't have sprayed them like a real skunk, because horn-swoggles have no scent glands."

I said "what if he disguised himself as a five-legged catawampus?"

Vern crouched down to get a better look at whatever scuffed pebble or trampled pine needle had caught his attention. He

---

4 Hornswoggles have been known to steal domestic chooks right out of the chicken coop (and sometimes right off the dinner table). But no predator is foolish enough to prey upon vicious wild chooks. Well, except for muddle-headed bunnikins — but there aren't too many of those left. No one is quite certain why.

didn't see the catawampus padding around thirty yards downhill, carefully lining us up for an unobstructed uphill charge. He said "what about it?"

"Could he still attack?"

"I suppose he could — but he wouldn't. Because what if we stood our ground and called his bluff? Hornswoggles have almost no natural body mass. Even if he rammed us at full speed, he'd bounce off us like a red balloon."

"So what you're saying is, if a catawampus were to charge us right now, then we can be pretty sure she's not the hornswoggle. Is that what you're saying?"

"Yes. That's exactly what I'm saying." Vern looked up. "Why?"

I pointed downhill.

The catawampus bellowed and surged in our direction.

Vern said "uh oh."

INTERLOGUE:

The Silence of a Single Forgotten Voice

TODAY, in the swamps of Sogbottom and the jungles of Morainia, there is a silence.

Mind you, it's not an absolute silence. It does nothing to inhibit the cacophony of a billion life forms competing to be heard. No, this is the silence of a missing sound — the hole in the midst of a symphony where the virtuoso is meant to play. It is the silence of a single forgotten voice.

The silence has persisted for a thousand millennia. That's when the last hollow-toed canard piped out a mournful dirge as it sank into the bubbling mire. It was an appropriate send-off... hollow-toed canards had always excelled at dirges. But oh! when the jungle put on a festive mood, no bird in the world could pipe a more sprightly tune!

You see, the hollow-toed canard had tubular bones and a neck like a chanter. To make music, the canard simply puffed up its belly and played itself like a bagpipe. Tell you true, no modern-day songbird can ever hope to produce such an exuberant, spine-tingling sound. Canaries croon and warblers warble — but the hollow-toed canard could make the forests *reel*. When the canard sang, the mountains themselves tapped their feet.

Alas, no fossil record has ever been found. No prehistoric DNA sequence has ever been mapped. The legend of the elusive hollow-toed canard is all but lost.

But there is a witness yet living... a man who has walked this Earth for a million years... who heard the music way back when, and remembers it still. The witness's name is lost to history. Very few people even suspect that such a witness exists.

Of those few, there is one who calls him Pedestrio.

CHAPTER 6:
Beware the Five-Legged Catawampus

THE five-legged catawampus is one of the strangest-looking creatures under Blue. She's got horns like a bull and a head like a block of cement, mounted on the body of a mountain lion. Not a lean, graceful, agile-looking mountain lion, but a stocky, sturdy, barrel of a mountain lion. I mean to say, she's built more like a battering ram than a spring-loaded wildcat, with two legs in the front and three in the back.

Her back legs are massive. They're like kangaroo legs, only she doesn't bounce around on them. Her front legs are smaller and shorter — which means, if you happen to catch her on the flats, you'll see she tends to walk a crooked line. I mean to say, her front bits'll be marching along, setting what she thinks is a reasonable pace, when all of a sudden, she'll look to one side or t'other and see her caboose go rumbling on by. So she'll take a moment to get herself straightened out, but it's only a matter of time before it happens again: first on one side, then the other, till eventually she gets where she's going. It's a comical sight to behold, but trust me on this: you don't ever want to be caught standing uphill from a five-legged catawampus.

So there we were, standing at the top of a ridge, when the catawampus bellowed and charged.

Good thing Vern was there. He knew what to do. He yelled "havoc!" and took off running — but he ran downhill, straight at the catawampus.

I ran after him. At the last second, Vern jumped one way, I jumped t'other, and the catawampus threw both horns at the empty space between us!

Her momentum carried her all the way to the top of the ridge, and then some. She was eight feet in the air before gravity brought her back to earth. She landed spitting mad and ready to charge — but this time we had the advantage, on account of she was uphill and we were halfway down.

She didn't like that. She snarled and snorted and pawed the ground. We didn't scare off. We just stood there and waited. She tried to circle around us, to come at us again from the downhill side, but we didn't let her. We blocked her every move, until finally she bellowed a raging bellow and charged us from the uphill side.

Big mistake. We stepped aside and watched her tumble on by. She looked like she was trying to climb onto her own back. She practically left footprints behind both ears.

Vern and I hiked back up the hill. We still had a hornswoggle to catch. But by the time we found the tracks, the catawampus had gotten herself sorted and was lining us up again.

I said "how many times do you think we're going to have to do this?"

Vern shrugged. "Could go on all day."

"Maybe we should find a bigger hill. Or a steeper one."

"We could run her up and down the steep side of Precipice Peak, and it wouldn't matter. She doesn't get tired. Not as long as she's got a clear path and an easy target."

The catawampus charged. Vern and I countercharged. Same tactic, same result. Vern said "how attached are you to that hat of yours?"

Now, between you and me, I loved that hat. It was only a weather-stained, slouch-brimmed, crusty and battered old bush hat — not much to look at, but it was a good hat. Plus, it had the advantage of being so ugly, it put all but the hungriest mozzies off their feed. I felt naked without it — but was I attached to it?

Not anymore, apparently. "I spose I could get along without it," I said. "For the time being."

"Then I have an idea," said Vern. "Let's see if we can lead this critter over to Crikey Creek."

CHAPTER 7:
Crikey Creek

CRIKEY Creek is slow going for any traveler: the whole valley is overgrown with dense thickets of swaddle bush.[5] Swaddle bushes have long, shiny green leaves that like to wrap themselves around you till it's almost impossible to move. The foliage is so dense, you feel like you're unwrapping a present from the inside out, and you're trying to be very careful not to tear the shiny green wrapping paper, on account of you might want to use it again someday, until it finally begins to dawn on you: there's about a million layers of it. I said to Vern, I said "you think we're safe yet?"

Behind us, the catawampus growled and grunted. She'd hit the swaddle with all the momentum of a bull moose charging into a clothesline full of sheets — but the clothesline didn't break, and now the sheets were fighting back.

Vern said "she's causing a lot of damage back there."

I'd have gladly done some damage myself, if it helped us get out of there. A few swipes with a machete could have blazed a trail all the way to the creek. But I didn't say that out loud. Vern believes that kind of bushwhacking is disrespectful to plant life, not to mention the mark of a greenhorn. Or a Town Sider.

"Pity she doesn't eat swaddle fronds," I said.

---

5 *Myopus claustrophobus* is the binomial sobriquet. But nomenclature aside, swaddle bushes have not been studied all that extensively by the scientific community. Whenever anyone gets close enough to start taking measurements, it's not long before they're swaddled so tightly, they can't reach their instruments. More than a few aspiring botanists have chosen to pursue careers in geology after such an encounter.

Vern pushed forward another half a step. Then he stopped and listened. "That's the creek. Can you hear it?"

No, I couldn't. "Sure I can. How far?"

"Hundred feet."

Behind us, the grunting and snarling and thrashing stopped. "I think she's finally clear," said Vern.

"Probly setting an ambush for us."

Vern shook his head. "She'll find easier prey upslope. Still, it might be a good idea to keep going."

I used the front of my shirt to wipe the sweat out of my eyes. "At this rate, it'll take us an hour just to get creekside."

I was wrong. It took two hours. The sun was dangling low in the sky by the time Vern stopped and scanned the bank, looking for a good place to cross.

Then he froze.

I said "something wrong?"

"Somebody's been through here," he said. "No more than an hour ago."

"That's impossible." We would have heard them. We'd have seen something: a broken stem. A bruised blade. Not even Vern can push through the swaddle without leaving a trace.

He said "there's a footprint."

I couldn't see a thing. "Maybe it was the hornswoggle."

"I doubt it. They like open areas where they can see the chumps coming."

I don't think he meant that as an insult. A lot of people have been taken in by hornswoggles. That doesn't make us chumps. But Vern doesn't always express himself in the best possible way. He talks to trees more often than he talks to people.

The trees don't answer, of course. Leastwise, they haven't yet. Only people I know of who can engage a tree in conversation are the Wodewosen — the wild folk who live up yonder in the Sea of Green. But Vern keeps trying.

I said "maybe it was your cross-breeze."

He didn't bother to answer. He was examining the ground intently. All I saw was a mat of dead swaddle fronds.

I tried again. "What do you think it was?"

"Human," he said. "It's a human footprint. Adult male. And he's barefoot."

INTERLOGUE:
Like a Dancer Sliding Past a Silk Curtain

LOOSE-LIMBED and sure-footed, Pedestrio glides through the swaddle like a dancer sliding past a silk curtain. He touches a branch — not to push it aside, but to listen with his fingertips. The swaddle tells him its story: how long it's been here, how many relatives it has, what the weather was like when it was young.

Pedestrio listens. He hasn't set foot on this patch of ground for many years, but he knows its contours like no other living being. He remembers when this valley was nothing but a meadow, and the grass reached up high enough to tickle his nose. Back then, the creek looped around the Wandering Hills and missed this valley completely.

He recalls the time, long ago, when The Void dug a tunnel through the creek bank — a dozen miles upstream, just at the bend where the creek slams into Sacree Ledge. He remembers the floodwaters that rose up the following spring. The torrent pushed its way through that worm hole, deepening and widening the passage, until it had carved a new bed for Crikey Creek.

He wonders where The Void is digging now.

The creek has grown older. It meanders more than it used to. In a few years, it will cut a new, deeper channel to the west, and this creek bed will be left high and dry.

With a touch, Pedestrio tells the bush where to drop its seeds. Then he excuses himself, and the swaddle relaxes just enough to let him pass.

Pedestrio moves on. In minutes, he has crossed the creek and climbed up the opposite bank. He does not hurry, but neither does he linger. After all, he has many steps to go before sunset.

The swaddle bushes, it's safe to say, are forever changed by the encounter. They know what they need to do now. Change is a constant — but knowing its direction is a blessing.

In human terms of intelligence, swaddle bushes would be classified as vegetables. But that's not how it works on Wild Side. The truth of it is this: swaddle bushes are survivors. And when survivors know what's coming, then they can plan…

CHAPTER 8:

A Morning Stroll up Mount Exile

VERN waded all up and down both sides of the creek, searching in vain for more sign. He never found so much as a drop of water shed beyond the creek's edge. The whole scenario minused him, which is to say he was nonplussed. Finally, he led us up the opposite bank and back into the swaddle, directly across from where he'd spotted the mystery print.

The going didn't get any easier. Vern kept on twisting his body like he was trying to slide sideways through the tangle, but the swaddle fronds only wrapped him up tighter. I half expected him to fetch out his knife and start cutting a path. He didn't, of course. But it was a measure of his frustration that I thought he might try.

By the time we pushed through, it was full dark and the mozzies smelled blood. They gathered in clouds just beyond reach of the outermost fronds, waiting for us to come out.

Mosquitoes and swaddle bushes don't get along. I think it's the buzzing — it drives the bushes crazy. Not that they can hear it, but the vibrations cause some kind of physical spasm which makes them appear to swat at the mozzies with their oversized leaves. Anyway, Vern and I decided to spend the night swaddled at the edge of the thicket.

The plants didn't seem to mind. In fact, they gave me the rather strong impression they enjoyed our company. I had the weirdest feeling they were trying to tell us something — but you know how hard it is to listen to somebody who's standing a little too close. I kept on trying to inch away, to no avail.

It rained overnight. The swaddle bushes didn't exactly keep us dry, but I had a poncho up my sleeve, and Vern is pretty close to waterproof. He made a pillow out his little sack of chook feathers, curled up inside the swaddle leaves, and drifted off to sleep.

We stayed warm enough. When you spend a lot of time out in the Wild, you get acclimated. Your internal furnace works harder out here than it does back in town, and you start generating your own heat. I'm not saying the difference is huge — I mean, you can't sleep naked in the snow, or anything like that — but your comfort level tends to be a few degrees cooler than most Town Siders can tolerate. Vern probly found the accommodations a bit on the toasty side.

Anyway, it was still dark out when Vern shook me awake. He said "come on, we gotta go."

My feet were numb. I wished I hadn't got them wet while crossing the creek. I said "where's the Ballerina?"

At this season of the year, you can tell time by the location of a constellation known as the Ballerina. She leaps into the sky in the wee hours of the morning, hovers for a moment above the horizon, then gracefully descends back to earth. When you see her getting ready to stick the landing, then you know sunrise is just 'round the corner.

Vern said "I don't know. I can't see the stars from here."

I didn't feel like moving. I said "well, why don't you go check it out, then come back and tell me?"

Vern kicked my soggy feet. I drew them closer under the swaddle. "Come on," he said. "We've got to follow the track from last night."

I thought he meant the hornswoggle. I said "that was two ridges ago, and I'm not keen on going back."

"Not the hornswoggle tracks. The one we saw creekside."

I wriggled away from the sound of his voice. "One track doesn't make a trail, Vern."

"I think I know where he was heading. It's got to be Mount Exile. Come on, we've got to get to the summit by dawn."

"Bring me back a sunbeam."

He kicked my feet again. I curled up like a roly-poly bug.

Vern gave up. "Fine," he said. "See you in a day or two."

I couldn't tell if he was bluffing. Not without opening my eyes, and that seemed like a drastic and unnecessary measure. I resolved to postpone it for as long as I could. But then Vern moved beyond the swaddle and everything got quiet, and I thought about the chooks, and the catawampus, and I supposed I was being selfish, allowing Vern to face such hazards alone. So, with great effort, I unswaddled myself and stumbled after him.

Mount Exile isn't really a mountain. Mountains rise up suddenly out of the ground like fists answering a polite beg-to-differ. Mountains take your breath away with their steep inclines and towering heights. Technically speaking, Exile is really just another hill — although I readily admit the summit is the highest point for miles around.

And it's a long trek to the top: at least a couple of hours, assuming you can see where you're going. I thought Vern was being overly optimistic if he imagined we could get there before daybreak.

I said to Vern, I said "what's the rush? We haven't even had breakfast yet."

"I thought you were the self-proclaimed Supervisor of Sunrises?"

"That's true," I said. "But here's the thing: the sun doesn't like to be micromanaged. It doesn't like being watched all the time. That's why I try to limit my involvement to occasional spot checks."

"What happens when something goes wrong and you're not there?"

I thought about that time the sun tried to wriggle through an unfortunately-placed hole in the ground — potentially showing itself ten minutes ahead of schedule. Also, there was the time it forgot to bring the colors, and I had to send it back to get them.

Frankly, the sun needs somebody like me to keep things running smoothly. Otherwise, it might forget where it is and what it's supposed to be doing. But take it all around, such lapses are pretty rare. And if I miss one every now and again… well, the fallout would only make the sun more likely to pay attention next time, wouldn't it?

So I said "what could go wrong?"

"There's a difference between delegation and abdication, that's all I'm saying."

Well, I didn't know Vern was such an expert on management styles. But his chiding still didn't explain why he was dragging me and my soggy feet all the way up Mount Exile in the dark.

I tried again. "You know, if we just hunker down and wait a while, I think I can get the sun to kind of sneak around that crag for us. Then we won't miss the sunrise, and when it comes, we can dry our socks and save ourselves a blister or two."

"But don't you want to see him?"

I tripped on a root of small evil and plunged headfirst into a shadow of doubt. "See who?"

Vern scanned the ground while he waited for me to pick myself up and wipe the mud off. "Nobody I know can walk through the swaddle bushes like that. Not even the Wodewosen."

"Look, I'm not saying it wasn't there, but I couldn't see any kind of track at all."

"It was subtle," Vern admitted. "I almost missed it myself."

"Maybe you imagined it."

Vern didn't answer. He just kept on striding up the rain-sodden slope, cutting sign as he went. I didn't see how he could spot anything in the dark, nor how any footprints could have survived the overnight downpour.

I said "what's the hurry? Wouldn't a ray of daylight make tracking a mite easier?"

"There are no tracks," he said. "That's the whole point."

"Then how do you know we're not just stumbling around in the dark for nothing?"

Vern didn't say anything for a long while. We trudged on. Vern kept looking up at the sky. The stars faded, and the firmament turned from black to purple.

"We're not going to make it," I said.

Vern knew it. He slacked his pace. A minute later, he spotted a fallen log and headed for it. "Let's rest."

I could tell by the way he sat down that his shorts were beginning to chafe. We'd been pushing pretty hard through rain-soaked vegetation, getting more and more saturated with every step.

"What's this all about?" I said.

Vern pulled a small jar of salve out of a pocket and began treating his hot spots. "Maybe nothing."

"How come it was so important to climb this mountain before daylight?"

"Just had a hunch, that's all."

"So did I," I said. "I had a hunch those mozzies were planning a dawn raid. But I reckoned we could have waited them out."

"I didn't imagine it," he muttered, frowning. "Someone passed through the swaddle without making a sound, leaving almost no trace. There's only one person in the world who can do that. And until yesterday, I didn't think he was real."

"Who's that?"

Vern glanced at the sky again. The birds were beginning to sing. The last few stars winked out, one by one. Vern took a deep breath.

"I call him Pedestrio."

CHAPTER 9:
Pedestrio

————————

THE lower slopes of Mount Exile are dominated by pine trees. But about two-thirds of the way up, the pine belt gives way to a wide, treeless swath, as if somebody mowed a ring around the mountain a hundred yards wide. Above that are the coven trees. Unsettling creatures, coven trees: you rarely find two of them standing within a dozen feet of one another, and you never find them mixed in with any other arboreal species. Most birds won't go near them, and after spending an hour in their presence, I didn't have to wonder why: it felt like breathing poisoned air. It felt like being trapped in a very small room. It felt like telling a tale to a stone-faced audience, and one by one they all turn away. But even the coven trees thinned out as we climbed higher.

The sun did beat us to the top, though not by much. The summit was a rocky dome sprinkled with tussocks of old, brown grass. At the center, a weathered granite outcrop stepped into the sky like a stairway leading nowhere. Vern looked around. "No sign of a camp," he said.

"Were you expecting one?"

"It's where I'd spend the night. Wouldn't you?"

Not if it meant hiking up through a belt of coven trees. But Vern didn't seem the least bit fazed, so I shrugged off my lingering disquiet and peered down at the valley below. The morning mist dragged itself along the creek's path like an injured cloud.

"It is a nice view," I said. "Are those the Graymatters out there to the west?"

Vern didn't answer. He wasn't interested in landmarks. He was on hands and knees, scouring the ground for bent blades of grass and overturned pebbles. Eventually, he worked his way over to the granite outcrop.

"Hmm," said Vern.

Beside the outcrop, a handful of small pebbles formed a familiar pattern:

"I've seen this pattern before," he said.

"Yeah, so have I."

"In the sky, at night."

"Nope. On a countertop, at breakfast."

Vern looked up. "How's that?"

"Some folks were talking about it the other day, down at Elmer's Café," I said, circling around the stones to get a different view. "If you look at it from over here, it looks kind of like a snake wearing a party hat."

Vern shook his head. "It's not a snake."

"You have to look at it from just the right angle."

"You're thinking of a completely different constellation," he said. "This one is called Pedestrio."

I sensed a story, but Vern needed a bit of prompting. "How's that for a coincidence?"

"Hmm?"

"That's what you called the stranger in the swaddle."

Vern didn't answer. He sat down next to the pebbles and scratched his head. "Looks like a person caught in midstride, doesn't it?"

"Looks like a lot of things. Could be a lopsided letter M, or a W. Not to mention a snake wearing a party hat."

Vern ignored me. He does that sometimes. He said "he can't be real, though."

"Who can't be real?"

"Hmm?"

Like pulling frog's teeth. "Who can't be real?"

"Well, there's a story… I can't remember where I heard it… about a man who walks the Earth by day and the sky at night."

"Do tell," I said.

"That's it. There's a man who walks the Earth by day and the sky at night."

Nobody will ever mistake Vern for a storyteller.

"You're gonna need a little more than that, Vern."

"He's as old as the mountains, and there isn't a patch of ground anywhere on the planet that he hasn't walked across too many times to count."

"Better."

"And at night, he walks among the stars — which is why I call the constellation Pedestrio."

I nodded. In my experience, the best yarns always teeter just on the edge of believability. "So you figure that's who we almost ran into down by Crikey Creek."

"Can't be. It was just a story, that's all."

"Yeah, I hate it when stories come to life."

He bent over the pebbles again, saying "give me a minute."

I gave him an hour. He spent all of it with his nose to the ground, personally interviewing every blade of grass. I sat on the granite stoop and watched him work. Occasionally I threw a pebble in his path, which irritated him just enough to make his eyebrows twitch. Still, he didn't bother to look up. It's possible his Undivided Attention Syndrome could be getting worse.

Finally, he sat back on his heels. "Not much to go on," he said. "But somebody was here last night. They sat almost exactly where you're sitting and deliberately put those pebbles in place."

"Wasn't me."

"No, it wasn't," he said. "It had to be the same person who made that partial print down by the creek."

I reckoned he was probly right. After all, if a jungle of swaddle bushes can't stop you, how's a copse of coven trees going to turn you away? But just for fun, I said "how do you figure?"

"Same hunch as before," he said. "The creekside track points in this direction. Mount Exile is a good place to camp for the night, if you can reach the summit before dark. And I cut some sign up here that I missed on the first once-over. Nothing as clear as a print, but enough to indicate somebody took a pretty direct route from the swaddle bush to this outcrop."

"Then what?"

"I don't know." His face screwed up in frustration. "After that, the trail simply vanishes."

I shifted around and regarded my throne with renewed interest. "You think I'm sitting on the entrance to a secret passage?"

Vern looked at me, then looked away. "No."

"You sure? I mean, a secret passage could add a little zing to the story, don't you think?"

"What story?"

See, that's the thing about Vern. He doesn't recognize that his whole life is a story, and he could improve the telling of it by adding the odd secret passage to the narrative. "Never mind," I said. "I'll sketch one in later, if necessary."

"Tell me more about the discussion you heard back in town. Are you sure they weren't talking about the stars?"

I stared at him. "When's the last time you've been to Elmer's Café?"

"Don't think I ever have."

"Well, then, take my word on it: the conversations are hard enough to follow without trying to figure out what everybody's talking about."

"What does that mean?"

"See, that's my whole point," I said. "Water flows downstream. You see it happening. Sometimes you can even hear it. But what does it mean?"

"Means the head is upstream and the mouth is downstream."

"Yeah, well… down at Elmer's Café, sometimes the mouth is upstream from the head."

"I don't know what that means, either," he said. "Just tell me, did anybody mention stars?"

"Nope. Somebody mentioned shopping lists, and somebody else brought up the snake with the party hat. Then the conversation sort of moved on."

"Hmm."

"Rosetta might have had more thoughts on it, but she didn't get a chance to tell us."

"Who?"

"Rosetta Stone," I said. "She's the one who showed us the symbol. She said she found some rocks stuck in the ground out by Nothing Flat, arranged in this pattern. She thought it might be a signal."

"A signal from whom?"

I shrugged. "The planet?"

"The planet?"

I could tell Vern wanted to ask *what does that mean,* but he didn't want to get caught in another upstream current. "Rosetta's an academic," I said. "A professor of terralinguistics and ecosystemic communication. Something like that, anyway. Basically, she thinks the world is trying to tell us something, so whenever she sees patterns in nature, she assumes it's a message."

"From the planet."

"Well, maybe not the planet. But she's pretty adamant that something Out There is trying to communicate. And she's collected a dragload of evidence to support her theory.[6] I could introduce you, if you like."

Vern tossed his head at the pattern of pebbles. He said "she's not the one who thought it was a party snake, is she?"

"Nah. That was Elmer. Or maybe Stanley, I forget which."

"Hmm." Vern gave the pebbles one last hard stare, as if committing the visual to long-term memory. Then he took a deep breath and gave his head a shake — same as if he'd just woken up. "Do you still want to get your hat back?"

---

6 A dragload is very simple: it's more than anyone can carry, but less than no one can move.

INTERLOGUE:
Escape Routes

THERE is, indeed, a secret passageway beneath the summit of Mount Exile. Several, actually. But they don't go anywhere.

The original passage was excavated many years ago by a field mouse desperate to save her family from the clutches of a ravenous great horned scowl.[7] The entrance is well-hidden, but a mouse in a hurry could find it with both eyes closed.

The plan worked; the family survived. The scowl moved on, unable to cope with the depression brought on by roosting too many nights in a coven tree.

The Mount Exile field mice have re-excavated their primary escape tunnel many times over the years, adding numerous side tunnels with multiple access points. The colony is now well protected from aerial assault. But they are trapped on the summit, as even the bravest field mouse will not undertake to dig a tunnel past the toxic roots of the coven trees.

Even if the tunnels *did* go somewhere, it's important to remember this: mouse tunnels are far too narrow for most humans to crawl through.[8] In other words, the person who rearranged those pebbles before vanishing from the summit must have found another way off the mountain.

And there is no other way. Unless, perhaps…

No. No, that's silly. I don't care if that granite outcrop *did* look like a stairway — there's no way it could have taken him all the way to the stars.

---

7 Scowls are nocturnal birds of prey. They are closely related to owls, but grumpier. They are the only birds who will go anywhere near coven trees — not that the association does anything to improve their disposition.

8 Although there are certain narrow-minded individuals who *think* they can do it…

CHAPTER 10:

The Old What's-in-the-Bag Trick

"**I** EVER tell you about the time I climbed a decision tree?"

"Yep," said Vern. "Heard that one before, too."

Vern lay on his back and stared at the clouds. They'd started rolling in shortly after noon. By evening, there wasn't a single patch of sky that wasn't stuffed full of cumulus. They weren't rain clouds — but Vern didn't care about rain. He just wanted to see the stars.

I said "well, how 'bout the time I woke up backwards, and spent the whole day walking around inside my own dreams?"

"… and the only way out was to wait for your dreams to come true. Yep. Told me that one last year." Vern turned his head just enough to catch me with the corner of his eye. "Guess you're still waiting, huh?"

If I didn't know Vern, I might have mistaken that for a gibe at my expense. But Vern doesn't have a sense of humor, so the way I figured it, there must be some other interpretation. Didn't take me long to settle on his true meaning.

"Hah!" I said. "You see, you've forgotten the ending already! Maybe I should tell that one again, just to refresh your memory."

"You hear that?"

I shut up. That was Vern's way of telling me I was talking over the music.

The air was full of birdsong. Crickets chirped and peepers peeped. The odd mozzie buzzed our ears, but Vern had found some pennyroyal and crushed it up to make a tolerable mozzie repellent. They were just part of the orchestra now.

We'd set a roundabout course back to the spot of the catawampus attack. It took the whole day, but we avoided the swaddle. We saw no sign of the catawampus — Vern reckoned she'd be clear the other side of the Wandering Hills by now. That left us free to wander and forage and supervise the coming of spring.

I listened for the sunset. They say you can hear it, if you know what to listen for. They say it's like somebody very quietly took a pan full of sizzling bacon off the fire, only that somebody is ten miles away. You know how hard it is to hear bacon sizzling from ten miles away? Well, hearing the sunset is even harder. It's almost impossible even on a sunny day, much less on a cloudy spring evening in a forest full of tweeters, chirpers, peepers, and whiners. Still, you never know unless you try.

I said to Vern, I said "have you ever heard the sunset?"

Vern didn't answer. *Probly listening to it right now.* I stole a glance in his direction.

His eyes were closed. He looked content.

I listened a while longer. Then I rolled over and went to sleep.

"Three or four weeks," said Vern. "Assuming nothing goes wrong."

"That long, huh?"

Vern shrugged. "He's got a four-day head start. Takes a while to catch up — especially when the tracks keep changing. Then there's a chance the rain could wash out the trail just when he hares off in a different direction. Or he could climb on a log and float a mile or two downstream. I'm not saying I can't track him down; I'm just saying there'll be obstacles."

I threw a rock at a rotting tree stump. "What does a hornswoggle want with my hat, anyway?"

"That's just their way," said Vern. "They take everything they can, even if it's old and ugly."

"It's got character," I said.

"Yes, it does. Character leaking out the frayed bits."

"I don't care," I said. "It's my best hat, and I want it back."

Vern looked at me with his chin lowered and his eyebrows raised. Last time he gave me that look, we spent the next month eating bugs and wiggly things out in Bleckphooey Swamp. That didn't end well. Turned out the notorious Bleckphooey Willow-wisp was really just a shy old woman whose real name was Marsha Gass, and those eerie green lights that travelers always talk about? Why, those were just made by the glow of her jade smoking pipe.

Marsha was a very nice old lady, once you got to know her. She made cookies for us. So that part of the ending was okay. It's just that, after a month of eating bugs and wiggly things, I rather expected to close the story with a more dramatic finish.

Anyway, Vern gave me that are-you-sure-you-know-what-you're-getting-into look. "So," he said. "You're okay with spending the next three or four weeks on the stalk?"

I thought about it. "Can't we just set a trap or something?"

"Could do."

"Great! How do we do that?"

Vern looked off into the distance. "Well, you've got several options. You could try a net, but you need something to bait the trap. You don't happen to have any live chooks in your rucksack, do you?"

"I'm not that reckless." Live, domesticated chooks tend to attract vicious wild chooks. Even if you manage to fend off the wild ones, the domesticated chooks could suffer the kind of trauma that can lead to some really bad eggs. "Anyway, I don't have a net. Do you?"

"No."

"So that option's off the table," I said, wondering why he'd brought it up in the first place.

"What about tar?" he said.

"What about it?"

"You got any?"

"No."

"Too bad. We could have made a baby hornswoggle out of tar."

"Does that really work?"

"Sometimes."

Hornswoggles are ruled by their instincts. In theory, the sight of a baby hornswoggle sitting all alone out in the Wild might bring an adult hornswoggle close enough to try to steal its lunch money. But I'd never heard of such a plan actually working in practice.

"Any place around here where we can get some tar?"

"I don't know of any source this side of the black stump."

I groaned. The black stump was all the way out near the border of Tar Nation. I said "are we running out of options yet?"

"I spose you could always try the old what's-in-the-bag trick."

He looked away as he said it. I couldn't cipher out why he was being so cagey all of a sudden. I said "how's that work?"

Vern untied the sack full of chook feathers from his belt and handed it to me. "You'll need this."

"Okay. What do I do with it?"

"First, you scatter the feathers."

I turned the bag upside down and shook it inside out. Feathers went flying. Vern grabbed his head with both hands. "Not all at once!"

"Oh."

"The feathers are meant to get the hornswoggle's attention. You scatter a few here and a few there, like breadcrumbs."

"Oh," I said again, as I pounced on a grounded feather.

"Never mind," he said. "Let it go. Just look around for some good-sized rocks."

Vern spent the next hour drilling me on the finer points of how to run the old what's-in-the-bag trick. You see, what you do is, you get yourself an old gunnysack, and you put a couple of rocks in it. Three or four rocks. Then you walk around like you're going somewhere, but really, you're just walking around. The important thing is, you've got to keep both hands on the sack. You do that because you want to give the impression that whatever's in the sack, it's too important and valuable to be swinging it around with one hand. And every so often, you stop and put the sack down — very carefully, mind you — and you open it up and reach inside and pretend you're checking to make sure all the contents are still there, and nothing is damaged or broken. You count the rocks, and then you rearrange them a little bit, and then you close up the sack and continue on your way.

Hornswoggles are very curious, especially if they think you might be toting around something worth stealing. So if there's a hornswoggle anywhere in the immediate vicinity, it's even odds he'll sneak in for a closer look. He might even try to steal the whole sack. That's why you have to be extra vigilant whenever you take one hand off the sack, like when you put it down to rummage around inside it. Also, if you're carrying it over your shoulder, you have to make sure he doesn't sneak up behind you and cut the bottom out of the sack.

You also have to remember that a slick-fingered hornswoggle could be disguised as anything, so you don't want to set the sack down too close to any rocks or trees or bushes. Basically, the what's-in-the-bag routine is a two-person job — one to carry the sack, and one to keep on the lookout. That's what Vern told me. But somehow, he always got to be lookout, and I was always left holding the bag.

"It's getting heavy," I said, putting the sack down for the millionth time.

"Who are you talking to?" said Vern from behind a tree.

"You."

"I'm not here, remember? You're all alone, out in the woods, and you've got something valuable in a sack, and it would be a terrible shame if somebody were to come along and steal it."

"How do we know the hornswoggle is even out here?"

"That's my job. Your job is to carry the sack."

"Why can't I be lookout for a while?"

Vern abandoned his hiding place and stomped over. "You don't even know what to look for."

"I bet I do," I said. "Furry little guy, wearing my hat."

"Not what I meant," he said. "You have to know how to read the mood of the forest. Look at this tree, for instance: you see how its bark is wrapped even tighter than usual? Classic arboreal defensive posture — same as people do when they know there's a pickpocket lurking about. You've got to pick up on these things if you want to be a lookout."

I glared at Vern. "You look like you just woke up from a nap."

"Nonsense," he said, looking away. "Now listen: we need to work on your bag-holding technique. Try it this way…"

He spent the rest of the morning showing me different ways to hold the sack — telling me sometimes to hold it straight out in front of me, and sometimes to hold it over my head like I was fording a river. Sometimes he'd say the rocks weren't big enough, and we'd stop, and he'd empty out the sack and load me up with bigger ones.

That sack got heavier and heavier, but the hornswoggle remained at liberty.

We hunted into the afternoon, and Vern kept disappearing for longer and longer periods. "You're doing fine," he said, looking more rested with each reappearance. "You just need practice, is all. Tell you what: you keep at it. I'm going to scout the next watershed."

I said "hold on! I thought you said this was a two-person job?"

"It is," he said. "But let's face it: it doesn't matter how good the lookout is, if the sacker doesn't have his technique down pat."

"But you haven't even shown me what to do if a hornswoggle comes."

Vern almost smiled. That surprised me. I didn't think he knew how. He said "we'll cover that in the advanced class. For now, you just keep practicing what you already know."

He wandered off. I bared my teeth at his retreating back. *All this work, and he still didn't think I was ready? I'll show him.* I set the sack down and practiced rummaging through it.

As soon as Vern was out of sight, I dumped out all the big, heavy rocks and replaced them with smaller ones. What did it matter, if it was only practice?

CHAPTER 11:
Larcenous fraudulentus

VERN was gone a long while. My mind wandered. Maybe it went looking for Vern. Anyway, I was rummaging inside the sack for the million, umpteenth time when a voice called out from behind me. It said "hello there!"

Quick as a flash, I whipped around and brought the sack down over the voice's head.

"Ow!" said the voice.

"Hey!" said another voice.

"Ow!" said I, as somebody walloped me over the head with a blunt instrument.

"Let her go!" said the second voice. The walloping continued.

That's when I remembered: hornswoggles can't talk. Also, they don't travel in pairs. Plus, I forgot to take the rocks out of the sack.

"Ow!" I said, trying to fend off my attacker and set my victim free at the same time. "Sorry, I thought — Ow!"

Turned out I'd bagged a young day hiker. She was dressed in improbable colors. Town Side colors: pinks and purples and spotless whites. She looked like it never rained where she came from, and there was never any dust nor dirt to speak of. Apart from the fact that somebody had just thrown a sack full of rocks over her head, she looked brand new.

"Are you okay, Brooke?" said my assailant. She looked brand new as well, only she had a few more sharp edges and dangerous bits about her. Her hair was spiked. Her eyes were hidden in the shadows, like a raccoon's. It never rained where she came from, either. It wouldn't dare.

She carried a pair of binoculars, and her daypack sagged heavily. No doubt it was full of maps and field guides and signal mirrors and emergency first aid kits. The first buds of spring always bring out the sightseers.

She caught me staring and threatened to whack me again with the binoculars. I looked away.

"That hurt!" said Brooke. She whipped off her stylish black leather cap and rubbed the top of her head. "What did you do that for?"

"My apologies," I said. "I thought you were a hornswoggle."

Brooke's friend had no use for apologies or explanations. She said "what kind of a creep tries to throw a bag over someone's head?"

Brooke wasn't ready to forgive and forget, either. "It wasn't just an empty bag, River. There was something in it."

River growled at me. "What was in the bag, creep!"

"Just a couple of rocks, that's all."

"You dumped a bag full of rocks on my friend?"

She advanced a step in my direction, brandishing the binoculars. I backed away. "No, not a whole bag full. Just a few small ones. I forgot they were in there."

Brooke didn't believe me. "You forgot all about them, huh?"

"Yes."

"But you were counting them when I walked up."

"Yeah, well… what I mean is, you startled me. I wasn't expecting anybody to sneak up on me and holler in my ear like that."

Brooke glanced at River. "Did I holler?"

River stepped back warily and threw an arm around Brooke's shoulders. "No. And you didn't sneak, either. You walked right up and said hello." She threw me a scowl. "Even though I told you not to."

"You were right," Brooke admitted. "It was a mistake. He just looked so lost and helpless."

That hurt. "Lost? *Helpless*? Why, I know these hills as sure as I know my own name."

"You're too trusting," said River. Her tone was gruff, though I spose it was meant to be soothing. "You can't just walk up and say hello to everyone you meet. Especially not the kind of weird, creepy old men who lurk in the woods." Her eyes flicked back at me.

"It's Abner, by the way. Abner Serd. And I'm not that old."

"No, just weird and creepy," said River. "What are you doing out here, creep?"

"Hunting."

River looked at Brooke. "Told you he was a creep."

Brooke stood a little taller. "River and I are philosophically opposed to killing wild animals for sport."

I threw my palms out in front of me, same as saying *whoa, slow down*. "Oh, hey, I don't want to kill anything. I just want to get my hat back."

"What hat?"

"Exactly! As you can plainly see, I'm not wearing one. That's because it was stolen from me, and I aim to get it back."

River and Brooke looked at each other. River shook her head. Brooke couldn't help herself. "Stolen by whom?"

"Not by *whom*. By *what*. And the *what* is a devious little critter known as a slick-fingered hornswoggle. *Larcenous fraudulentus*, if you want the scientific name."

Brooke scratched her head. "Did you say Larson's Frog?"

"No. *Larcenous fraudulentus*. Never mind, it's probly an assumed name, anyway. The point is, hornswoggles are the sneakiest creatures on the whole planet. They steal things, and they play tricks, and they're almost impossible to catch, because they can disguise themselves to look like almost anything from a mouse to a marmalade moose. They can even take human shape."

River gave me the fish-eye. "So how do we know you're not one?"

"Well, they can't talk, you see."

"But I talked!" said Brooke. "I said hello, and next thing I knew, you threw a bag of rocks over my head."

"Yeah, sorry about that. I should have taken the rocks out first."

"That's not the point! Why did you think I was a hornswoggle if hornswoggles can't talk?"

"Maybe he thinks you stole his hat," said River.

"I didn't steal your hat!" Brooke flourished her black leather cap at me. I was willing to bet it had never been worn out-of-doors before. There were no sweat stains, and the mice and squirrels hadn't started gnawing on it yet. "This is *my* hat. I bought it three days ago, at That's Hats."

River backed her up. "It's true. I was there."

Brooke lifted her chin defiantly. "I bet it doesn't even fit you."

"Don't let him try it on. He looks like he's got bugs in his hair."

I wasn't listening. I could have sworn I saw something… "Did that boulder just move?"

River looked at Brooke. "He's trying to change the subject."

Brooke nodded. "I bet there isn't any such thing as a hornswoggle." She glanced down at River's hands. "Hey, what did you do with the binoculars?"

"Ow!" said River, as I dumped the remaining rocks onto her foot.

"Sorry!" I dove at the boulder — but I missed. The gray stone skittered away, morphing into a red-handed cheetah as it ran. One of its crimson claws held my hat. The other clutched a pair of binoculars.

"Hey!" said Brooke and River in unison.

Before I could heave myself up off the ground, all three of them galloped over a low ridge and disappeared out of sight, with River and Brooke shouting various exclamations of "stop, thief!" and "tally ho!" and such.

They kicked up quite a racket. As for me, I just followed the sounds of the chase.

Oh, I'm sure I could have easily outrun the lot of them, if I'd wanted to. But hornswoggles are a tricky breed: they can double back on you at any time. They can duck behind a tree and turn themselves into a burl on the other side and cling there until you've scooted on by. And so, for purely strategic reasons, I thought it would be best if one of us lagged a considerable distance behind the other two.

But I've got to give credit where it's due — Brooke and River never let the hornswoggle out of their sight. They worked as a team, not running single file, but spreading out in a two-person skirmish line. Gave them better sight lines. Also kept the varmint from ducking and dodging.

They chased him all the way to Jagged Creek. Never gave him a chance to catch his breath.

By contrast, Brooke and River weren't even breathing hard. Somehow, between the two of them, they'd sucked all the oxygen from the air and kept it for their own personal use. I don't know how they did that. All I know is, I staggered up to the showdown, wheezing like an old, broken bellows.

Jagged Creek was in full flood, on account of all the rain lately. The girls had the hornswoggle pinned against the torrent. By the time I rumbled up, he was trying desperately to assume the form of a great-clawed wunderbear — but he was panting so hard, he couldn't hold the shape. He reared up with every inhale — a towering menace, with eyes like fire and teeth like almighty vengeance. Then on the exhale, he slumped back down to the size of a cowering dog. Over and over again, he bloomed and withered, swelled and shrank like a spring peeper trying to outduel a bullfrog.

Vern was right — hornswoggles just aren't that good at bluffing.

"That's weird," said Brooke.

"Reminds me of the last time I tried to make a soufflé," said River.

"You think he's dangerous?"

Of course he's dangerous! I tried to say. *He's a wild animal cornered!*

I tried to tell them. But due to the lack of oxygen, I just couldn't seem to get the words out.

River said "he doesn't look dangerous. Anyway, there are two of us."

Huh. Only two of you? Well, okay then. I guess you don't need my help. That's fine. If you don't mind, I'll just stand over here and watch.

"It's okay, little fellow," said Brooke. "We're not going to hurt you."

"That's right," said River. "Just give us the binoculars and we'll let you go."

Upon my honor, I could see the hornswoggle laughing behind his disguise. He was up to something — they always are.

"It's okay, little one," cooed Brooke. "You can trust us. We're your friends."

"Yes, and we just need the binoculars back. Okay?"

River edged a little closer. Brooke followed. The hornswoggle grew puppy dog eyes.

"Do you think he knows what we're saying?"

"I think he understands our tone, if nothing else. Just keep talking softly."

The hornswoggle played for time. His panting gradually ceased. He assumed the form of a cute little furry beast that might have been a cross between a lamb and a monkey. Tentatively, he inched forward. I could almost hear him purring.

"Aw, he's so adorable!"

"Don't get emotionally attached, Brooke. At least, not until we get our binoculars back."

"Don't worry, he'll give them back. Won't you, mister fuzzy-wuzzy?"

The hornswoggle nodded shyly. He shuffled forward another half a step… and cautiously offered the binocs. Brooke reached for them.

The hornswoggle sneezed.

Pandemonium ensued.

Startled by the sudden uproarious, full-bodied, spittle-soaked convulsion, the girls jumped. The hornswoggle seemed to be everywhere at once. Even standing off a ways, I found it nigh on impossible to keep track of all his movements. I did, however, feel a plucking sensation in the vicinity of my back pocket.

I let it go. I may not be ready for Vern's advanced bag-wielding lessons, but I know this much: always carry a fake wallet in hornswoggle country.

The little guy skimmed my hat out over the creek, threw the binoculars straight up into the air, and took off downstream, cackling like a hyena with a duck in its mouth.

My hat lost altitude and landed smack dab in the middle of Jagged Creek. River snatched the binoculars just before they hit the ground and crowed triumphantly.

"Ha! Got them!"

"Nice catch," I said.

"Where did he go?" said Brooke.

"You, umm… you let him get away."

River shot me a contemptuous look. "Who cares? As long as we got our binoculars back." She waved them at me, as if to show me what she was talking about.

Brooke jumped in. "And your hat is right over there. See?"

"Yes, I see it. Thanks. By the way, where's yours?"

Brooke felt around the top of her head with both hands. "Hey! Where did my hat go? Did it fall off during the chase?"

"No, it didn't," said River. She pointed an accusing finger at me. "What did you do with it?"

"Me? I've been standing way over here the whole time. Say, I could have sworn you had a backpack. Didn't you?"

River reached an arm behind her back. Nothing there. "My backpack is gone!"

"Oh no!" wailed Brooke. "Did you throw it off at the start of the chase?"

"I don't think so."

"But where could it be, then?"

"Probly about a half-mile downstream by now," I said.

Brooke looked at me like I'd just told her the world was coming to an end, and even though she knew I'd just said something important, she couldn't for the life of her figure out what a "nend" was, nor why the world should be approaching one. She turned to River. "Did you drop it in the water?"

"No, of course not," said River. She looked at me, uncertain for the first time in our brief yet busy acquaintance. "Did I?"

"Nope."

"Then why did you say it's a half-mile downstream?"

"I tried to tell you," I said. "Hornswoggles are a tricky lot. They'll make you think you're getting the better deal, and next thing you know, they're wearing your shirt."

They still didn't get it.

"The sneeze was a diversion," I said. "If I were you, I'd check your pockets as well."

I left them to their inventories and waded out into the creek. Only my hat wasn't where I thought it would be.

I looked downstream. Given the current, I figured it couldn't have drifted more than twenty or thirty yards. Unless it sank.

Puzzled, I sat down on an island of shale. *More sleight of hand? That varmint didn't toss a fake hat into the creek, did he?*

River said "if you're looking for your hat, it's up there."

She pointed upstream. There was my crusty old bush hat, just bobbing along, riding swiftly and mysteriously and inconveniently against the current. I watched it sail further and further away till it disappeared around the bend.

"Huh. I've never seen it do that before."

Brooke gasped. "My necklace is gone! The silver one with the triskelion design."

"Which I told you not to wear out here."

"I know, but it's supposed to be good luck."

"Not so lucky now, is it?"

"It must have fallen off. I can't imagine that cute little furry thing taking it."

I couldn't help myself. I laughed out loud. River glared at me.

"Sorry," I said. "You've got a lot to learn about hornswoggles."

"But why would he take it?" said Brooke. "It's of no use to him."

"Was it shiny?"

"Yes. So?"

"Never mind that," snapped River. "Let's get after him. He can't have gone too far."

For a moment, I thought Brooke was going to ask me to come along. I hated to say no. They were greenhorns. They'd need all the help they could get out here. But they were going downstream, and my hat — against all known physical laws and statutes — was sailing away in the opposite direction. Sometimes a man's got to make a choice.

"Excuse me…" Brooke showed me her most charming smile. "May we borrow your burlap sack?"

INTERLOGUE:

In the Beginning, There Was a Garden

IN the beginning, there was a Garden.

It was a very big Garden — a vast and variegated Garden, spanning fields and forests and lakes and mountains and oceans and continents. Indeed, the Garden covered almost the entire planet.

Beautiful flowers of every shape and color blossomed in the Garden, and their sweet fragrance filled the air. Trees of every height and hardiness stood watch over shady glades, and creatures of every description frolicked and gamboled among them. There were glaciers, and waterfalls, and scorching deserts, and boiling mud. There were jungles and prairies and lush tropical islands, and there were places where the topsoil had been scraped clean down to the bedrock. The Garden contained a life zone and an ecological niche suitable for almost every living thing. But the Garden had no people, for they did not belong.

The Garden was a sculpture… a play… a symphony. The Garden was a living work of art — a dreamscape given form and substance and spirit.

And who made the Garden? Who sculpted the cliffs and the clouds? Who painted the sea and the sky? Whose decision was it to create six hundred species of oak tree (genus *Quercus*), and not name a single one of them *schmercus*?

It was the Old Ones. Well, except for the *Quercus* bit. They didn't have anything to do with that.

The Old Ones made all the world has to offer. They made the sun, the wind, the rain, and the snow. They made scent and sound, taste and texture. They made color. The golden ratio. Gravity. Electromagnetics. Biosynthesis. Life. They made everything we know to be real — and yes, that includes oak trees. But the Old Ones are not responsible for the naming of things. That was people.

People love to name things. It's a bad habit, and it's also rude. Imagine if you had constructed a beautiful landscape, with all the plants and animals working together in perfect harmony, only to have someone else come along and hang a label on everything?

Such outrageous behavior! What next? Alphabetizing all the names? Sorting by type? Collecting metadata? Information warehousing?

The naming of things is one of the reasons people were banished from the Garden. Those who name things will go on naming them until there is nothing left to name — at which point they will conclude they know everything there is to know. Such a path can only lead to trouble.

The Old Ones do not like trouble, by and large. They (mostly) have no use for it. And yet, trouble exists.

Why is that, do you suppose?

CHAPTER 12:
Snagged on a Buck Salmon

I CAUGHT up with Vern about a mile upstream. He was roasting moue-lipped mussels over a small campfire. I said "Vern, where've you been? You missed all the hullabaloo."

"I didn't miss it. You almost caught a day hiker. Not bad for your first day as a sacker."

"Even better than that," I said. "I almost got my hat back. But the hornswoggle threw it into the creek before I could grab it. Did you see it come floating by?"

"No."

"Because it was headed this way, is what I'm saying. You notice anything peculiar about that?"

Vern didn't say anything. He just looked at me like he was standing at the point, waiting for me to get to it.

"You ever heard of a hat floating upstream before?"

"No."

"Why would it do that?"

"Might have got snagged on a buck salmon."

I hadn't thought of that. Buck salmon would be spawning this time of year. If my hat got stuck on a salmon's antlers, it could be halfway to the spawning ground by now. Might even be stuck on the rack permanently, on account of the barbs.

Of course, antlers don't have barbs. But then, the spiky things growing out of a buck salmon's forehead aren't really antlers. Some folks say they resemble straightened-out fishhooks, and that they evolved as a defensive countermeasure against prehistoric fishermen. I don't know about that. All I know is, you don't ever want to catch a buck salmon with your hands.

I've seen what can happen. Once I saw a buck salmon jump an eight-foot waterfall, right under the nose of a giant grizzly bear. The bear couldn't resist — he took a swipe at the fish and got a paw full of salmon spikes for his trouble.

Howling in pain, he reared up and tried to shake the fish loose. That's when lost his footing and tumbled backward into the creek. Last I saw, the salmon was swimming away upstream, towing the poor, struggling grizzly along behind him.

Now, spawning salmon can be quite aggressive, but they aren't known to be carnivorous. What I'm saying is, don't worry about the bear. I'm sure he came to no lasting harm. But I'll bet he never again tried to catch a buck salmon… umm… how shall I say it?

Bear-handed.

Vern said "you still want to go after your hat?"

I said "well, yeah. But it's probly a hundred miles upstream by now."

"Not that far. Not yet, anyway. Give it a few more days."

I glanced at the sky. The clouds were bunching up again. "I hate walking in the rain without a hat."

"You could make one."

"Out of what?"

"You still got that sack?"

I shook my head. "Gave it to the day hikers."

Vern grunted. He'd have done the same — assuming he could have summoned the courage to show himself. Vern's a mite shy around folks he doesn't know.

"Could make one out of grass," he said. "Might take a while, though. Too early in the season."

I tried to imagine what I'd look like wearing a grass hat. "Nah. I'll just pick up a cheap one in town — something to last me till I get my own back."

"Suit yourself."

"Want to come? Your britches are looking pretty raggedy. Maybe it's time you traded up."

Vern didn't even look. "Nothing that can't be repaired."

"When's the last time you came to town, Vern?"

"I visit folks, from time to time."

"I mean to resupply."

Vern took a swig from a plastic water bottle that had seen better days. Then he put his finger through a hole in his shorts where a triangular flap of fabric had torn away. "I've lost my needle and thread."

I let it go. No sense dragging him all the way to town for a sewing kit. "No problem. I'll bring you back something."

He looked relieved. "Much obliged. Meantime, I'll keep scouting upstream for your hat."

CHAPTER 13:
The Mystery of the Stolen Pancake

T HE morning broke cold and drizzly. I hauled some water away from the creek and shivered through a quick sponge bath, but I needn't have dried myself off. By the time I got out of the Wandering Hills, I was soaked through. Praise Blue, I had a clean, dry shirt stashed at the edge of town.

Flora Caprifolia and Rosetta Stone were talking about earthquakes when I walked into Elmer's Café. It was a disjointed conversation. Rosetta, being an expert in global communications, thought there must be hidden messages in the tremors. But Flora's not anything like that. She's a junior vice president of marketing ploys. She couldn't help pondering whether earthquakes could be used to sell products.

"Don't get me wrong," she said. "I'm not saying anybody should make money off a natural disaster. But if there are hidden messages, I'd like to meet whoever sent them. Perhaps we could schedule a small quake to coincide with our fall 'Roll Back Prices' campaign. It doesn't have to be a really powerful one — nothing big enough to cause injuries or property damage. But at the right moment, a tiny tremor could generate a lot of buzz."

Rosetta said "one earthquake alone doesn't convey anything. You have to look at the whole, worldwide pattern of seismic activity in order to get the entire message."

Flora waved her off. "One is all we need. We don't want to oversell it. And we'll provide the message — the quake is just for emphasis."

"What's the product?" I said. "Milk shakes?"

"I'm not speaking to you," said Flora.

I glanced at Elmer. He refused to clue me in. He just gave me a curt nod and said "welcome back."

"Have I done something wrong?"

Flora said "you owe me a pancake. And you owe Elmer for a landfill and a cup of coffee."

I tried to remember what I had for breakfast last time I stopped in at Elmer's.

I do like a good dumpster now and then, but I don't usually order the landfill, on account of my limited financial resources. For the price of a landfill, I could have gotten *two* dumpsters — *and* saved myself the trouble of guessing which mystery meat went into the landfill.

Rosetta said "oh, yeah, I heard about that. It really wasn't all that funny, Abner."

I said "what are you talking about?"

Doc glowered at me over his coffee mug. "You skipped out on the check."

"And stole my pancake on the way out the door," added Flora.

"No I didn't." I looked to Elmer for help. "Did I?"

Elmer said "don't worry about it. I figured you'd be back sooner or later, to settle up."

Whatever had happened, Elmer was being a nice guy about it. But there was a trace of disappointment in the way he looked at me, like I'd taken a practical joke just a little too far. Ironic, coming from a guy who used to drive new customers away by hiding an eerily lifelike plastic eyeball in the bottom of their oatmeal bowls.

Flora said "I was really looking forward to that pancake."

Elmer said "I made you another one."

"That's not the point."

"Wait a minute," I said. "If I inadvertently walked out without paying, then I'm very sorry. But why would I steal Flora's pancake?"

"Beats me," said Elmer. "You were acting pretty strange that day."

Doc snorted. Elmer apparently felt the need to elaborate. "I mean, stranger than usual. You never said a word all morning. You just pointed at the menu board, wolfed down your food, tipped your hat, and disappeared out the door."

The morning sun chose that moment to break through the clouds and come streaming in the plate glass windows. *I tipped my what?*

"When was this?" I asked.

"Couple days ago."

Uh huh. "So you're saying I was in here two days ago, and I tipped my hat before I left?"

"You always were a good tipper."

I dished out a round of dirty looks. *How dare they accuse me of strange behavior?*

"For your information, I've been out on Wild Side for the last..." my brain took a second to count them up... "four days. And if you can remember that far back, you might recall I wasn't wearing a hat when I came in four days ago."

Flora looked confused. She said "but you always wear a hat."

"Do I have one on right now?"

"No..."

Rosetta said "I remember now. You said something about getting it repaired."

"Well, I lied. The truth is, it was stolen."

"So was Flora's pancake," said Doc.

I growled in frustration. *Geez, couldn't these people put two and two together?* "Obviously, whoever stole my hat is the same bandit who came in here two days ago and stole Flora's pancake."

Elmer looked dubious. "How do we know your hat was stolen?"

I stared at him. "You don't believe me?"

"You just said you lied. Now you're asking if I believe you?"

"My hat was stolen right off my head! The day I got chased out of the woods by vicious wild chooks!"

Rosetta and Flora exchanged glances. Doc shifted around in his seat. He said "this ought to be good."

"Oh, come on!" I said. "You know it wasn't me who stole Flora's pancake! When have I ever sat in here for more than five minutes without saying a word?"

"That did seem out of character," admitted Elmer. "'Course, at the time, we had no idea you were busy planning the heist of the century."

I collapsed on my stool. These people were sposed to be my friends. "I bet he didn't even look like me."

"Spitting image," said Flora. "Better posture, though."

Elmer said "is that what it was? I thought maybe he'd grown an inch or two."

"That does it," I said. "I'm getting my hat back, if it's the last thing I do."

Elmer said "you want some breakfast before you go?"

"Yes please, I would like two rocks and a mudslide." That's what Elmer calls biscuits and gravy.

"Coming right up. I hope you don't mind paying in advance."

"Very funny."

Doc said "so tell us all about how you lost your hat while running away from a chicken?"

INTERLOGUE:
The Old Ones

AND who are the Old Ones?

Call Them guardians. Call Them spirits of the Earth and Sky. Call Them the dreamers who made the world. Call Them the essence of everything real.

Call Them anything you want to, for They have no names — which of course means They are called by many names. Define Their responsibilities however you wish, for Their responsibilities are unknowable — which of course means They are praised and/or blamed for just about everything. Such is the life of an immortal supernatural Being.

In Morainia, the people believe in a Sky spirit called The Gray, whose job is to blanket the heavens all day long, thus preventing the sun from burning everything in sight. But in cultures where the cloud cover is more sporadic, that very same Sky spirit is commonly referred to as Old Blue. Like The Gray, Old Blue is a constant, steady presence; He is the sky at rest.[9] Blue is generally regarded as a passive spirit, content to cede His domain to the supernatural forces in command of the sun, the moon, the wind, and the stars. Still and all, the odd pilgrim will occasionally beseech Old Blue to send down some favorable traveling weather.

It won't work, of course. The Old Ones almost never grant such favors. Not anymore, anyway. But no harm in trying.

---

9 Earth and Sky spirits have no gender — and yet, nearly all of Them are referred to as He or She by long-standing convention. These pronouns help to humanize the Old Ones in a way that makes Them ever so slightly less intimidating. Of course, there is one exception… but no. We will get to that One later.

In Regaltown Palace,[10] the First Bard has collected well over a million Cozener tales from around the world. In most traditions, The Cozener (also called The Trickster, or simply Mischief) is the only Earth spirit known to have regular contact with humans. The Cozener loves to play tricks on people and often appears in disguise — sometimes taking the form of a raven, sometimes a fox, and sometimes a hornswoggle. Certain lesser talents have speculated that the First Bard of Regaltown Palace may herself be The Cozener, since anybody who claims to know a million Cozener tales by heart is either lying or has first-hand knowledge.

But most of the Old Ones are never heard from at all, except perhaps in the rarest of circumstances. This is just as well, since the Old Ones are Beings of immense power who do not like to be bothered. It is one thing to say a quick prayer for blue skies. But a reckless demand for a personal audience with Old Blue is likely to bring the sky itself crashing down. Millions of lives would be lost, and civil engineers from all over the world would have to labor for many generations in order to put it back. Investigations would be called for. Fingers would be pointed. Muck would be raked.

Word to the wise, is all.

---

10 Regaltown Palace is in the Kingdom of High Falutin, on the Coast of Gristmas Pass. There are no direct flights to that part of the world. There aren't even any indirect flights. To get there, you must sail for a month of Sundays across the Uphill Sea. It's a long, steep voyage — bring grappling hooks.

CHAPTER 14:

An Irresistible Hook and a Bang-Bang Ending

IT took four drizzly days to track Vern down again. By that time, I'd gone a mite hollow 'round the middle, tell you true. Vern's an expert forager — he can survive indefinitely almost anywhere on Wild Side. Me, I'm lucky to scrounge up a handful of cress for dinner. By the time I found the inukshuk out near Thinker's Dam, my legs were getting wobbly and my head felt like dandelion fluff.

The little stone figure stood on a ledge where the tumbling waters of Jagged Creek couldn't reach it. It pointed up in the direction of the Mulls. Grousing like a goosed jay, I filled my canteen and started uphill.

The Graymatters aren't the world's tallest mountains, but they're all scrunched up and creased and folded like somebody tried to shove them into place. Climbing them is a bit of work. Time and again I crested a ridge, only to find yet another gorge between me and the next peak.

Several million lumbering footsteps later, I finally caught up to Vern. He was sitting cross-legged under a ponderwood tree. His eyes were closed. He said "I found another symbol."

"Good for you."

Vern opened his eyes. "Something wrong?"

I plopped my tired bones down on an opiñon pine stump and shrugged off my pack. "You could have met me down by the creek. What'd you drag me up here for? And where's my hat?"

"Vanished. Did you see that buck salmon? In the pool right below the inukshuk."

"No."

"Huge rack. Pink stripe. Charged me when I caught one of the does. I don't know how you could have missed him."

"I wasn't looking for salmon," I said. "I was looking for you."

He smiled unapologetically. "Well, you found me. Come on, I'll show you the symbol."

"Hang on, there! What do you mean, my hat vanished?"

"No sign of it. My guess is, that big buck had it, but he got rid of it somehow."

"So you lost the trail."

Okay, that line came out a lot sharper and more pointed than you normally hear in polite discourse between friends. But Vern showed a surprising knack for letting the edgy bit fly by and launching a counterstrike at the heart of the problem instead.

"It happens," he said. "You hungry?"

It wasn't the best smoked salmon I've ever had. The meat tasted all worn out, and there were too many bones. Still, I could feel my sharp edges growing duller as I scraped the last bits of flesh off the blackened skin. "So that's the end of it, then," I said. "Just like that, it's over."

Vern said "for now. We can catch another one tomorrow."

"Not the fish. My hat."

"I thought you were getting a new one?"

"I don't need a new hat. I need a new story. Something in the action-adventure genre, with an irresistible hook and a bang-bang ending."

"I don't know any stories."

Vern knows thousands of stories. He just doesn't know how to tell them. And he doesn't mind if I tell them, which is one of the reasons I let him drag me Hitherin yawn searching for uncommon beasts and botanical rarities.[11]

"You know what could have done the job?" I said. "The Tale of the Stolen Hat. Now, that one had potential: vicious wild chooks flying every which where! Five-legged catawampuses charging about like avalanches with claws! Slick-fingered hornswoggles roaming the countryside, misappropriating headgear and stealing pancakes. But then what? *Then the hat simply vanishes without a trace.* What kind of an ending is that?"

"It's got an air of mystery to it."

"Nobody likes mysteries. Especially unsolved mysteries. What can you give me in the way of a resolution?"

Vern said "it's just a hat, Abner. Things like that come and go."

"That old hat was full of stories," I said. "It's the same hat I wore when my friend Jimmy Fingerbutton accidentally sent me back in time."

"And you got into an argument with your past self, and you punched yourself in the face. You told me that one before, too."

"He punched *me*," I said. "All I was trying to do is follow in his footsteps, so as not to change history."

"The way he told it, you kept getting underfoot."

"I don't know why you always take his side."

Vern stood up. "Well… good luck finding your hat, Abner. I wish I could give you more to go on."

"Where you going?"

---

11 Hither is a remote southern province on the Somniak frontier. The locals are famous for their siestas, which often begin right after breakfast and generally last until bedtime. These legendary naps are usually preceded by a crocodile-style unhinging of the jaw and a full-throated bellow that sounds like a hippopoceros in pain.* To the uninitiated traveler observing this ritual for the first time, it can be a frightening experience. Indeed, the Hitherin's jaws are separated by such a great distance that the term "Hitherin yawn" has become a synonym for far-flung destinations.

   * A hippopoceros is a cross between a hippopotamus and a rhinoceros. Sadly, every time a hippopoceros opens wide, it pokes itself in the back with its own horn. This is very painful; hence, the bellow.

He started walking uphill. "Going to take another look at that symbol."

He was almost out of sight by the time I unfolded myself and got to my feet. "Wait up," I said, and lumbered after him.

Just above the furrowed brow of the Graymatter mountains is a spidery network of trails called the Mulls. They are a popular hiking destination, even though the Graymatters are miles off the Yonder Track. Something about how the footpaths wind back and forth around the Pate in apparently random patterns, one trail leading to another, seems to give certain philosophically-minded folks the impetus they need to reach beyond the clutter of everyday thought processes. Many a theorist, after spending days wandering through the Mulls, has returned home with a most extraordinary hypothesis all fleshed out and ripe for testing.

I can understand the attraction. It sure beats a month of hard labor down in the idea mines.

We ignored the trails and climbed straight up to a flat shoulder about two hundred feet below the Pate. Then we pushed through a bulwark of nogginberry branches. Nogginberry thickets can be a hundred yards wide, but the whole patch is really just a single bush. New shoots come up every year in an ever-expanding outer ring, while the old growth at the center withers and dies, leaving a secret, well-hidden clearing in the middle. Usually, the dense outer ring discourages most folks from ever finding it. Vern must have seen something that drew him in.

At the center of the clearing, five sparrow-sized chunks of feldspar marked a familiar pattern. But this time, the placement was off: the striding figure's back leg was far too long, and the trailing arm swung back at an unnatural angle.

I said "it looks out of kilter."

Vern nodded. "I reckon it wasn't meant to last forever. The stones were probably kicked loose by a deer or a betchacant."

"How old is it?"

"At least three winters. Probably no more than ten."

I said "so, now we've got two symbols in two different places — three, if you count the one Rosetta found. Question is, what do the locations have in common?"

"Nice views."

The nogginberry bush was ten feet high. We'd have to stand on each other's shoulders to see past the thick green leaves and waxy red limbs — but Vern's eyes weren't on the horizon. He was looking at the sky.

I said "have you been up to the Pate?"

"Covered in ponderwood. Can't see the stars from up there."

I looked around. Somebody had cleared the deadwood from a patch of ground just big enough to lie down in. "You spent the night here, didn't you?"

Vern nodded.

"See anything?"

He frowned. "Seed moon's about full. Clouds broke up a little after midnight."

"You saw Pedestrio?"

"I saw the constellation."

"Any sign of the barefooted stranger?"

Vern shook his head. He started pacing the clearing.

"You still reckon he's the one who's making these symbols?"

Vern didn't hear me. He was too far lost in thoughts of his own. When he finally spoke, he wasn't really talking to me — though it didn't stop me from talking back.

"What if he's real?" he said.

"Who?"

"It was just a story I once heard. But what if it's true?"

"You mean the one about Pedestrio?"

He gestured at the rocks with an upturned palm. "You know, I've probably seen this pattern hundreds of times without ever noticing it. I mean, it's just a few stones, right? Not worth a second look. But it all fits together: the footprint in the swaddle. This symbol. The constellation."

"Don't forget the hornswoggle."

"If he's real, I've got to meet him. He can't be real. But if he is… imagine walking the Earth for a million years. Imagine knowing the ground that well. No wonder he doesn't leave a trace."

"Maybe he's got some kind of swaddle repellent." I winked at Vern. Not that he noticed.

"This symbol could be the only way to track him. But how often does he make it?"

"Whenever he's bored, is my guess."

"What?"

"I'm just saying, maybe he likes to doodle with rocks."

Finally, the fever broke. Vern left his thoughts behind and turned his attention to me. "What are you talking about?"

"I'm saying, if you want to know more about the symbol, we should talk to Rosetta. She's studied it. She can tell us all the places she's seen it — and she might even know something about whoever made it."

Now, I don't know if I mentioned this or not… but Vern's not comfortable around people he doesn't know. I could see him rassling with himself: was it better to make the trip into town and get it over with, or spend the next ten years trying to solve the mystery all on his own?

"All right," he said, fingering the rip in his shorts. "Then let's go Town Side."

CHAPTER 15:
The Bat Signal

WE took the Yonder Track back to town. It's faster than going cross-country, especially if you're not poking around in a futile search for vanished articles of clothing. Even so, Town Side is a long day's march from the Graymatters.

My cache at the Yonder end of town had two shirts in it — both dirtier than the one I had on. My little cake of soap had worn so thin, it barely qualified as film. We freshened up as best we could, but… well, let's just say we didn't need a bloodhound to tell us everything was in odor.

Vern hung back. In Town Side adventures, he was content to let me take the lead.

It was evening by the time we got to Rosetta's house. Rosetta lives in a small stone cottage out by the college. The house is hidden away behind great blooming mountains of lilac and honeysuckle. I was hoping the sweet bouquet of uninhibited efflorescence would help to mask our own whiffy presence — but it was way too early in the season. The flowers had not yet come into bloom.

Rosetta answered the door and immediately wrinkled her nose. I hoped I hadn't overestimated her charity.

I said "hi Rosetta! Can we use your shower?"

Rosetta's the kind of person who likes to bring her work home with her. Every bookshelf, table, and countertop is piled high with precarious stacks of research materials and geological specimens, all of which allegedly confirm her theory that the Earth itself is trying to talk to us. She dug a couple of kitchen chairs out from underneath a rolling sea of paperwork and set them up near her desk. I sat on one while Rosetta leaned back in her swivel chair. Vern hadn't come out of the shower yet.

"So let me get this straight," she said. "You and your disheveled friend saw somebody walking barefoot out in the woods, and you think that person is responsible for making the bat signal?"

"Yes and no," I said. "Or, rather, no and yes. We never saw the guy, but we cut his sign and tracked him to a fresh signal we found on Mount Exile."

"And you think that same individual is traveling all about the countryside, making bat signals everywhere she goes?"

"Hang on," I said. "You keep calling it a bat signal. Are we talking about the same thing?"

From the tidewrack of odds and ends washed up on the shore of her desktop, Rosetta grabbed a piece of lightning glass, a weathered stone, a knot of wood, a dragon's tear, and a pine cone with a pronounced spiral twist. She pushed everything else to one side and arranged the five items like so:

She said "is that what you saw?"

"Yep, that's it. Vern said it looks like a constellation."

"It is a constellation. It's called the Bat. You see how the right wing is banked higher? That's because it's just about to swoop off to one side — as bats have been known to do."

"Vern called it Pedestrio, on account of it looks like a man walking."

Rosetta frowned at the desktop arrangement. "I don't see that at all. I see a bat."

I glanced in the direction of Rosetta's bathroom. *What's taking him so long?* "Well, whatever. We agree that somebody's been tromping around making rock patterns in the shape of a constellation, right?"

"No."

No? "But you just said —"

"I agree the bat signal is in the shape of a constellation. Your premise that some barefooted stranger is responsible for its creation is unfounded."

"But we tracked him right to it."

"And where is your evidence?"

"It's in the shower."

Rosetta raised her eyebrows. "Your evidence is in the shower?"

"Well, Vern is. He's the evidence. I mean, he did the tracking."

Rosetta gave me the kind of look you give the guy who hired the guide who led you into a box canyon. She took a deep breath and tried a different route. "And what are your friend's qualifications? Where did he go to school? How many degrees does he hold?"

"You might say he's a graduate of the Wild Side Academy of Natural History, and as far as I know, he's got 98.6 degrees."

"So he has no formal training in the scientific method?"

Confidentially, I wasn't sure what she meant by the "scientific method." I tried to picture Vern in a white lab coat and goggles, hovering over a neat row of test tubes and writing things down on a clipboard. "I don't know how formal it is," I said. "But he's got a lot of field training."

"Thought so." Rosetta swept the bat aside and leaned forward. "Abner, I like you. You're irresponsible and ill-informed and you don't make sense half the time, but you're harmless. So don't take this the wrong way — it's nothing personal. Your friend is misguided at best."

I didn't know what to say, so I said "… huh."

"At worst, he's toying with geo-ontological forces he couldn't possibly understand."

I decided to clarify my previous remarks. "I mean… huh."

"The bat signal out at Nothing Flat is a million years old. Nobody alive could have made that signal. I don't know what your friend thinks he's doing, but you should know that it's dangerous to attempt to reproduce or to amplify a terralinguistic message — especially if you don't understand what it means."

It took me a second to unwrap that passel of words. "Now, hold on," I said. "Vern couldn't have made the symbol on Mount Exile, on account of I was there when we found it."

"He led you to it, didn't he?"

"Well, yeah — "

"And you never saw the person who made it, did you?"

"Well, no — "

Rosetta sat back and folded her arms. She said "I've been doing this for a long time, Abner. I've investigated all kinds of phony signals. Not all of them were maliciously fraudulent — some were created by well-meaning individuals having nothing but the best of intentions. But a true signal can only be created by the Earth itself — or a physical manifestation embodying some aspect of the Earth's spirit. My advice is, until you know more, you should remain skeptical."

I thought about that. Then I jumped into the weeds. "But Vern couldn't have made that symbol, because that would mean he's the one who made the footprint down by Crikey Creek. Otherwise, we'd have had no reason to climb Mount Exile."

"Did you see the footprint?"

"Well, no. But it was a very faint impression, and you'd have to be a really experienced tracker to spot it."

"So says your friend."

The weeds were getting taller. *It was Vern's idea to go into the swaddle in the first place. It was Vern who led us right where the catawampus wanted us. Maybe Vern stole my hat!*

But then… if Vern made that footprint, then he's really only chasing himself.

I said "I don't think Vern wants to see phony signals, either. That would only muddy the track."

Rosetta squinched her eyebrows. "What track?"

"I mean, you both want to preserve the evidence, but for different reasons. To you, the bat pattern is a signal — a message. You want to know what it says. But Vern, on the other hand — Vern is more interested in what it can tell him about the person who made it."

"Your barefoot stranger."

"Exactly."

"And what if your barefoot stranger turns out to be a fraud?"

I put on my best shire reeve persona, tipping an imaginary hat and hooking my thumbs behind an imaginary pair of suspenders. "In that case, ma'am, we'll find him and bring him to justice."

"You're a goof."

Right on cue, Vern came out of the bathroom, trailing a puddle of water behind him. He'd showered in his clothes. They probly needed it worse than he did.

Rosetta jumped to her feet. "What are you *doing!*"

Vern froze. Rosetta advanced on him. "You're getting water all over my floors!"

He looked down. "Oh. Sorry."

"Get back in the bathroom!"

Vern did as he was told and shut the door. Rosetta fixed me with a look that hovered somewhere between anger and disbelief. "What was that all about?!"

"Sorry about that," I said. "I thought Vern was housebroken."

"What is he, an idiot?"

"No, he's just more at home out in the Wild than he is here in town."

"That doesn't explain why his clothes are soaking wet!"

I tried to explain. "All I can say is, he was nervous about meeting you. He didn't want to come tonight, because he didn't have any clean clothes to wear."

"Maybe you should have taken him to a laundromat first."

"Maybe I should have," I said — silently calculating how many coins a trip to the laundromat would take, then mentally adding up the coins in my pocket and wishing we'd done a rinse and wring before we left Jagged Creek.

She said "well, go in there and tell him to wrap his clothes in a towel and hand them out to me. I'll throw them in the dryer."

"Thanks, Rosie. Um… while we're at it, do you spose we could run my clothes through the laundry, as well?"

INTERLOGUE:
The King of Jagged Creek

AT the base of the Graymatter Mountains, not far from the headwaters of Jagged Creek, a slick-fingered hornswoggle crouches in a catclaw tree and watches a buck salmon toss his rack.

The salmon is magnificent — long and strong, as they say, with a flashy pink stripe running from gills to tail. He is the King of Jagged Creek, handsome and virile enough to attract an entire school of potential spawning partners — so he is understandably upset to reach this deep pool, only to find himself crowned with the most ridiculous-looking hat in fishdom.

The King leaps and thrashes. He spins. He dives. He stands on his tail. He swims backward. But try as he might, he cannot dislodge the hat.

The hornswoggle watches all this with rapt attention. An astute observer might come to the conclusion she is rather amused by the salmon's struggles. And indeed She is, for She is no ordinary hornswoggle.

The morning sun climbs higher. Shadows recede. The surface of the pool sparkles.

The other salmon are catching up. The King can sense them downstream, pushing and fighting their way through the rapids just below the bend. There are females among them — good, strong females. The King gathers himself. Now or never. Do or die. Fish or cut… no, sorry — wrong idiom.

The surface of the pool explodes. The King shoots out of the water and into the thin mountain air. For one glorious moment at the absolute pinnacle of his mighty leap, the King becomes a superstar, soaring higher than any uncaught salmon has ever leaped.

It isn't quite high enough. The hat doesn't fly off—it remains firmly fixed on the King's rack. But just as the King turns to begin his downward plummet, the Hornswoggle reaches out a slender paw and pushes down on an overhanging catclaw branch.

A catclaw thorn hooks the hat. The branch bends. A single thread in the crown of the hat gives way, and that's enough. The branch snaps back. The hat sails into the air and lands on the gravel bank. And the King, yanked backward by the unexpected arrest of his momentum, executes a perfect triple backflip before hitting the pool headfirst with nary a splash.

It is an extraordinary feat, unmatched in the history of salmon-kind. And none of the King's schoolmates are there to see it. They are still struggling through the rapids. No one will ever know. But the King doesn't mind — no, not a-tall. Truth to tell, the amazing stunt has left him feeling a bit queasy. He is grateful for a few quiet moments alone to catch his cool.

Well! thinks the Hornswoggle who is no ordinary hornswoggle. *That was fun. What game shall we play next?*

CHAPTER 16:
A Pocketful of Obstinite

ROSETTA made it plain she didn't have any room to put us up, and it was true: what with all the stacks of books and papers, even just blazing a trail from the front door to the kitchen felt like pushing your way through a crowd of one-legged porters, each one carrying a basket of eggs on his head. The slightest jostle from an errant elbow might scramble the lot.

So we spent the night in the greenhouse out behind the School of Agriculture.

It's not an ideal location for an overnight stay, on account of farmers and agricultural students tend to be up and about rather early in the morning. Plus, you can't see the stars. All that being said, the greenhouse had a warm, cozy, earthy kind of atmosphere, and I reckoned we were both too clean to sleep out-of-doors — I mean, seeing as how we'd showered off all the layers of dirt and mud and dried sweat we'd been using for insulation.

I woke up to find Vern munching on lettuce leaves from one of the starter beds. I said "hey! No! Bad Vern!"

He looked up in surprise. "What?"

"Don't eat those!"

He looked down. "Why not? They're not poisonous." He looked up again, as if suddenly realizing he was Town Side now, where all the rules are different. "Are they?"

"Never mind. Let's get out of here before somebody comes."

We vacated the premises not long after first light. The streets were quiet, except for a handful of brightly attired folks who appeared to be running in random directions at a fairly leisurely pace for no apparent reason. I kept a wary eye on them, in case they formed themselves into a posse of angry agronomists, but they showed no interest in us.

"So, what's next?" I said.

He'd gone quiet following the debacle at Rosetta's place — that is to say, quieter than usual. But this morning he didn't seem any the worse for it. I took that as a sign he'd decided to give up his pursuit of information related to the barefoot stranger. Turned out I was wrong.

"Reckon I'll head for the library," he said. "Then out to Nothing Flat."

"To see Rosetta's bat signal?"

"It's not a bat," he said. "It's Pedestrio."

"Library won't be open for a few hours yet."

"That's okay. I've got an errand to run first."

"Yeah, sorry about that," I said. "I meant to buy you that sewing kit, but my cash flow ran into a logjam."

"No worries. Time I traded out, anyway."

"Good on ya," I said. Vern's usually down to skin and patches before he splurges on a new outfit. "You got money?"

"Should have, soon enough."

"Enough to buy us breakfast?"

I'd been steering us in the direction of Elmer's Café, in hopes Elmer would front us a pancake or two on credit.

"I'm really not that hungry," he said.

"You shouldn't have been grazing, back at the greenhouse."

"They won't mind. They'll probably think it was grasshoppers."

"Yeah, right. A plague of grasshoppers appeared overnight and ate all the lettuce. How do you spose they got in?"

"Well, it's not like the place is vacuum-sealed."

"It will be now," I said. "They might even put a lock on the door. Thanks for tipping them off to that vulnerability, by the way."

But Vern wasn't there anymore. He'd taken an abrupt right turn down a side street. I hustled to catch up with him.

I said "do you know where you're going?"

"Think so."

He led us away from downtown, through a neighborhood where the houses looked about as long-suffering as a boulder covered in dry-leaf.[12] We hopped a fence, then cut across a narrow sliver of Wild Side on the edge of the barrens — a lonely neighborhood of idle factories and forgotten warehouses.

Vern doesn't get lost. But I had to wonder if there might be some kind of Town Side airborne static interfering with his sense of direction.

Finally, we stopped at a low tin building that seemed undecided about whether to walk away or stay put. It was leaning in the direction of option number one, but something kept holding it back. Cold feet, perhaps. A clanging noise came from inside the building, and a metallic tang hovered in the air.

Vern pushed a buzzer. The clanging stopped. Then started again. Vern pushed the buzzer again. The clanging ended in a clatter, like iron tools being dropped into a tin bucket. Muffled sounds of movement came from behind the door. Somebody hawked and spat. The door opened a crack.

Then it closed again.

It stayed closed. Vern sort of nodded to himself, turned to me, and said "it might be best if you waited over there."

He pointed at nothing at all, unless he meant for me to stand on the horizon and wait for the sun to come up and burn my backside. I said "over where?"

"Just out of sight somewhere. She's not really a people person. I'll be out in a few minutes."

He might as well have reached out and put a cap on my glottal stop. *Not really a people person? Coming from Vern?? She's gotta be shier than a turtle raised by ostriches.* I pumped my jaw for a second, but the well was dry — not a single drop of sound came

---

12 Dry-leaf is a kind of lichen that's brown and peels away at the edges — like very old paper placed too near the fire and come away scorched, but not charred. To put it in boring old Town Side terms, the houses all looked as if they needed new paint jobs.

out. Finally, I turned and faded into the background. Behind me, I heard Vern rap a knuckle lightly against the tin door. When I looked around, he was gone.

I loitered a while, got bored, and sank into a cross-legged sitting position.

I may have dozed off.

Then I heard footsteps, and Vern's voice a few yards out, saying "okay, we're all set."

I pretended I was meditating. Without opening my eyes, I said "what was that all about?"

"Just cashing in some tender," he said.

So much for meditation. I cracked an eyelid and squinted at Vern. "What sort of tender?"

"Bit of obstinite."

Whoa. "How'd you get that?"

"Dug it up a while back."

"Just like that, huh?"

Obstinite is a common mineral, but its unyielding nature makes it very difficult to pull out of the ground, and even more difficult to work with. I've heard tell of miners who tried blasting their way into an obstinite deposit. Raised up a dust cloud a mile high. Next day it rained miners.

Vern shrugged. "You just need to have the right touch, is all."

I stood up and dusted off my backside. "What'd you trade it for?"

"Cash. He needed the obstinite, and he didn't have anything else to trade."

"He?"

"That's right."

"A minute ago, you said she."

Vern looked uncomfortable. "It's complicated. Anyway, it's not important. Point is, she's an alchemist."

"Ah."

Vern seemed to be laboring under the misapprehension that I was missing something — when, in point of fact, I was missing almost everything. He switched pronouns again. "They use obstinite to make bendable steel."

"That sounds… counterintuitive," I said.

"That's because you've never studied ironics."

"As you say." I favored Vern with a slight bow, same as saying *the field is yours. The game is out of reach. Alas, to think that I should be driven from the battleground by a cruel twist from such a familiar weapon! There's gotta be a word for that…*

Vern turned his gaze eastward. It would be at least an hour yet before we saw the sun. "What time do the stores open?"

"Oh, ages from now."

"Good. Then we've got time to forage. I thought I saw some wild mushrooms back there…" He started heading back to the sliver of meadow we'd just come through. I grabbed his arm.

"Great idea," I said. "I know just the place. Follow me."

Vern caught on pretty quick. He dragged his heels. He fussed and fretted. He insisted he couldn't eat store-bought food. You'd think I was dragging him to the dentist instead of breakfast.

I said "look: we've got at least two hours to while. We might as well while them away down at Elmer's."

"You walked right past the chicory."

"Love chicory. Love coffee even more."

"Shouldn't we save our money for the outfitters?"

"You worry about the necessaries. I'll handle the things that give life joy and meaning. Like coffee. Good morning, sir!" I said to a burly man in a plaid shirt. "May I spin you a yarn guaranteed to amuse and enlighten…"

The man filed by without so much as a sideways glance. I said "have a nice day, sir. Thank you for your time."

Vern said "cut it out."

"I'm just trying to drum up some business, is all."

"You're bothering people."

"Hey, I didn't stop you from doing business with your alchemist friend. Just give me a chance to rustle up a few coins… Good morning, ma'am! Shall I tell you a poem? I have a sale on mismatched limericks, chock-a-block with unrhymable words…"

The woman stomped by, still talking on her phone. "You tell him I'll break his fingers if he tries that again. No. You know what? He doesn't get a second chance. I'm heading over there right now…"

I watched her go. Three of four gangly, overgrown urchins rounded the corner a block away. When they saw the woman barreling toward them, they crossed the street. "On second thought," I said, "this isn't the best neighborhood for busking. Downtown is better."

I headed toward Main Street. Vern tried to make a break for it. I cut him off. "You want to know about Pedestrio, don't you? Well, Elmer's Café is a great place to gather information. All I need is enough money for a cup of coffee."

"Here." He fished a couple of bills out of his pocket and pushed them at me. "Go have coffee. I'll meet you on the way out to Nothing Flat."

I pushed the bills away. "Come on, Vern. You know there were stories in that warehouse that I'll never get to hear, let alone tell. But I waited outside because you asked me to. If I can do that, you can come inside and have a cup of coffee with me."

"I don't like coffee."

"Breakfast, then. Take a little more scrounging, but I can manage. Hello, kind soul! May I interest you in a salad of chopped plots and shredded themes?"

"Stop," said Vern, squaring his shoulders. "Okay, fine. I'll buy you breakfast."

"That's really not necessary. Just give me an hour to busk up some change."

"Please," he said. "I insist."

CHAPTER 17:

What Does a Whispering Moonboggle Say Before It Eats You?

THE café wasn't officially open yet. But the door was unlocked, and Elmer doesn't mind if you pop in early to watch him prep. He was just taking four loaves of bread out of the oven when we got there. Elmer makes good bread. Cuts the slices nice and thick. I think he gets about four slices per loaf.

Elmer looked me in the eye and said "this is the moment I've breaded."

I said "quit loafing around."

He said "are you trying to get a rise out of me?"

I said "that's the yeast of your problems."

You can tell when somebody's never been to Elmer's Café before. Vern looked about ready to turn and run. He leaned in close and whispered "what are you guys talking about?"

"Nothing," I said. "Just playing tennis, that's all."

Elmer set a pot of coffee to brewing. "Did you ever get your hat back?"

I shook my head. "I decided to send it on a world tour. It was getting restless. You know how it is when the daily routine gets to be old hat. So I told it to go, have fun, meet some new people…"

"In other words, you passed the hat."

"I just hope it comes back full."

Now, there's one thing I forgot to mention to Vern…

No, sorry — let me try that again. I didn't forget. I purposely didn't mention it, on account of Vern gets all shades of quiet when other people are around. He's shy, but that's only part of it.

You see, Vern doesn't spend a lot of time in town, so when he does get to be around people, he doesn't know what to talk about. He has no common frame of reference when it comes to small talk, even if it's about something as mundane as the weather. He doesn't understand when Town Siders complain about how cold it got last night, or how they should have brought an umbrella this morning. He knows what they mean: they mean it was so cold, they almost had to turn the thermostat up another notch or two. They mean there's an ever-so-slight possibility that a few raindrops might land on them as they sprint from one building to the next.

He knows all that. It's just not part of his reality.

To Vern, cold is when you wake up with ice in your beard and your fingers won't work. You don't have an extra blanket to throw over yourself, and even if you were capable of moving your digits, there is no kindling dry enough to build a fire, and so you get up and stamp around for an hour or two. You jump up and down. You go for a walk. You do whatever you need to do in order to fire up your internal furnace. As for rain… well, rain is unavoidable, so why would anybody try to hide from it? Unless it's a really violent thunderstorm, or one of those cold, heavy, early spring downpours that leaves you shivering with hypothermia. Anything less than that is hardly worth a mention.

So Vern sometimes prefers to keep his thoughts to himself in the company of other people. But the thing I neglected to tell him is… at Elmer's Café, keeping your thoughts to yourself really isn't an option.

It's a small place — meaning there's nowhere to hide. You can't sit quietly in a corner, pretending nobody can see you. There aren't any quiet corners. You can't be a spectator at Elmer's Café. You've got to participate.

The good news is, there is no such thing as mundane small talk at Elmer's Café. If Vern found himself dragged into a conversation about the weather, and told everybody about the time he got caught in a horizontal thunderstorm, they'd likely take it in stride.[13] If not, I figured I could help him out by pushing the topic into safer territory.

I didn't tell Vern any of that, on account of I didn't want him to get nervous. I didn't want him to overthink the ebb and flow of logic that governs most conversations down at Elmer's Café. Sometimes it's better just to ride with the current. But Vern, he surprised me. He blurted out "do you know anybody who doodles with rocks?"

Vern does not lack subtlety. But sometimes he forgets where he put it.

Elmer said "I knew a caveman once. But that was a long time ago."

"Was he barefoot?"

Not the follow-up question I would have chosen. But Vern must have decided I'd handled the Rosetta Stone interview all wrong, and he was determined to reverse that trend.

Elmer thought about it as he lifted the lid off a pot and gave the contents a stir. The thick aroma of sausage gravy wafted in my direction. I practically drooled on the countertop. "I wouldn't call them bare," he said. "Furry, is more like it. At first glance, you'd think he had socks on."

I said "socks?"

"You know, the kind with toes."

Vern broke in impatiently. The words tumbled out of him like a flash flood ripping through an arroyo. He said "we're looking

---

13 True story: this one time, the wind blew so hard, even the lightning got blown sideways. Raindrops never got a chance to land, and the ground stayed dry as a bone. When the sun finally went down, the wind stopped so suddenly the rain just hung there in midair, like it forgot what it was doing. Hung there a good three or four seconds, until somebody turned the gravity back on, and the whole storm fell out of the sky at once. Made an ankle-deep puddle, stretching as far as the eye could see...

for a man who can walk without leaving a trace, almost. He probably spends a lot of time outdoors, and he's barefoot, and he likes to make the sign of Pedestrio as he watches the sun go down."

Elmer said "well, that puts my caveman out of the mix. He had an aversion to sunsets. Kept howling and jumping up and down like the world was on fire."

I felt a blast of cool air, and a voice behind me said "is it?"

I turned to see Stanley standing in the doorway. "Is it what?"

"On fire," he said, taking off his jacket. "If so, I need a new coat."

Vern clammed up. Stanley's entrance had rattled him. I got the impression he'd been trying to get his interview with Elmer all wrapped up before anybody else came in.

I said to Stanley, I said "what kind of coat would you get for a world-on-fire event?"

Elmer took the question instead. "I'd get me a coat of arms, and form my own bucket brigade."

Stanley said "I'd rather have a coat of legs. Then if the flames got close, I could run away."

The regulars were beginning to drift in. Flora nodded and smiled at everybody, then grabbed a seat down near the grill.

Elmer set a mug down in front of Flora and reached for the coffee pot. "'Course, if you had a coat of paint, you could just paint over the fire."

"Or a turncoat," said Stanley. "If I had a turncoat, I could turn off the flames."

"No, you couldn't," said Flora. "You'd only get roasted evenly on all sides."

I stole a glance at Vern. He kept looking from Elmer to Stanley to Flora and back again, the way a dying man tracks a trio of buzzards circling overhead.

He wanted to bolt. He wanted to get back to safer ground. But he'd come this far, and I could tell the moment he decided he had to see it through. He said "has anybody seen a barefoot stranger?"

"Ah," said Stanley. "Now, feet are another matter. If the world were on fire, I definitely wouldn't want to be caught barefoot."

Elmer said "why is that?"

"Because shoes attract shoe flies. If I can round up enough shoe flies, I figure they can fly me out of there."

"I think there's been a mistake," said Vern. "We were talking about a man who walks barefoot through the wilderness. It's possible he can talk to plants. There's no fire involved."

Stanley shrugged, without moving his shoulders. He did it by raising his eyebrows, pursing his lips, and tilting his head slightly to one side. Whatever the topic had been before his entrance, it wasn't his concern. To Elmer, he said "give me two rocks and a mudslide, when you get a chance."

"With you in a minute," said Elmer. He removed the counter cutout, stepped through the gap, and flipped the sign on the door from Closed to Open. Then he stepped back behind the counter, grabbed the coffee pot, and worked his way down the counter with it. When he got to Vern, he gestured with the pot.

"Babadee zoom, gadabing?"

Vern looked at me. I said "he wants to know if you want some coffee."

Vern said "what language is that?"

I waved Elmer away, telling him "neh bada zoom, gadabing." To Vern, I said "forget about the words. The words are irrelevant. You have to read the gesture."

"But what was he saying?"

"Out loud? Nothing."

"He said something. I heard him."

"What does a whispering moonboggle say before it eats you?"

Vern opened his mouth, then closed it again as he thought that one over. As everybody knows, whispering moonboggles don't say anything at all — they just go "psst!" to get your attention. Then they make a series of meaningless, breathy, low-pitched sounds while they gobble you down.

"Tell you what," I said. "Let me see if I can bring the conversation back around."

Elmer had wandered down to the other end of the counter. He started telling Stanley and Flora this unlikely story about a pear-shaped egg. I bided my time.

There is a strategy involved in steering a conversation at Elmer's. You can do it, but you have to be patient. You can't just come straight out with a list of questions. First, you have to wait your turn. You have to let the current topic run its course. Then you have to get the crowd's attention.

You start by spinning a little yarn. You add just enough color to get people interested, and you wrap it all up into a little ball. But you don't wrap it too tightly — you want a few loose ends poking out. The more loose ends you have, the more likely some other spinner will move to tie a bit of their own yarn onto yours.

Then you roll out your little ball of yarn, with the loose ends dangling and the bits of color flashing, and you hope it turns somebody's head. If one person takes a swipe at it, then it's good odds another person will take a swipe, until pretty soon the whole crew is batting it around.

So I waited until Elmer wound up his unlikely tale with a conclusion so ludicrous, you could almost hear the jaws dropping onto the counter.[14] Then I jumped in.

I said to Vern, I said "you know, I think I might have actually seen somebody like your barefoot stranger once. Out by the Bored Rock. He was too far away to tell if he was barefoot or not. But he sure didn't act like any tenderfoot I've ever seen."

I had to kick Vern's ankle to keep him from interrupting. Couldn't he see this ball of yarn wasn't meant for him?

"Do tell," said Elmer.

---

14 He claimed the egg was pear-shaped owing to the fact that it was laid by two different birds, working as a team. Unfortunately, the birds failed to agree on a uniform set of dimensions before embarking on their joint egg-laying project.

"Well, I was on my way out there to turn it around," I said. "Because, you know, I figured maybe the reason the Bored Rock is so bored is on account of it's always facing the same direction. It's got nothing new to look at. Anyway, I was about a mile away when I saw this little old man sitting there on top of the rock. He looked like he was talking to it. Telling it jokes, I think. I swear, I could see the Bored Rock shaking with laughter, and the little old man bouncing and sliding around like a bean on a hot griddle. I don't know how he managed to stay up there. 'Course by the time I got close, the old man was long gone. And the Bored Rock lay there, quiet as ever — only just as I turned away, it gave a little shiver, as if to keep from laughing out loud."

For a moment, there was nothing but silence. I waited for somebody to take up the tale: now, about this little old man… who was he? Why was he telling jokes to a boulder? Ah, I see. Now you mention it, I saw somebody like that a while back, talking to the cattails up on Babbling Brook…

Instead, Flora said "may I have bug eyes and a beard, please?"

I have got to get some more colorful yarns.

Elmer cut a generous slice of bread, then cut the slice in half diagonally. He buttered the two triangles on both sides and threw them on the grill. Then he shaved a potato onto the grill and cracked a pair of eggs into a bowl. Timing is everything: the eggs don't go on the grill till after the bread is turned.

"Big ears, bug eyes, and a beard, coming right up," said Elmer.

Stanley started talking about the weather. He said "it sure was cold last night. It was so cold in my house, I almost wore my hat to bed."

Vern glanced at me. I grinned and rolled my eyes. The outside temperature never even got close to freezing. I'll wager it was quite a bit warmer inside Stanley's bungalow.

Doc walked in, growled at everybody, then huffed himself down on his favorite stool, up against the right-hand wall. Elmer poured him a mug of coffee without saying a word. Elmer's favorite hobby is harassing Doc — but even Elmer knows not to start anything until Doc's been reasonably caffeinated.

Stanley and Flora chatted on about the weather. I decided to float the barefoot stranger down a different fork of the river.

Another strategy for advancing a particular topic at Elmer's Café is to attempt to engage in a private conversation. I say "attempt," because the quickest way to attract Elmer's attention is to pretend you're ignoring him. So I turned to Vern and mumbled "so, if this guy really is who you think he is, what then? I mean, how do we catch him?"

Vern said "well…" and shut up. Because right about then, Rosetta walked in.

Vern didn't even turn around. He just knew, almost before the door even opened. He'd been halfway facing me, but he swiveled and faced forward almost as if the door and his stool shared a pair of hinges.

Rosetta said "morning, boys."

I said "morning, Rosie!"

I flashed her a charming smile, but she'd already moved down the row to sit next to Flora. Vern didn't say anything. He sat there with his shoulders hunched and his head down, as if the ceiling were about to fall.

Elmer set the tea kettle on the back burner. He said "hey, Ro. How many universes are there?"

"Six," she said without hesitation.

Stanley put down his coffee mug and scratched his elbow. "Gotta be more than that, hasn't there?"

Rosetta exchanged hellos with Flora, ignoring Stanley. She didn't care to defend her position, which meant she probly knew for a fact exactly how many universes there are — and you can bet they didn't add up to six.

Doc said "there's only one universe. By definition."

Elmer tried to adopt an innocent expression, but the expression made it plain that it didn't want to be adopted. Didn't stop Elmer, though. He said "you think so?"

Doc said "the universe contains everything. Nothing exists outside the universe, because there is no 'outside' the universe. Therefore, there can only be one universe."

Elmer said "but there can be different poems."

Doc said "don't start."

Elmer said "no, I'm serious. Literally speaking, the word 'universe' means one verse. Basically, we're living in a limerick."

Flora said "speak for yourself. My universe is a haiku."

Rosetta said "I think you're all thinking of a unistanza. A universe would be like singing 'Row, Row, Row Your Boat' over and over again."

I glanced at Vern. He'd already given up. Too much traffic on the river. Too many balls of yarn being batted around. We weren't gonna find any answers here at Elmer's.

But that didn't mean we couldn't fortify ourselves with a spot of breakfast before continuing our quest. I said "nope. If it repeats itself, then it's a unicycle. May I have a stack of pancake, please?"

INTERLOGUE:
The Bored Rock

THE Bored Rock is not its real name, of course. Its real name is something that cannot be expressed without a deep understanding of crystalline lexicology. Nevertheless, ever since the first hominid thought to describe the world through a series of meaningful grunts and fricatives, men and women have given this particular outcrop of horizontal stone a name that can invariably be translated as "the bored rock."

It's the posture, more than anything: the way the boulder slumps against the hillside like a minute that has dragged on so long, it can no longer summon the energy to crawl away into the past. The rock's downhill side is covered in moss and lichen, giving it a back-of-the-head appearance. Its uphill side stares blankly at a featureless cliff, uninhabited by so much as a blade of grass. The elements have conspired to carve a short, narrow tunnel through the northwest corner of the stone. When the wind blows just right across the mouth of the tunnel, all those within earshot are left with the impression the stone is heaving a great, melancholic sigh.

Also contributing to the Bored Rock's persistent anthropomorphic appellation is a failure to understand basic mineralogical kinesics, coupled with a complete misapprehension of geo-emotional response patterns. Rocks do not have a single face in the animalian sense; they "face" as many directions as they choose. Their external sensory inputs are not receptive to sight and sound, but to pressure and vibration. When the sun shines upon them, they do not feel its warmth. Instead, they feel the internal tension as each of their constituent grains begins to expand. Likewise, when the snow falls, they do not feel cold. They simply feel a different kind of pressure, as the contracting grains of stone are squeezed by expanding molecules of ice.

Rocks are quite stoic about this process. After all, they're not going anywhere. One day they may eventually be weathered down to a fine sand, but sooner or later, they will be reborn as a magnificent layer of sandstone. In the meantime, they amuse themselves by "listening" to the rumbling sermons emanating from the greatest rock of all: the Earth itself, speaking from its very core.

In short, the Bored Rock was not bored. It simply had little interest in the affairs of short-lived hominids.

It did, however, look forward to the occasional brief visit from a certain barefoot stranger. He was funny. He understood rocks. He knew how to listen.

Of course, he never stayed long. But before he left, he always "sang" a particular song, whose vibrations resonated through every last pore and sent echoes deep beneath the surface. The Bored Rock was not accustomed to feeling any emotion beyond contentment, but this particular song had an unusual effect: it tickled. The vibrations pulsed and tingled until the Bored Rock couldn't help but shiver and squirm with delight.

Thank magma, the sensation never lasted very long. It might have caused a catastrophic reorganization of the rock's constituent grains. But whenever the Earth's fiery sermons droned on just a little too long, the Bored Rock would think back on the last visit from Pedestrio, and answer the seismic pontification with a slight tremor of its own.

CHAPTER 18:
The Legend of Midi Wigi

AFTER breakfast, Vern ran the gauntlet at Wild Siders — Bill O'Sale's trendy backcountry gear and clothing emporium located paradoxically in the center of town. The way he dodged the friendly and knowledgeable sales staff reminded me of my recent adventures among the vicious wild chooks. I did my best to run interference for him, lest he get overwhelmed by the onslaught and go to ground behind a wall of backpacks or underneath an overturned canoe. There was a tense moment when I got momentarily distracted by a breezy young huckster who tried to sell me a witstone, but Vern pulled me away. He said store-bought witstones don't work so well for some people.[15] Anyway, we eventually made it all the way back to the fashion section. I mean (sorry) outdoor apparel.

The prices came like to turning my head inside out, but Vern didn't seem to notice. He was more concerned about putting together an outfit that didn't come in all the colors of a performing circus troupe. Vern likes to blend in when he's out tracking. Less chance of getting spotted by a swivel-headed lukbehind.

He offered to buy me a new hat. I declined. I didn't like any of the models they had on display. Half of them looked as if they'd go limp on impact from a single raindrop, or slide off to the leeward side if a butterfly got too close. In the end, I picked up

---

15 Witstones are used for sharpening minds. Many people swear by them, but they are not recommended for anybody who has difficulty concentrating. You have to keep your thoughts straight while using a witstone; if you keep changing your mind — or worse, approaching the same thought from different perspectives — well, that's like changing the angle of a blade against a whetstone. All you do is dull the blade.

an old pork pie from a rummage shop on Bitter Street. It had less character than a penguin in a monkey suit, but the brim was in good condition, and I could make it fit if I had to.

It was midmorning by the time we crossed the library threshold. As we sidled past the front desk, a very tall woman in a blue suit glared at me and said "shh!"

Vern jumped like he'd just gotten buzzed by a rattlesnake. He leaned in close and whispered "but we weren't even talking!"

I shrugged. "She knows me."

We found the books on stars and planets without any trouble. Strangely, not one of them listed a constellation called Pedestrio, nor even the Bat. Vern finally located the grouping on a star chart, but the constellation's proper name left him puzzled.

"Cathy o' Pia?"

He squinted at the name, as if narrowing his field of vision could somehow make sense of it.

"Never heard of her," I said.

Vern thumbed to the back of the book. "It says here she was a queen."

"Of what?"

"Some country out beyond the Insolven Sea, I think."

"Did she do a lot of walking?"

"Doesn't say. The constellation is supposed to look like her throne."

"Her throne?" My eyebrows contorted as I tried to recall the exact pattern.

"Well, she's sitting on it, obviously."

I slid the book away from Vern and flipped back to the star chart. "Looks more like a steel-jaw trap than a chair," I said. "Is she being punished for something?"

Vern pulled a book called *Multicultural Interpretations of Celestial Bodies* from the stack and began leafing through it. "Either that, or venerated. The ancients never seem entirely clear on which is which. This book says the constellation is called Midi Wigi in Hinterland."

"Who's Midi Wigi?"

"It's not really a who," he said. "Midi Wigi refers to a legend about a mountain that disappeared overnight, and a valley that appeared in its place. There's a paragraph about how the constellation can look like a mountain range in the evening, then by dawn it flips over to look like a series of valleys."

I spun the star chart around. "Or a capital M and a W."

Vern cocked his head, his eyes still on the text. "I've been to the Midi Wigi valley," he said. "Unusual geology."

"You know, I've heard tell of a land out beyond Fargone where they've outlawed Tuesday. They did it so long ago that nobody remembers why anymore, but I bet it had something to do with this constellation. What if they looked up in the evening and saw a big M in the sky, and said to themselves 'oh! It must be Monday.' But then the next morning they got up before dawn and went outside and the M was now a W, and they said 'oh! Is it Wednesday already?' I mean, that would explain the whole outlawing Tuesday thing, wouldn't it? Vern?"

Vern's Undivided Attention Syndrome had him paralyzed. I'm used to his episodes, but this one was the worst I've ever seen. I waved my hand in front of his face. He couldn't see it. I whistled and barked. He didn't hear a thing. He couldn't spare a thought for anything other than the book in front of him. Then, suddenly, his head snapped up. He looked around wildly, then practically ran to the section on myths and legends.

I dodged a sharp glance from the tall woman in the blue suit and followed Vern into the stacks. He scanned the shelves like a snakebit bibliophile searching for a good book on antivenin. "What's wrong?" I whispered.

"The Legend of Midi Wigi," he said. "Help me find it."

I pulled a big, gray, cloth-covered tome off the bottom shelf. The spine read *Tales of Old Hinterland.* Vern grabbed the book away from me and threw pages aside till he found the index. "Page 974," he muttered, tossing pages back and forth, same as wielding a machete through the jungle. "Here it is: 'Now, the Midi Mountains were sacred, and every Hinterlandian knew from childhood that it was forbidden to climb those hallowed slopes. But one day a stranger was seen wandering in the foothills… the Hinterlandians called to him, but he ignored their pleas and continued up the mountain…'"

Vern looked up. "Doesn't say if he was barefoot."

"What about his head? Did he have a hat on?"

Vern looked at me like I'd asked him if he had any spare same.[16] "What?"

"Hats are important," I said. "Almost as important as shoes."

He just kept staring at me.

Finally, he shook his head and reached for another book. "On second thought," he said, "I'll find you a witstone first chance I get. After all, how much harm could it do?"

---

16 This is, of course, impossible. Anyone can have spare change, but the amount of same to which a person has access is, by definition, always a fixed quantity. If you give any of your same away, then what you have left — obviously — is no longer the same.

CHAPTER 19:
Handing a Match to a Bonfire

W E lingered in the library for a while, as Vern wanted to look up stories about barefooted strangers. I left him to it and lost myself in another tale of Old Hinterland — something about a young Hinterlandian who couldn't find his way home and was cursed to wander the Earth for all eternity, or until he'd worn his feet all the way down to his knees. Then the tall lady in the blue suit suggested in rather stern terms that I was welcome to leave if I couldn't refrain from telling the story out loud and acting out all the lively bits. I said but what about the oral tradition, and she said you can't call it a tradition if you keep changing all the details. I said well, every storyteller is bound to dress up the tale according to his or her own style, and she said you can't just add dragons any time you want to. I said I didn't add a dragon just because I *wanted* to. The presence of a dragon was implied in the text. She said she'd read the text. In fact, she'd known that story ever since she was a little girl, and there was never a dragon in it. I said well, you have to admit, the tale started dragon toward the end.

One time I fell off a cliff. Hundred feet from the top of the cliff to the rocks below. All the way down, I got pummeled by fist-sized hailstones and lacerated by lightning claws, but the injuries I sustained that day were like mild sunburns compared to the scorching I got from that blue-suited woman's glare.

So I gathered up Vern and we lit out. I could feel the back of my head smoldering all the way to the edge of town.

We took the Arcadian Road, traveling light. I carried a small rucksack full of water bottles and other necessaries. For short trips, I don't generally bother with a full pack — except in the winter, when it's tough to get by without a cold-weather kit. Vern, per usual, carried everything he needed in his pockets. He doesn't need much. Plus, he makes a point of having a lot of pockets. Back at Wild Siders, he'd bought himself a vest that sported more pockets than a trilliard table.[17]

We did bring a modest supply of victuals this time. Ordinarily, when Vern and I go a-wandering, we stick to the backcountry and forage as we go: meandering from berry patch to fishing hole, traveling in the roundabout fashion of nomads and vagabonds. 'Course, if I'm traveling alone, that's different — I always haul a day or two's worth of food, on account of I lack Vern's particular talent for squeezing morsels of nutrition out of every leaf and root. But Vern was in a bit of a hurry to get out to Nothing Flat, so we mainly stuck to the fastest route, which happened to be the Arcadian Road. Even then, it's a two-day trek just to get to Fathom River.

The Arcadian Road heads due east, following a more or less straight line through the low country between the Wandering Hills and the coast. On this side of Fathom River, the soil is a little too salty for any kind of serious farming, though a handful of hardscrabblers keep trying. A few years ago, a man by the name of Spud Rumbledethump bought up all the arable land and planted nothing but potatoes. He figured they'd be the perfect ingredient for making potato chips, on account of the taters would already be salted. Unfortunately, he planted one of the lesser-known varieties. Turned out it was a new kind of potato that had no eyes, and so naturally, they got lost on the way to market.

Anyhow, we were a few leagues beyond the city limits when Vern, he said "I guess we ought to take a swing past the Bored Rock."

---

17 A trilliard table is like a billiard table, only with an order of magnitude more pockets. It's almost impossible to hit a bank shot in trilliards. In fact, it's almost impossible to hit any shot without scratching. This is not so much because of the many, many pockets along the side rails and at the corners — those are easily managed — but the holes in the middle of the table are very hard to avoid.

I said "hmm?" He'd caught me daydreaming. Something about mermaids, and whether they might have a preference for salt-free potato chips.

"Back at Elmer's. You said you saw Pedestrio sitting on the Bored Rock. I don't know why you didn't mention that earlier, by the way."

"Oh, that. I was just trying to get the conversation going, is all."

"Even so, we should probably make live sightings a higher priority. I mean after all, anybody can set a bunch of rocks down in a pattern."

I shot Vern a sidelong glance. I'd told him Rosetta's theory about pranksters making the Pedestrio symbol. It sorta sounded like Vern may have taken offense. Generally speaking, Vern takes his cue from the wild beasts — most of whom aren't capable of holding a grudge[18] — but nobody likes having their expertise called into question. Anyway, I reckoned it might be best not to scratch that scab. So I ignored the swipe. I said "Vern, it was just a story."

"I know that. But until we catch up to this guy, that's all we've got."

"Right. Look at me. How long have you known me?"

"Almost as long as I've known myself."

"And what do I always say about stories?"

"You say they grow better with a little fertilizer."

"That's right," I said. "Not all of them, of course. Most stories do just fine on their own. But some of them need a little help."

"Are you telling me your story isn't true?"

"Not at all," I said. Then it occurred to me he might interpret that statement in a couple of different ways. "I mean, no, I'm not saying that. I'm just saying, when I saw that guy sitting on top of that rock… well, it was a long way off, and maybe what I thought I saw wasn't really the way it happened."

---

18 The most obvious exception being the Bezurkish waka mole, which the Bezurks tried to exterminate way back when. It is said that the waka moles fought back. Unfortunately, the story cannot be corroborated, since there are no Bezurks left to tell the tale. Travelers to that region are nevertheless advised to leave the mole population alone.

Vern nodded, the way you do when somebody asks if you can keep a secret, then tells you something everybody else has known for years. He said "don't worry, Abner. I've heard you spin yarns before. I know how it works."

We walked on a ways. Presently, I said "there really was a guy sitting atop the Bored Rock."

"Oh, I bet there was."

"I didn't make that part up," I said.

"No, of course not."

"That would be lying," I said. "I can't abide liars."

Just then, a figure appeared on the horizon. The figure sauntered toward us, his shoulders back, his arms swinging free and easy. He walked like he owned the road. He could have been barefoot — from that distance, I couldn't tell. But he certainly wore the air of a man who could cakewalk through a swale full of swaddle bushes without touching green.

I admit it: just for a passing second, I found myself thinking *it can't be this easy, can it? The barefooted stranger can't just come walking right up to us, can he?*

Then the figure drew near, and my heart sank.

It was my old friend and nemesis. He of the Outrageous Fiction. He of the Unsubtle Falsehood. The one person I know who couldn't tell the truth if his life depended on it. Who fills the air with so many lies, they block out the sun. Who once told a lie so big, it took a year to tell — and once it was told, it took a team of six graduate students working 'round the clock in shifts almost an entire month to believe all of it.

He said "top of the morning, gents! How do you do this fine day?"

I said "Stretch! what are you doing out here?"

"Me? Oh, not much. I'm just taking a walk, that's all."

"That's stealing!"

Okay, so maybe I jumped straight into accusatory mode where a simple "how do!" is all the situation warranted. Fact is, I was already miffed at Stretch for making me think he might be the barefoot stranger, so it wasn't out of my way to find additional cause.

He said "I beg your pardon?"

I said "you can't just go around taking walks that don't belong to you. That's grand theft amble."

Vern looked confused. He said "Abner, what are you talking about?"

Stretch put on a show of looking hurt. He said "as a matter of fact, I do own this walk. It was given to me by my late, great Auntie Diluvian, who won it in a card game."

I glared at Stretch. "You made that up."

"Did not."

Vern said "hi, I'm Vern."

I stared at Vern. Some things are bound to take you by surprise, like the first time you see a cactus crowned with snow. Vern grew up Town Side; he must be familiar with the basic rules of social interaction. It's only that I haven't seen that side of him for a very long time.

"Sorry, I thought you two knew each other. Vern, this is Stretch. Don't believe anything he says. Stretch, this is Vern. He's a human lie detector. Don't even think about dumping any of your hogwash on him."

"A pleasure to meet you," said Stretch. "And you're welcome to share my walk any time. What brings you out this way?"

Vern said "we're looking for a million-year-old man who walks the Earth by day and the stars at night."

Well, I just about fell over. It's one thing to tell folks you're looking for a barefooted stranger. But a million-year-old man who walks among the stars? Even I didn't believe that part of the tale.

Neither did Stretch. He nodded approvingly. "That's a good one!"

"I call him Pedestrio," said Vern. "Though his real name is a mystery lost in time. We don't know that much about him. We're not even sure what he looks like, except he may not have any shoes on. Anyway, we're wondering if you've seen anybody with an unusual set about them."

Talk about handing a match to a bonfire. Stretch looked off into the middle distance and scratched his ear thoughtfully.

"Covers a lot of ground, you say?"

"Yes. Without leaving much in the way of track or sign."

"Well, it's not much to go on. But I did see a guy out here yesterday. He was carrying a pair of boots."

Vern's face lit up. "So he was barefoot?"

"Not exactly. He had socks on. Matter of fact, he tried to sell me the boots."

"Don't listen to him," I said.

"He said they were seven-league boots," said Stretch.

Vern said "what are seven-league boots?"

"They looked like fancy Town Side cowboy boots: black, with a lot of magical symbols stitched in silver. No, sorry, not just silver. Quicksilver, is what Pete called it."

"Don't listen to him," I said.

Vern said "Pete?"

Stretch said "yep. Pete Estrio. That's the name he gave me. Anyway, he said all I had to do is put on the boots, and I could travel seven leagues with every step."

"Don't listen to him," I said. "There's no such thing as seven-league boots."

Vern said "did you buy them?"

"Oh, I thought about it. But I didn't really trust him all that much. He had a shifty look about him. In fact, he looked a bit like Abner."

I glared at Stretch.

Vern said "so what happened?"

"We negotiated back and forth for a while. I told him, I said 'if the boots are really magical, how come you're selling them?'"

"And what did he say?"

"He said he had to sell them, on account of his feet couldn't keep up."

"What does that mean?"

"Well, you see, all he had for socks were three-league socks."

I said "there is *definitely* no such thing as a three-league sock."

Stretch said "that's what I thought. So I said to myself, I said *this guy is definitely up to something. Everybody knows socks are measured in feet, not leagues.* So I asked if I could take the boots for a test walk to make sure they worked. But Pete said they'd only start working for a new owner when the old owner was far enough away. He said I should pay him for the boots first, then wait for him to get at least seven leagues down the road before I put them on. He made a big thing about how that would be a day's walk for him, but only one giant step for me, once I had the boots."

Vern said "well, he had a point there, didn't he?"

"Maybe," Stretch conceded. "But I still didn't trust him, so I told him I had no intention of sitting around while he walked away with my money. I told him he should be the one to do the waiting and I would do the walking."

"Good thinking," I said. "If you like, we'll wait while you do it again."

Vern said "what did he say?"

"He agreed. Reluctantly."

"So you bought the boots?"

"He gave me a good deal."

"And did they work?"

"Of course they worked."

"Really? So you were able to walk seven leagues in a single bound?"

"Oh, sure, easily. Yep, I sure did owe Pete an apology. Those boots were everything he said they were."

Stretch gave me a look as if to say maybe I should apologize, as well. And maybe next time, I shouldn't think so little of my fellow travelers.

I said "so where are the boots?"

"Pete's got 'em. I had to return them."

Vern said "why?"

Stretch said "they weren't broken in. You should have seen the size of the blister I got. It was bigger than my whole foot."

"What a shame," I said. "Can we see the blister?"

Stretch favored me with a big old grin. Then he turned to Vern and said "Abner doesn't believe me. What do you make of that?"

Vern allowed as how my lack of trust did seem to be a tiny bit rude.

"All I'm saying is, if you can't show us the boots, maybe you could show us the blister. You know, just to punctuate the story."

A shadow of a smirk curled Stretch's lips. He tamed it quickly. He doesn't like to give up the game. "I can see you don't know anything about magic blisters."

"Illuminate me."

"The thing about magic blisters is, once the shoe that caused them is no longer in your possession, they just sort of fade away."

"Ha!" I said, filling the syllable with all the scorn I could find.

Vern said "yes, I've heard about those. You were lucky he didn't take off in the other direction the minute you turned your back. Then you'd have had to take *two* steps to catch him, and you'd have blisters on *both* feet."

Stretch nodded. "Now, whether Pete's a million years old or not, I couldn't say. But I think he might be the character you're looking for. What do you reckon?"

Vern said "maybe. Where did you say you saw him?"

"Just this side of Fathom River. If you hurry, you can probably catch up to him somewhere out in Arcadia."

"Thanks. We'll certainly keep our eyes out," said Vern.

INTERLOGUE:
Dawn on the Tundra

Dawn comes in agonizingly slow motion out on the tundra. The frozen wind rushes across the permafrost, blowing from west to east, charging at the horizon like a stampede of bison, determined to knock the sun backward into yesterday. The sun battles back, throwing bands of color into the sky like grappling hooks, pulling itself closer and closer to daybreak.

One by one, the stars fall back to the light of day. The Ballerina makes her brief, belated appearance before disappearing behind the big blue curtain.

The curtain rises higher and higher, until it fills the entire sky. Meanwhile, directly overhead, Pedestrio says goodbye to his nocturnal companions. He steps down from the heavens as if walking down a staircase. The journey doesn't take long. The staircase exists on the astral plane, where distance is relative. And just as Pedestrio steps off the last step, he crosses over into this world…

The tundra is home to a race of indigenous, seminomadic people who call themselves the Shiverboots. The Shiverboots often roam the frozen expanse for days in search of the scarcest and most valuable of commodities: firewood. They have been known to travel many hundreds of miles to investigate a spurious rumor of driftwood washing up on some distant, ice-packed beach. On this particular morning, the people are crowded into a communal lodge not far from Lake Neverswim. They are still basking in the warmth of the previous night's celebration. The venerable larch tree that grows nearby had finally dropped a branch, and a ceremonial bonfire had been lit. It had been a very small bonfire, seeing as how the branch was not that big. But the glowing coals had been brought inside, and the fragrance of woodsmoke still permeates the lodge.

If any Shiverboots had been awake and alert on this particular morning, they would have marveled at the sight of Pedestrio materializing out of thin air. They would have been awed by his magical abilities. They would have wondered where he came from.

Howbeit, there is magic, and then there is madness. Had there been witnesses to Pedestrio's sudden appearance, they almost certainly would have put aside their own sense of amazement in their haste to explain that only a fool leaves home without his boots, and that Pedestrio would be wise to go back right away and get them.

But on this particular morning, no one sees Pedestrio gain his full substance just as his foot touches the ground.

He stands for a moment, taking in his surroundings. He is dressed lightly for that time and place, wearing only a sealskin jacket and a hat and leggings made of wool. He is barefoot, but that doesn't seem to bother him much. The tops of his feet are matted with hair, and his calluses are an inch thick. He pulls his hat down over his ears, takes one last look around, and sets out, heading directly into the wind.

A thousand miles away, in a remote section of the taiga, a rather large, empty, malevolent supernatural Being stops chewing through the Precambrian shield. The Being has no eyes. All the same, It turns in the direction of Pedestrio, bringing Its other senses to bear.

A single thought blasts its way out of the Being's mind. The power behind the thought is so great that it takes physical form — raking through the air and defoliating several nearby spruce saplings.

Trespasser! the Being thinks.

Then, slowly, the Being sinks into the bedrock to renew Its pursuit.

CHAPTER 20:

Emmett Roll

WE said our farewells to Stretch and continued east. The road wended its way through boggy marshes and mossy woods. I was glad of the season: the greenflies hadn't quite taken hold of the place yet. In another week or two, they'd be swarming like tiny airborne piranhas.

I said "well, that was a colossal waste of time."

"He seemed like a nice guy."

"He's a flat-out liar," I said. "I don't know why you even bothered to talk to him."

"He tells a pretty good story, though, doesn't he?"

"No."

Vern clocked me with a curious look. "I don't know why you're letting yourself get so worked up over him."

"I can't abide liars."

"You've been known to pull one down from the ether yourself, from time to time."

"That's different."

"How's that?"

"I'm a storyteller. He's just a liar."

"An important distinction," said Vern diplomatically.

A cold, gusty breeze blew from the west. Mostly it pushed us along, but every once in a while, it swooped in sideways to knock my hat akilter. I said "and speaking of pulling things down from the ether, you might not want to mention all that stuff about Pedestrio being a million years old and walking among the stars.

I mean, even Stretch wouldn't bite on those, and he once told me Gilda Moshe owes him seventeen shekels. Plus interest."[19]

Vern eyed me with that sidelong look again. "It took me a while to get accustomed, as well."

"Don't get me wrong, I think you've got the beginnings of a first-rate yarn. I'm just saying, the wilder the claims, the more evidence you need to back them up."

He said "I've got evidence."

"What, the symbol at Nothing Flat? We haven't even seen that yet."

"No, I'm talking about evidence I got from the library. All those stories about mysterious travelers. The Midi Mountain Stranger. The Outlander at Outer Downanout. The Wigtown Wanderer. It's the same legend, over and over again: a rootless vagabond passing through town and country, cursed by the Gods, distrusted by the locals. The same character pops up in a thousand tales from around the world and all across time."

"Doesn't mean it's the same guy."

"It's him. He's always on foot, and there's always something that sets him apart."

I straightened my hat again. One good thing about a strong westerly: it keeps the mozzies grounded. Greenflies wouldn't have cared; they'll fly as long as the tall trees can stand without bending. I said "Vern, did I ever tell you about my friend Archie Tipe?"

"No."

"He had a rugged jaw. That's what stuck out the most about him: the rugged jaw. Some folks thought he had a set to his eyes that made him look focused and determined, but really, he was just sensitive to bright sunlight. So he squinted a lot. But because of the rugged jaw and the determined squint, folks kept asking him to do battle with horrible, cranky, sleep-deprived

---

19 Gilda Moshe was an ancient hero who tried (and failed) to find the eternal secret of life. Ironically, though she died many thousands of years ago, her name lives on in that timeless literary classic, *The Epic of Gilda Moshe.*

monsters and invincible bureaucrats. Archie didn't want any part of that. He just wanted to sit in the backyard and drink lemonade. So that's what he did. And eventually, all those folks that kept coming around… well, they found someone else to bother."

Vern looked at me.

I looked at him.

He looked at me some more.

I said "what?"

Vern said "… and?"

"And he lived happily ever after."

Something splashed out in the marsh. Vern looked away. "So no point to the story, then. No lesson. No moral. No relevance whatsoever."

"Of course it's got a point," I said. "The point is, there's always another rugged-jawed, squint-eyed guy out there."

"There's only one Pedestrio."

"Okay, fine," I said. "Let's say there really is only one million-year-old barefoot stranger. How does he get to walk among the stars?"

"I don't know. There wasn't anything about that in the library. But you've seen the constellation."

"That's just a bunch of stars, Vern. You're not claiming it's really him, are you?"

"No. But it's a sign that he's up there. It's his mark."

I could feel myself channeling the blue-suited librarian. I tried to block the channel. The words came spilling out, anyway. "Vern, you can't add a dragon to the story any time you feel like it."

"I didn't add any dragons."

"No, you added an astronaut."

"Did not."

"Then how does he get up into the sky? Jet pack? Trampoline?"

"Where did he go that night on Mount Exile? Huh? He didn't stay the night, and there was no trace of his leaving. So where did he go?"

"My money is still on the secret tunnel."

"There was no tunnel. Plus, it doesn't explain the stones."

"Nothing explains the stones," I said. "The stones are a great mystery, and any tale about them is just as true as any other."

"Exactly," said Vern. "Don't you hate it when stories come to life?"

We reached the river late in the afternoon of the second day. Fathom River provides drainage for all of Arcadia, the Wandering Hills, and the Sea of Green — that endless expanse of forest north of the Wandering Hills. Some folks say the reason it's called Fathom River is on account of you can sail a thousand miles upstream, and the depth will never drop below a single fathom. Seems likely the folks who say that never tried to sail up the river during the dry season. Why, I once bought a ticket on a packet boat heading upriver to Three Point Landing. That was back in the days of the Great Drought. Ugliest trip I've ever taken. The water level was so low, the entire crew and every able-bodied passenger had to climb out of the boat with buckets, and scoop all the downstream water from behind the boat, and pour it out in front of the boat, over and over again, just so we could keep sailing.

Now, that was hard work. On the other hand, several of us became quite good friends with a litter of mudpuppies that had been abandoned by their mother. We would have adopted them and brought them home with us, but the captain wouldn't allow it. He said all that barking gave him a headache.

Of course, this close to the ocean, the river is considerably deeper than one fathom. The floodplain alone is almost a mile wide.

At Bridgetown, we debated whether to pay the troll and take the bridge across, or swim for it. Frankly, I thought Vern could stand a good soaking. I even offered to buy him a miniature personal flotation device in the form of a bar of soap. But the day was getting on, and the late afternoon air was beginning to feel a bit crisp. Shadows fell across the river, making it look dark and cold and uninviting. Besides, the troll stated quite plainly that if we swam, he was contractually obligated to throw rocks at us.

Okay, fine. He's not really a troll. And yes, I have been duly informed that it is rude to call somebody a troll simply because of his name and/or occupation. But honestly, when your name is Emmett Roll, I really believe you should think twice before electing to become a professional toll collector.

Not to mention, you probly shouldn't threaten anyone who comes near your bridge. I mean, talk about playing to stereotype…

I said "come on, Emmett. That's not really in your contract, is it?"

Emmett said "yep. Paragraph 9(c). Right under the part where it says, if you try to cross the bridge without paying, I get to hit you with a club."

Vern said "that seems a little harsh, don't you think?"

Emmett thought about that. It took a long time. I began to wonder if his contract had a clause in it that prohibited thinking. Finally, he said "if you wanna cross the bridge, you gotta pay the toll. If you don't pay the toll, I get to hit you with my club."

I said "where is your club, by the way? I mean, not that we're planning on not paying, but I should think you'd want to have it at the ready, just in case."

Emmett said "I would, but somebody stole it. I wish they hadn't done that. If I have to get another one, it comes out of my own pocket."

Vern said "are you sure you didn't misplace it?"

Emmett said "yep. I'm sure. I know, because I had it in my hand when it was stolen."

I said "you had it in your hand? What was it, an armed robbery?"

"Nope. It was a paragraph 7(f): Confronting a Suspicious-Looking Bridge-Crosser. I shook my club at him like it says I can do, and that's when he made a grab for my coin purse. I grabbed it back, and he ran away, and that's when I noticed my club was gone."

I looked at Vern. Vern nodded back at me. "Hornswoggle."

Emmett said "what's a hornswoggle?"

"Never mind," I said. "What did this suspicious-looking bridge-crosser look like?"

"Little brown hairy guy. Carried a lunch pail. Wore a hat down over his eyes. Looked a lot like that old hat you used to wear, Abner."

"Dang it!" I said. "Which way did he go?"

"That way," said Emmett, pointing in the direction of Arcadia.

"How long ago?"

"Day and a half."

I said to Vern, I said "he's got my hat again."

"I doubt it's the same one, Abner."

"The hat, or the hornswoggle?"

"Yes. Both."

Emmett was getting impatient. He waved an imaginary club at us. "Are you guys gonna pay, or what?"

"I want my hat back."

Vern said "I know you do. But he's got a day and a half on us."

"Well, keep a lookout, anyway," I said, eager to push on.

It was the same hornswoggle, I knew it. The same hornswoggle, and the same hat. There couldn't possibly be two of them.

"Pay up," said the troll.

CHAPTER 21:
Johnny Callcrow

—————————

ARCADIA is home to some of the best farmland in all the world. The topsoil goes down so deep, the worms living in the bottommost layer speak with a different accent. And it's so rich and fertile, even the crabgrass can't help being cheerful. The farmers in Arcadia have learned to plant their crops in circles, on account of by the time they've made it all the way around the circle, the seeds have sprouted and borne fruit, and the crops are ready for harvest.

As long as we were in the neighborhood, Vern and I decided to pay a visit to our friend Buford Colic. Buford's farm is on the other side of the Coin, about five miles east of the river.[20] He and his wife, Melanie, are easy-going country folk; Vern gets along well with both of them. Melanie is a mite shy, but Buford knows just about everybody from Piggy Bank to Nothing Flat. We reckoned he'd be a good person to ask about Pedestrio sightings. Plus, Buford's got one of those scary, old-fashioned clawfoot bathtubs, and Vern was sorely in need of a bath.

Old Buford is famous for his hospitality — and notorious for his ability to put visitors to work. Of course, he never comes right out and asks anybody for help. He's always more than willing to stop what he's doing and chat a while. Then somehow, before you know it, he's turned back to his chores and you're standing there with a rake in your hand.

—————————

20 The Coin is a small farming village on the east bank of Fathom River. That's the side they call Piggy Bank. About half the villagers grow fiddleheads, and the other half grow cattails. When you meet somebody in the Coin, the standard greeting is "heads or tails?" Technically, Piggy Bank is part of Arcadia, but the more serious farmers like to be a bit farther away from the river, as insurance against the occasional flood. Needless to say, Buford is a serious farmer.

We found Buford out in the back forty with his tractor, pulling a big seeder around in a circle.

I said "howdy, Buford! Whatcha doing?"

Buford stopped his tractor and climbed down. "Howdy boys. Just getting this season's crop in the ground."

Vern said "what's the crop?"

Buford said "myta beans."

I said "what are myta beans?"

"They're a new, experimental variety of legume. Bit tricky to grow — I'm already wishing I'd planted something else. But you know what they say: once they're in the ground, there's no sense worrying about your myta beans." He took a moment to wipe his brow with a red-checked handkerchief. "What brings you boys out this way?"

Vern said "we're heading out to Nothing Flat. Just thought we'd stop in and say hello."

"Well, you're more than welcome to stay the night. I know Mel would love to see you."

"Thanks," I said. "We'll do that."

"Yeah, thanks," said Vern. "Abner really needs a bath."

I glared at Vern. Buford grinned. "I think we can scare up enough hot water for both of you."

I said "how is Melanie doing, by the way?"

Melanie Colic is one of the saddest people I've ever known. It breaks your heart to see her, sometimes. But Buford swears that secretly, she enjoys being sad. She's a poet, you see — it's almost an occupational requirement.

"Doing great," said Buford. "Wrote a poem about a teardrop the other day. One lonely tear, cried in the dark and wiped away before anybody could see it. One lonely tear, cried in silence and dried in haste. Made you feel more sorry for the teardrop than for the person who cried it."

I caught Vern giving me a strange look. He said "you got something in your eye, Abner?"

"No, of course not." I turned away and blinked furiously. "Must be some pollen in the air. It's making my eyes all watery."

Buford said "well, if you'll excuse me, I've got to get back to work. When you're done with that hoe, you can take it over to the barn. Tool room is on the left. And while you're there, you can throw a few bales of hay down from the hayloft and fill up the feed bins."

I looked down at the long-handled hoe in my hands. I wasn't sure how it got there. I didn't remember picking it up. Oh well, might as well put it to use. "Where do you want me to start?" I said.

"Pedestrio?" said Buford. "Nope. Can't say I've heard of him."

We had finished the outside chores and were sitting around Buford's kitchen table, working on the dinner chores. Vern shelled walnuts. I peeled the taters. Melanie chopped onions, while Buford played the eight feet of counter space between the stove and the sink like a one-man percussion orchestra — now stirring a pot, now grating the cheese, now pounding away with a meat mallet.

Vern said "that's just what I call him. You might know him by another name, or only just by sight."

I let Vern do the talking. It was good practice for him. He said "have you ever spotted a stranger way off in the distance, hiking along where there is no track?" Crackle crackle, went the walnuts.

"That sounds so lonely," said Melanie, wiping away a tear. Chop chop, went the onions.

Vern said "he would have stood out. If you saw him out walking in a field, you'd think to yourself, *nobody walks like that.*"

"Got a funny walk, does he?"

"No, not at all. What I mean is, according to the stories, he walks like he's walking across his own backyard — even when he's out in the middle of nowhere. You know, making it look easy, no matter what the terrain is."

"Sounds like Johnny Callcrow," said Buford, pounding away with the meat mallet. Bam! Bam! Bam! "Sure, I've seen him once or twice. He's not from around here, but I've seen him jump an irrigation ditch like only a farm boy can. Didn't even give himself a running start — just walked right up, same old sauntering pace, and hopped across like it was two feet wide instead of ten. Never saw the like. Yes sir, most of the folks around here have a tale or two about old Johnny."

"Do tell," I said.

Stir stir. Grate grate. "Well sir, Pastor Al calls him Johnny Trespass, but I think that's a tad uncharitable. It's true, he never asks permission to cross our fields, but there's never any harm done, and possibly some good."

"How's that?"

"Well, you know, we count our blessings every day for the natural abundance all around us. But it seems to me, nature's bounty is ever the more when Johnny passes through. Grass grows taller. Corn stands prouder. And the fruit trees always yield a few extra bushels of fruit."

I said "so he fertilizes as he goes?"

Vern shot me the kind of look you give the blackbird who keeps screaming and diving at your head long after you vacate the nesting area.

"Don't rightly know how he does it," said Buford. "Russ Tick, who lives over there in East Arcadia, he says he's seen old Johnny scattering seeds from some kind of seed sack. I never saw him do any such thing, but that would explain the crows."

"What about them?" I said.

"They follow him around like he's got handfuls of grain in one pocket and chocolate-covered mice in the other. That's why I call him Johnny Callcrow — always got one perched on either shoulder, and more in the air. Anyway, the crows disappear when he does. Where he leads them, I don't know — but it's days before they find their way back."

Vern leaned forward. "What does he look like?"

"Hard to say. He sort of blends into the landscape. I might not have seen him a-tall if it weren't for the crows."

"When did you see him last?"

"That'd be the time I saw him jump that ditch."

"And how long ago was that?"

"About five years ago, I reckon. It was early summer, just before the first haying. I remember, on account of that was the year I baled the hay too soon after cutting it. Baled up a mess of fireflies along with the hay. Almost burned down the barn that year."

"What time of day?"

"Morning. Spotted him wading through the timothy, about three hours past dawn. I remember wishing he'd gone around the edge of the field, but I checked later: not a single patch was trampled."

"Hmm," said Vern. "Anything else you can tell us?"

"Well sir, I was too far away to hear anything, but I'd swear he was talking to himself. Or the crows."

I said "did he have any shoes on?"

"Funny you should mention that. I couldn't see his feet. But Claude Hopper calls him Johnny Unshod. Swears he walks around barefoot."

Vern's eyes lit up.

Buford noticed. "That sound like your man?"

"Could be," said Vern. "I didn't see any stories about him attracting birds, but it fits with everything else we know."

I said "maybe he was stealing corn, and the crows were escorting him off the premises."

Buford said "more likely t'other way 'round. Anyway, they can ride him all the way to Neveryoumind, so long as it gets them out of my hair for a few days."

Melanie put down her cleaver, stared off into the middle distance, and began to recite:

Caw! Caw! Cries he:
The corvid speaks
The language of loss
And bitter remorse.

Caw! Caw! Cries he:
The black bird speaks
His tragic ode
To death, and worse.

"Hey, not bad!" said Buford. "That one even almost rhymes!"

He beamed at Melanie, who lowered her eyes, smiled a sad, pretty smile, and picked up her cleaver again. "Thank you," she whispered. Chop chop. Sniff sniff.

"She makes them up all the time," Buford boasted. "I tell her she oughtta write them down, but she just can't stand the thought of holding all those lovely poems prisoner on little scraps of paper."

The onions were getting to me. I dabbed at my eyes with a corner of my shirt sleeve. "Beautiful," I said. "Just beautiful."

Vern was oblivious. "Actually," he said, "crows are quite jolly about death and corpses and all. They've got quite a morbid sense of humor about it. I guess that comes from being around it all the time, scavenging at kill sites and whatnot, hoping to be the first one to pluck out the eyes."

I cleared my throat, loudly. Vern looked around, surprised. "Is something wrong?"

I glared at him. "You could have said something nice about her poem."

"Oh. Sorry."

I risked a glance over at Melanie. She was horrified, and trying very hard not to show it. She —

No. No, I can't even pretend. Her eyes were brimming with tears, but only on account of the onions. The rest of her face wore a grin as big as a canoe.

She said "that's such lovely imagery!"

Vern blinked. "It is?"

She said "you just gave me an idea for an even sadder poem! Tell me again the part about plucking out the eyes?"

INTERLOGUE:
In the Beginning,
There Was a Valley

IN the beginning, there was a valley.

It was a very small valley — a narrow and desolate valley, kept separate from the Garden by the Tallest Mountains in the World. The mountains were so high that the full light of the sun reached the valley for no more than a few minutes at midday — and at night, only a single star could be seen.

It was the same star every night — for the star did not move, but kept its place in the sky. A few of the valley dwellers called it the Wishing Star. They believed it was watching over them, and said prayers to it. But most took the star for granted, because it was always there. The sun, who appeared so briefly and shone with such blinding radiance that it was nigh on impossible to look at, made a much more powerful and interesting symbol of divinity.

There were no animals in the valley, other than people. There were no cats, nor dogs, nor fish, nor lizards, nor chimpanzees. There were no birds in the valley — although large raptors could often be seen high overhead, flying from one peak to the next, like guards on patrol. For some reason, the raptors liked to use the valley for target practice.

There were only three forms of plant life in the valley. There was a sort of moss that grew everywhere, but couldn't be walked on because it had sharp spines like a cactus. And there was a species of tree that spit pitch at anybody who got too close. And there was a cross between a lichen and a tumbleweed that would wrap itself around boulders and roll them around and around the valley, intent upon chasing people down and rolling over them.

The valley dwellers subsisted on a thick, sticky kind of paste made from spit pitch and bird droppings. They spent their days dodging tumblerocks and pulling mosspins out of their feet. They spent their nights in dull, visionless slumber, for the valley was so remote and isolated that not even dreams could find their way in.

But the people loved their little valley. They called it Paradise.

Among the people, there were legends of a world beyond the mountains. Dim recollections, perhaps. Vestigial memories of a time before the beginning — a place before Paradise. And every day, the people counted their blessings, because it was understood that the outside world must be a wretched, horrible place. Who would want to go there? After all, nothing could ever be more perfect and beautiful than the valley they called home.

The Old Ones did everything They could to encourage this attitude, for They had no desire to share Their Garden. The people would only ruin it, They reasoned. The people were ignorant; they lived their entire lives in a coloring box full of gray crayons. They could not possibly appreciate the exquisite grandeur of a cherry tree in full bloom, nor the subtle simplicity of a drop of dew on a cabbage leaf. It was best to keep them safely contained in Paradise, where they could do no harm, and where no harm would come to them.

Well, no more than usual, anyway.

CHAPTER 22:
A Runway or a Crater

NEXT morning, Buford took us 'round to Aggie's Café and introduced us to the regulars. Some of them I recognized from Buford's annual harvest party, but that was different: anybody can show up at a party. At Aggie's, you don't get to sit with the locals without somebody vouching for you.

'Course, a seat at the table is no guarantee the yarns'll spin in your favor.

"Don't know what I can tell ya," said Buford's neighbor Claude. "Haven't seen Johnny Unshod in years."

"Had a good crop, year before last," said Ari Bell. Everybody looked around.

Buford lowered his voice and leaned in closer to Vern and me. "Good crop could be a sign of Johnny passing through. Just don't let Pastor Al catch you saying it."

"Sure did," said Russ Tick. "We didn't see you for a month."

Everybody laughed. Ari's cash crop is maize. Sometimes he gets lost in his work.

"Anybody ever talk to him?" I asked.

Blank looks. I tried again. "Can anybody describe Johnny? What he looks like? The clothes he wears?"

Head shakes all around. "He sort of blends into the landscape," said Ari.

And so it went. Nobody could add much to what Buford already told us, and the talk soon turned to more important things, like rain.

Vern mostly kept quiet, but he did ask permission to do a little wandering through the tractor lanes to the east. He didn't say why. That was probly for the best, as I found out later.

The definition of Wild Side is more complicated than I let on, sometimes. Broadly speaking, any place that sits outside the bounds of civilization is a part of Wild Side. But the border between Wild Side and Town Side can get pretty blurry. It's better to think of them as concepts rather than geographical regions.

Take Arcadia, for example. Now, we can all agree that in general, Arcadia is a civilized place — there's hardly a patch of ground between Fathom River and Nothing Flat that isn't cultivated or carefully managed. Every farmhouse is equipped with all the modern conveniences, and every farmer is highly educated and well-informed. And yet, there's more than a little Wild Side in every furrowed field.

The farmers know it, too: even the urbane, sophisticated ones who go around calling themselves agronomists never forget they have one foot in the natural world.

Bottom line is, it's possible to look at a farmer's field and see either a Town Side improvement or a Wild Side frontier, depending on whether your focus is on the cultivated crops or the glimpses of wildlife peeking around the edges.

Anyway, Vern and I, we headed due east for half a day or so, following the dirt lanes and tractor tracks, keeping our feet grounded on the Town Side routes while our eyes scanned the fields and frontiers for evidence of barefooted pedestrians.

I said to Vern, I said "what are we looking for?"

He said "a landing spot."

I stopped in midstride. "A landing spot?"

"Has to be," said Vern. "You heard Buford. He saw Pedestrio heading west about three hours after dawn. If he came down from the stars just at daybreak and set a brisk pace, then the place where he came down should be right around here."

"Vern, that was five years ago."

"If he leaves a sign in the evening, then maybe he leaves one in the morning, too."

"And the pebbles would have been plowed under long ago."

Vern's voice came from far away. He wasn't talking so much as thinking out loud. "You'd think somebody would have seen him touch down."

"Not necessarily," I said. "Not unless he came down with a flash and a bang."

"We know he favors hilltops in the evening. But elevation for its own sake may not be the goal. Could be he just likes the view. Question is, what kind of terrain does he fancy in the morning?"

"Good question," I said, trying to be helpful. "Does he need a runway, or does he just leave a crater?"

Vern thought about that. He was quiet for a long time. I began to suspect he was ignoring me. I said "did you hear me?"

"Hmm?"

"What kind of landing spot are we looking for?"

"Have you ever seen a sparrow do that before?"

He nodded off to our right, where a brown-eyed field sparrow stood on a clod of dirt beside a furrow. She was bobbing up and down in a quick, jerky movement: now hunching down, now standing tall, now hunching down again. She reminded me of a lizard doing push-ups. "I don't know," I said. "Maybe."

"Why do you think she's doing that?"

"Maybe she needs the exercise."

"It's like she's trying to peek over an invisible wall without being seen." Vern looked around. "You see any predators?"

"Just us."

"Point taken."

I said "I thought we were supposed to be looking for Pedestrio's splashdown site?"

"We are. But that doesn't mean we shouldn't keep our eyes open."

I tried to make sense of that.

Vern decided not to wait for me to catch up. "Every day I spend out here on Wild Side, I see something I've never seen before. Sometimes it's a bird doing a funny dance. Sometimes it's a pattern in the bark of a tree. There's always something different. That's one of the reasons I love being out here."

We kept walking. Vern had something on his mind. I tried to spot something I'd never seen before, but all I saw were sparrows doing sparrow things.

"I was just wondering if there ever comes a point when you've seen everything there is to see," he said.

"Wild Side is a big place," I said.

"But what if you live forever? Sure, it's a big place, but wouldn't you know the geography pretty well after a thousand years or so? How long till there's nothing left to discover?"

"Maybe he forgets where he's been."

"That doesn't make me feel better."

I sighed. "You thinking of taking up a new vocation?"

"What?"

"Getting tired of the same old routine? You could try accounting. I know a guy who needs an apprentice."

"That's not what I meant."

I thought for a second. No yarns in my repertoire covered this situation. I'd have to improvise. "Have I ever told you the Legend of Sissy Foot?"

"Yes."

"No, I'm pretty sure I haven't."

Vern kicked a stone out of his path. "It was worth a shot."

"Sissy Foot was a king who ruled half the world, back when half the world was unruly. He was famous for never walking anywhere. He used to ride around town in a sedan chair carried by four guys with arms like tree trunks."

"You mean tree limbs."

"Hmm? No, bigger than tree limbs. Definitely trunks."

"You're getting your metaphors mixed up. Legs are like tree trunks. Arms are like limbs or branches."

"Who's telling this story, me or you?"

Vern muttered "more to the point, who's listening?"

I decided to ignore that. "Anyway, the servants whose job it was to do all his walking for him started calling him Sissy Foot behind his back, and the name stuck. And the king really didn't mind all that much, on account of his real name was Eddy Puss, and he figured almost anything was an improvement over such a stupid name as that."

"He was mistaken," said Vern. "Does this story have a point, or is it another one of your maundering, incoherent fantasies?"

Maundering, indeed. I plowed straight ahead. "Sissy Foot thought being a king was the most boring job in the world. All he did was ride around all day in his sedan chair, and it's not like he had anywhere to go. He just did it so people could see him, because nothing gave a peasant's life more meaning than to be able to go home at the end of the day and tell everybody he saw the king. But, you see, the thing is, it didn't work the other way around — the king didn't derive any particular satisfaction from telling everybody back at the palace, 'hey, you'll never guess who I saw today: Hank the Peasant! Looking all fancy in his finest rags!'"

Vern said "never mind, I think I know the answer."

"The point is, he never got out of the chair."

"Ah. Now I see. Thank you for clearing that up."

I said "if we come through this way five years from now, do you think we'll see the same bird, doing the same up-and-down dance move?"

"Probably not."

"If we did, would you think it was boring?"

"I'd think it was highly improbable, and I'd worry that we'd got caught in some kind of time loop, and I'd have to endure this conversation all over again."

"Exactly. Everything is always changing. You're worried that Pedestrio might be getting bored. I reckon he's probly not thinking, *oh, man, I've got nine more eons to go before I can retire.* He probly comes down here every morning wondering what's changed. If he sees something he recognizes, it'll be like meeting an old friend. If not, well, there's your daily discovery. Either way, I doubt he gets bored."

We reached the edge of the field. Vern eyed the irrigation ditch and the newly plowed ground on the other side. "Maybe so. Although I'm still not sure what Silly Foot has to do with it."

"Sissy Foot," I said. "You really don't get it? I thought it was pretty obvious."

He backed up a few paces. "Enlighten me."

I threw my rucksack across the ditch, then backed up alongside Vern. "Well, at least Pedestrio isn't sitting in a chair all day, watching the world go by. Now *that* would be boring."

CHAPTER 23:
Chasing Camels

WE spent most of a day poking around fields and ditches, looking for signs of Pedestrio's landing spot. Naturally, we didn't find so much as a divot. No rock formations resembling stairways to nowhere. No magic invisible elevators. No five-year-old skid marks. But a steady, unrelenting afternoon rain turned the fields and byways into mud wallows. We got out of there before we lost our shoes.

Don't let anybody tell you the dry lake called Nothing Flat is named after the length of time it takes to get there. Fact is, it's about a ten-day hike east of Fathom River. The Arcadian Road can take you most of the way — but the farther you get from the river, the more arid the climate. Rain clouds dry up or double back to loiter along the coast. Wells get deeper. Farms get smaller and scarcer, until eventually the road simply turns to dust and vanishes from lack of use.

Beyond Nothing Flat, there is only the Great Empty Desert. Only a few outlaws and desert rats live out that way. Folks like that haven't got much use for roads.

I was in a crusty mood by the time we found the symbol. Sometimes I get that way — especially on days when my sweat dries before my shirt even has a chance to get damp, and I'm not sure where my next drink of water is coming from. So instead of taking an active part in the investigation, I sat in the relative shade of a thorn bush, up on what used to be the shore of the lake, and glowered down at Vern.

I said "you figure it out yet?"

Vern had spent the better part of a stifling afternoon taking measurements and scouring the ground for million-year-old man tracks. He said "the stones are local. I've seen examples of this same type of quartz all over the valley. And the pattern isn't random: they were placed here deliberately."

"A million years ago."

"More or less."

"For what purpose?"

"I don't know," he said, gazing down at the stone silhouette of Pedestrio marching off in the direction of the desert.

"Just for the sake of argument," I said "how do we know Pedestrio himself did this? Maybe some primitive protohuman came along and decided to lob a few rocks out onto the mudflat, just to watch them go splat."

"Then who made the symbol on Mount Exile, and the one in the Mulls?"

"My money is on a secret society of ancient and honorable protohumans determined to keep their ancestor's greatest artistic achievement alive."

Vern looked at me like I'd just accidentally dropped his doughnut on the ground. I looked around for the doughnut, but I didn't see it. He said "that seems highly improbable, don't you think?"

"At this point, improbable is all we've got. Can we get out of the sun now? I'm so parched, I could take notes on myself."

There wasn't any water out at Nothing Flat, so we backtracked to an abandoned farm a few miles west. Only a crumbling foundation and a windbreak of spruce trees remained. The trees looked about as out of place as a row of skyscratchers rising up from the plain. They weren't exactly thriving, but their roots had found enough moisture to keep them stubbornly hanging on.

The well still worked. The water wasn't bad. There just wasn't enough of it to keep the farm going.

A few hours later, Vern and I lay on our backs on a lawn gone to seed and listened to something small and fidgety rustling through the grass. The mice were probly hoping we'd rebuild the farmhouse and stock the root cellar with all kinds of mousy treats. It was a clear night, and a dark one — not so much as a sliver of moon lit up the sky. Pedestrio — the constellation — was almost directly overhead, facing west with his feet pointed north.

"You're not going out there, are you?"

"Out where?" said Vern.

"You know where. The Great Empty Desert."

I'd seen the way Vern had stared across the flats and into the hills that marked the Western Verge. They shimmered in the heat like a big, illuminated sign saying "Come In, We're Open."

"Pedestrio's mark was facing east. Maybe that's the direction we should be headed."

"The stars are facing west. Maybe we should head back to town."

"You want to go home? Already?"

I said "Vern, we don't even know where to start looking. We do know he doesn't always pick up where he left off — otherwise, we'd have caught him back at Mount Exile. He could be here today, and half a world away tomorrow. So the question is, do you want to die in the desert, or would you rather step back from the Verge until we can figure out which way the evidence is pointing us?"

Vern sat up and wrapped his arms around his knees. He took his time answering. "I think we should talk to more people."

"Good plan."

"Not the Arcadians. And not your Town Side friends. Someone new."

I raised myself up on one elbow. "Not the rats."

"Farmers see what a farmer would see. The rats might tell us something different."

"It's pretty late in the season, Vern."

"It's not even summer yet."

"It's a camel chase, is what it is."

Rumors of camels wandering around the Great Empty Desert have been circulating for decades. Camels are not native to this part of the world. They belong in the Great Shifting Desert, over there on the other side of the planet. The Shifting Desert has mountains of sand dunes that are constantly getting pushed up, pulled down, and blown around by the local breezes. By contrast, the Great Empty Desert is swept clean down to the pan.[21] It's almost as if the trade winds traded away our sand, and in return, we got the solitude of Great Emptiness.

Anyway, legend has it that a herd of wild camels once got caught in the biggest wind storm the Great Shifting Desert has ever seen. The locals called it the Kantsee Wind. Roughly translated, that means the I've-got-so-much-sand-in-my-eyes-I-need-a-broom-and-a-shovel-to-blink Wind. It blew for many many days, and the camels had no choice but to keep walking as a wall of sand blew all around them. When it was over, the camels found they'd walked halfway around the world.

That's the legend, anyway. 'Course, no trace of camels has ever been found, but that hasn't stopped several generations of wide-eyed, wet-behind-the-ears adventurers from wandering around the desert looking for them. Those of us who've got more sense than to go roaming around the desert on a lark refer to any insufficiently planned expedition as a "camel chase."

Vern said "we're not chasing camels. We're collecting field data."

"We are wandering around pretty much aimlessly. Which is fine in Arcadia, but not so much in the Great Empty."

"Two days, that's all. Just out to No Aces and back."

No Aces is a trading post and guide hangout situated about two days east of Nothing Flat. It's home base for a handful of

---

21 The desert floor in this part of the world is often called "the pan" — short for the frying pan. What isn't bare rock is a hard, sunbaked crust of dirt you could fry the whole chicken on, never mind the egg.

desert rats who prowl the Western Verge in hopes of hiring themselves out as professional camel trackers.

I said "you got any water? Food? A parasol, perchance?"

"We can travel at night and reach Youda Tank by morning."[22]

"Youda Tank, huh? Can you remember the last time it rained?"

"Sure. It rained a couple of days ago. Three days ago. You complained on account of you'd just taken a bath, and you didn't think it was fair because you had to get wet twice in the same day."

"Vern, just because it rained in Arcadia doesn't mean it rained in the Great Empty."

"I know that."

"Big chance to take. What if there's no water in the tank?"

Vern thought it over. Finally, he offered a compromise. "Tell you what," he said. "We can hole up here all day tomorrow, then camel up for a night hike tomorrow night."[23]

"What do you hope to find out there?"

"The rats might know something. We don't have to cut trail across the whole desert. But we can't come all this way and not talk to them. Maybe they've got the key to the whole puzzle."

I rubbed my head. The pork pie was giving me a headache. It was too small, and it tended to fly away in the slightest breeze — unless I yanked it down so tight, my brain couldn't think for wheezing. I took it off and glared at it. The brim was way too narrow; it barely offered any shade at all.

"I miss my old hat."

---

22 Youda Tank is a natural cistern — a hollow dug out of the bedrock where rainwater tends to collect. Similar naturally-occurring water holes are scattered throughout the desert, and they are absolute lifesavers — provided you know where to look for them, and provided they haven't dried up since the last time you passed through.

23 Not the same as chasing camels. To "camel up" means to drink as much water as possible before journeying through a country where the reliability of springs and other water sources is unknown.

INTERLOGUE:
Only the Old Ones Dreamed

IN the beginning, only the Old Ones dreamed.

They dreamed for different reasons than you and I dream. You and I dream in order to make sense of the world as we know it. When we dream, our brains are busy sorting and processing information. Our subconscious minds are hard at work making the free associations and intuitive leaps that will reshape our conscious understanding of reality. But in the minds of the Old Ones, all the information was already sorted and processed: the experiences of a thousand millennia had been catalogued, inventoried, and archived. The world of sights, sounds, smells, tastes, and textures had been sampled, compared, and graded. New sensory inputs were exceedingly rare, and were quickly placed into context. New thoughts were practically unheard of. The data had all been compiled and cross-referenced; there was nothing left to add up.

With a universe of knowledge neatly stacked and ready for rapid recall, dreaming for the Old Ones (most of Them) was a routine experience — like digging into a filing cabinet and pulling out the same piece of paper you've looked at a thousand times before.

This is not to say that Their dreams did not contain great power, for it is said that the Old Ones dreamed the truth. Or, to put it another way: when the Old Ones dreamed, Their dreams (most of them) became real.

Everything we know about the world today — every living thing, every natural law, every wisp of air, every color of the rainbow — exists because an Old One once dreamed it so. If an

Old One were to dream that the Earth had a core like an apple, and the core was filled with planet seeds, and the seeds could be scooped out and planted somewhere out in space, and whole new planets would grow from those seeds, then all of that would be true.[24]

In the beginning, the Old Ones dreamed nothing but new dreams, and the world around Them took shape. The Garden grew until it teemed with life. The seasons ebbed and flowed, the glaciers came and went, and the bustle of activity approached a point of equilibrium.

Then… one of the Old Ones dreamed of people.

Now, the Old Ones are not infallible. Some dreams work out, and others don't. Perhaps, if people had been created earlier in the process, they would have thrived in the hectic, unsettled environment. Perhaps they would have pleasantly surprised the Old Ones by helping the Garden to grow. But people were created late — long after the Garden had already matured and borne fruit. And they just never quite fit in. First, the people insisted on naming everything. Then they shifted everything around. Finally, they invented weeds.

Naturally, there are no "weeds" in the Old Ones' Garden — every plant has a purpose all its own. But the people decided that a well-tended Garden should consist only of "useful" plants, and the rest should be discarded.

The Old Ones tried to get them to stop. But since They were loath to appear in person, They had some difficulty in getting the message across. When They finally did deign to show Themselves, the people immediately started worshipping Them as Gods — which the Old Ones found embarrassing.

---

24 As of this writing, nobody has proved or disproved the existence of planet seeds at the Earth's core. However, that simply means there is work to be done. So much of modern science boils down to discovering the true meaning of the Old Ones' dreams.

Only one of the Old Ones thought people were a good idea. That was Mischief.[25] Of course, it was Mischief who created people. She dreamed of a curious species of apelike creatures with opposable thumbs and opposable minds, and people came to be. All the Others thought people were a mistake and should be undreamed. But Mischief refused, and since the decision was not unanimous, the creation could not be erased — it could only be contained.

So the Old Ones banished people to a single narrow valley, along with a few other dreams that just didn't pan out. For untold eons, the people lived in the valley, and they were as happy as they knew how to be. But people are designed to be restless; inevitably, they began to tell themselves stories about the world beyond the mountains. Maybe it wasn't so bad, after all.

Despite warnings and against all reason, they began probing for a way through.

---

25 Mischief (a.k.a. The Trickster, or The Cozener) has many names. She is called The Imp in some cultures. In others, She is The Raven or The Fox or The Coyote. The Stache people of Upper Lipp call Her Signified Sid, but they refuse to explain why. They just twitch their whiskers as if to say "why don't you chew on it a while?"

CHAPTER 24:
This Is How Your Story Ends

THE Great Empty Desert is as wild as Wild Side gets. Even buzzards make a point of settling all their worldly affairs before launching themselves on those blistering winds. Granted, No Aces is only about forty miles into the furnace, but those are forty hard, unforgiving miles. Traveling at night provides some respite from the heat, but not from the quiet terrors that lurk in the darkness, waiting for unwary travelers to blunder into their midst.

Not all the terrors are living monsters, either. The desert floor tilts and twists and plays tricks with shadows — sometimes throwing boulders out of nowhere, sometimes dropping away altogether.

First night out, I knocked my pork pie loose while leaping over a rattlesnark.[26] I landed a safe distance away, but the hat kept going. I lunged for to catch it — and came within a whisker of walking straight off a precipice. The pork pie wasn't so fortunate. It tumbled over the edge and fell into a canyon so deep, the echoes came back panting.

"Dang!" I said.

Vern dropped a rock into the canyon. On the count of four, we heard it bounce. It bounced again at six, rattled through the seven and eight counts, and kicked off a landslide that rumbled on for another four counts before coming to rest.

Vern looked at me. "Do you want to go after it?"

---

26 Rattlesnarks are closely related to rattlesnakes, but they don't shake their rattles until *after* they've bitten you. It's their way of adding insult to injury.

"I'm not that attached," I said. And I wasn't — the pork pie never really fit my character. Not to mention my head.

He nodded. Relieved, probably. "We'll find you another hat."

Even Vern had trouble with the terrain. By the second night, he was barking back at the shin-barkers. We'd slipped down into a wide canyon in search of an easier route. But there was less light to see by in the canyon, and the footing was occasionally treacherous.

"Dang tip toads," I grumbled as a boulder shifted suddenly under my feet. Tip toads are known for destabilizing canyon floors by burrowing under the rocks, making them tippy.

Vern said "I don't remember this route being so troublesome. Do you?"

"Maybe we're going the wrong way."

"Ha! That would be hilarious, wouldn't it?"

Good thing Vern doesn't have a sense of humor. If he did, I'd be worried about him.

"Not especially so," I said. "Do you know where we are, or not?"

"More or less. I'll know for sure when the sun comes up."

"Terrific," I said, as a Kalabian bayonet skewered my left knee.[27] "Ow."

"You okay?"

"More or less. How long till we get to No Aces?"

Vern paused to take a drink from his canteen. "I reckon we'll make it before the sun stops yawning."

"That's what you said about Youda Tank." We'd missed the tank by such a wide margin, we had to flag down a vulture and

---

27 Kalabian bayonet is a desert plant with long, thin, rigid leaves ending in a very sharp point. The leaves resemble the bayonets once used by the elite Kalabian air force, before they discovered how very nearly impossible it is to force the air to do anything it doesn't want to do.

ask directions. Naturally, the vulture didn't want to tell us. His beak pointed east, but his eyes kept flicking away to the south.

We followed his eyes instead of his beak. It's fair to say the vulture was rather disappointed.

"Well, last night we had to find a way around that chasm you almost fell into, and then we got turned around a bit when the dragons attacked.[28] But tonight's been pretty quiet, so far."

"What's that?" I said, pointing at a shadow blocking our path.

Vern stopped. "It's a shadow," he said doubtfully.

"Of what?"

"Good question."

The moon — a waxing crescent — had gone down hours ago. Somebody had come along and thrown a few extra shovel-loads of stars into the sky. Their combined light still didn't add up to a sputtering candle, but it was enough to see shades of darkness. It was enough to create pools of deep shadow.

But a shadow isn't supposed to be three-dimensional. It isn't supposed to rise up from the desert floor like… well, like a giant hole that somehow managed to climb up out of itself.

A shadow isn't supposed to reach out, as if to touch you — as if to pour itself into you, filling you with dark emptiness.

"Step back," said Vern.

I stepped back. The shadow advanced. I stepped back some more. "What's doing that?"

"I don't know. Go around that way."

We tried to edge around the left-hand side. The shadow moved with us. I heard a faint crackling sound, like sand shifting underfoot.

---

28 There are no actual dragons in the Great Empty Desert. Real dragons live far away, in the wretched wastelands of Grumbly Stitch. The small, fire-breathing lizards locally known as "dragons" are actually hot-headed skinks. The desert rats like to say they can be used to light cigars, but I wouldn't advise it. Hot-headed skinks are notoriously vicious for their size, and if you happen to wander into their territory, they tend to come at you in a swarm of tiny fireballs.

"Now would have been a good time to own a flashlight," I said. Neither one of us carried any such thing. Flashlights and headlamps can be handy in certain circumstances, but in general, they're more trouble than they're worth. They spoil your night vision. They focus your attention on a single tight beam, while putting your other senses on mute. And they tend to draw the attention of all sorts of bugs and beasts, most of whom you're better off not knowing.

On the other hand, their sudden, dazzling luminescence is occasionally enough to make shadows flee. So there is that.

"I don't think even broad daylight could penetrate that thing," said Vern. "Do you feel that?"

"The prickles? Yeah, I feel it."

It felt like something was crawling all over me, inside and out. It was a physical sensation without any physical cause — like the feeling you get when you sense somebody staring at you behind your back, only a thousand times magnified.

"We're running out of room," Vern said. We'd contrived to put a few steps between us and whatever caused that shadow, but the near-side canyon wall was looming in front of us. The shadow maneuvered to pin us against it. "Back up. We'll try to loop around the other side."

We executed a crescent-moon reversal, staying out of reach of the thing while circling around. If we hadn't been trapped in a canyon, it might have worked; the shadow didn't move fast, but it played the angles well.

"Why don't we just go back?" I said.

Vern didn't answer. His eyes were on the far-side canyon wall. He headed straight for it, even when it was clear we'd never get around. "What are you thinking?" I said — knowing full well what Vern was thinking.

"If we can get up to the rim, I think we'll be safe. Whatever it is, I bet it can't climb."

"Aren't we on the wrong side of the canyon?" The way to No Aces should have been up the other wall, unless I missed my guess.

"Doesn't matter. We get around that thing, we can cross again later. Anyway, the other side is too broken for night travel."

We retreated along the wall, looking for a way up. The shadow followed us. The prickling sensation intensified. It seemed to carry an undertone of suspicion and loathing. "What does it want with us?"

"I don't know."

About a hundred yards down the wall, we found a crack. Vern squeezed himself into it and began to chimney his way up.

I said "you're kidding!"

People who enjoy rock climbing enough to make a sport of it are a complete mystery to me. I figure there's almost always an easier way up. I was tempted to leave Vern to his folly and head down canyon looking for it. But that ominous, dark emptiness kept inching closer. Once again, I heard a faint crackling sound.

"Come on, Abner. Shake a leg."

"That's what I'm afraid of."

I squeezed myself into the chimney. My legs started trembling almost immediately. My brain sort of detached itself and commenced a disparaging commentary on what my body was doing. *You're gonna die tonight. You know that? One way or another. This is how your story ends: you're gonna die running away from a shadow. You're gonna fall and break your head open, all because you're scared of something you can't even see. That foot doesn't go there, you lumbering oaf. Your legs cold? You sure? They're shivering pretty bad...*

Slowly — too slowly — I clawed my way up the chimney. The crackling sound got louder. Then the sound turned hollow before tapering off. I didn't care anymore. My hands were slick. My eyes stung from the rivers of sweat pouring down my face. The canyon wasn't that deep — maybe twenty feet, maybe twenty-five — but

I was plumb exhausted by the time Vern grabbed my arm and hauled me up. "Come on," he said. "Let's get away from the rim."

The ground exploded not ten feet away. A thought that wasn't mine roared in my head like a bellowing catawampus. A tentacle of darkness shot into the air, hesitated, then reached in our direction.

"Run!"

CHAPTER 25:
The Great Empty

LET'S just say it was a long night.

Deserts aren't designed for running through — especially not by the dark of the moon. Before it was over, Vern was limping and my hands and knees ached from tripping over a cactus. Dawn found us miles off course. By the time we caught sight of No Aces, the sun had taken offense at our presence. It shot us a withering glance every time we stepped out of the shadows — and we were running out of shadows.

Vern said "there it is."

"Praise Blue." My head felt like candle wax, grown soft under the flame. We stumbled forward.

No Aces is built like a fortress: it's a single massive stone building set up against the base of a cliff. That's where the similarity ends, though. Shucks, there isn't even a door you can close. Inside, it's quite cozy. The common room takes up most of the interior. A few smaller chambers line the back wall. Mostly they're for storage, except for the one in the middle. That's the pump room.

You'd never guess from the bleached rocks and the brown and brittle landscape, but No Aces sits right on top of an underground river flowing deep beneath the surface.

Back in old man Noah's day, the place was called Noah's Ace — "ace" being short for oasis — although, in desert rat terminology, it can refer to any perennial water source. Youda Tank is an ace. It's open to everybody. But Noah's Ace belonged to Noah on account of he found the water, dug the well, and built the trading post around it.

After Noah died, the place went commune. Nobody really took over. People came and went, though a few stayed longer than others. As the years went by, the name gradually changed from Noah's Ace to No Aces. It's a play on words, you see: in the old days, a person who controlled an ace was himself called an Ace. So "No Aces" is just the squatters' way of saying none of us own this water hole. Still and all, as a matter of courtesy, it's best to ask permission before pumping your share.

Anyway, Vern and I dragged our withered carcasses through the arched entrance and stood for a moment like sentinels, one on either side of the threshold, giving our eyes a chance to get used to the gloom.

A voice called out from close by. "You need a guide?"

Another said "that's Vern. And… some other guy."

From across the room, a woman called out. "Hey, Vern. Who's the tenderfoot?"

That voice I knew. I still couldn't see anything, but you only have to hear Cinder's voice one time to remember it for the rest of your life. It's the voice of an opera singer — a sonorous contralto that would sound glorious no matter where you heard it, but especially so way out here in the Great Empty. Whenever Cinder speaks, it's like the desert coming to life after the rain.

Cinder herself is a tall, sturdy woman who looks like she's been set on fire and come out hardened, polished, and stronger than ever. When she's not hiring herself out as a guide, she tends a small herd of desert sheep out by Woolly Mountain. She — or someone in her household — probly made Vern's winter woolens. She also makes pulque, which endears her to every desert rat on the Western Verge.

I said "Cinder! It's great to hear you, wherever you are."

She laughed. The sound resonated like ringing a bell.

From the far shadows, a fourth voice said "come on in, boys! Grab a seat and tell us the news from beyond."

That would be Grudge — the big, burly, unfortunately named mule driver. I've never seen Grudge without a smile as wide as the crescent moon on his round, ruddy, sweat-streaked face. But then, I've never seen him angry. I hope I never do.

My eyes were beginning to distinguish shapes and shadows. Tell you true, it wasn't that dark in there — but the sun outside was so dazzlingly brilliant, it made the dimness of the common room seem a whole lot darker.

The common room contained a few stone slabs that served as tables or benches. A ring of sitting stones huddled near the door. Various corners were piled with the current occupants' personal possessions as if to stake out their sleeping billets.

A dusty old prospector named Kinglet occupied a table near the door. Kinglet roams the Great Empty Desert the way Vern roams all of Wild Side, only Kinglet never leaves the desert. He claims he's searching for the mother lode, but honestly, I don't think he cares a whit about gold, nor any other precious metal. He just likes being out there.

Two people I didn't recognize were sitting with him: a proud young man not much older than a boy, and a white-haired woman who looked like she'd been born in the desert and never left.

Kinglet said "that other feller looks like Abner, but it can't be. Abner's got more sense than to go wandering in the desert without a hat."

Grudge laughed. He and Cinder sat cross-legged on a table near the back, a pulque jug nestled between them. "If any one of us had a lick of sense, we wouldn't be out here to see it."

I said "funny story about my hat: you see, I was paddling it across Fathom River one day. Now, ordinarily I'd take the canoe, but my canoe had a hole in it, and my bicycle, for all its enthusiasm, just doesn't seem to understand the concept of staying afloat. So that left me with no other options but to turn my hat upside down, climb inside, and start paddling."

Kinglet smirked. "Ah, now I see the resemblance. Yep, that's Abner."

Vern said "does anybody mind if we pump some water?"

Grudge waved a hand in the direction of the pump room. "Sure, help yourself. Then you can tell us what's new in the world. Where'd you come from, the West?"

"Yes sir," I said, taking up the conversation while Vern filled his water bottles. "By way of Arcadia."

Grudge said "you bring anything to trade?"

"Got some stories."

"Anything else? Tools? Weapons? Livestock? Anything useful?"

"Nah. Didn't think of it. Didn't expect to be crossing the Verge this trip."

"You go much farther, you're gonna need a mule," Grudge said hopefully. He had a string of mules somewhere nearby. We'd seen the sign.

"Thanks. This is about as far as we plan to go." I added a few decibels to that last bit, just to make sure Vern could hear me.

Cinder pushed the jug forward. "Want some pulque?"

Pulque makes me feel woozy. "Maybe later," I said.

"You sure? It's a powerful good batch."

"I don't doubt it. But I spose I'd better rehydrate first."

I plunked myself down on a sitting stone. Grudge and Cinder came over to join me. So did Kinglet and the others. King-let introduced the kid as Hunter — a descriptive name, if not terribly imaginative. The woman's name was Wren. She stared at my hands, muttered to herself, and pulled a jar of salve out of her pouch.

"Wren's got a talent for healing," said Kinglet. "We're mighty glad of her society."

I smiled at her. She growled back. "What kind of fool thing you been up to, boy? Playing catch with a cactus? Put that on your hands, and anywhere else you got pricked."

"Much obliged," I said.

Grudge winked. "You and Vern get in some kind of adventure?"

I looked around at five expectant faces. It had been so long, I almost didn't recognize them for what they were: an audience. And an eager one, at that. So I said "we surely did, now you mention it. Happened about ten miles west of here." I paused to rub the salve onto my knees.

"Not too much," Wren snapped. "There's worse cases than yours."

Kinglet said "what happened, Abner?"

"Well sir, along about two o'clock in the morning, we came face to face with Midnight."

Hunter scratched his head. "You celebrated midnight at two o'clock in the morning?"

"No, not the hour of midnight. That's just what we decided to call it."

"Call what?"

"The deepest, darkest shadow you can imagine. Deeper than a hole in the bottom of the ocean. Darker than the shady side of space. We still don't know what it was, but it chewed a hole through a solid rock wall trying to catch us. We barely got away."

Something was wrong. The audience should have been on the edge of their seats. Instead, they were just on edge. *Am I telling it wrong? Have I forgotten how to spin a yarn?*

"Did It follow you here?" Cinder asked. She was deadly serious.

Vern came back from the pump room. "Did what follow us here?"

"I was just telling them about Midnight," I said.

Grudge got up and peered out the door. Hunter got up and strung his bow. Kinglet looked worried. Kinglet never looks worried. He said "you wouldn't be pulling our legs now, would you, Abner?"

I didn't know how to answer that. It's a question I get all the time, for some head-scratching reason — but I never got it this early in the tale before. So I said "'course not. Er... why do you ask?"

"Only two things that eat through solid rock: water, and the Great Empty."

He said it like it was a proverb — or a prophesy. Even Vern looked worried now. *What am I missing?* Out loud, I said "the desert eats rocks?"

"No," said Grudge, still peering out the door. "He means the Thing that made the desert. The Thing the desert is named after."

I looked at Vern. "I thought the Great Empty Desert got its name because it's big, and it's got almost nothing in it."

"Well, there are stories…" Vern said slowly.

Kinglet interrupted. "The Great Empty is an evil Earth spirit."

"It's not evil," Cinder countered. "But It's dangerous and unpredictable. It usually manifests as a void — an emptiness. Negative space. Some folks call It the Eater of Worlds. Others call It The Worm, on account of the way It travels underground."

Kinglet said "this part of the world used to be paradise. So the story goes. Used to be rivers and lakes and fields and fountains, till the Great Empty tore it all up. 'Course, that was a million years ago, but we've all heard the stories."

"I'm going to check on the mules," said Grudge.

"He'd better not try to bring them all in here," Wren muttered. "The place smells bad enough."

"If the Great Empty is on the prowl, it won't matter," said Cinder. "Nowhere is safe."

Hunter said "well, I'm not going down without a fight." He showed Cinder his best warrior face. Cinder smiled and shook her head, as if to say *How can you fight negative space?*

I said "how often does It go on the prowl?" I couldn't imagine anybody still living here, with an empty malevolent Void careening around the desert, laying waste to everything on a regular basis.

Cinder looked at Wren. Wren said "not in my lifetime."

"Like Kinglet said, the Great Empty is an Earth spirit," said Cinder. "It's always there, but you rarely see It. You might see signs of Its passing — some folks thought the rockslide up on Mount Molehill a few years ago might have been the work of the Great Empty — but nobody I know ever claimed to see the spirit Itself. What about you, Kinglet? Anybody talking up a Great Empty sighting out on the Eastern Verge?"

"Heard a campfire tale or two," he said. "But not from any credible source."

Everybody gave me the fish eye. I don't know why. "Don't look at me that way," I said. "You know I'm only telling you what I saw."

"Well, you've been known to tell a whopper from time to time, Abner. Not that we don't appreciate it. But the Great Empty is nothing to spin yarns about."

I said "Vern, back me up here."

Vern hesitated. That traitor. But finally, he said "it's true. We both saw It. I didn't remember the legends until just now."

More likely it didn't occur to him the legends could be real. Vern's a believe-it-when-I-see-it kind of guy. Though I did marvel at how there seemed to be a whole genre of tales that Vern knew and I didn't.

Cinder said "you'd better both tell us what happened."

So we told them — although, truth be told, Vern didn't do much more than nod and say "that's right." He had something else on his mind. Probly figuring out how to reconcile one more legend coming to life.

"Strangest part came when we finally got clear of The Worm." I reckoned I'd call It that, on account of it was easier to say than Eater of Worlds. I thought of that tendril of dark emptiness reaching blindly in our direction, and suppressed a shudder. "I told you about the roaring inside my head. Well, it became a thought. Only the thought wasn't mine."

"What's your meaning?"

"I mean, the roar didn't have any words to it, just emotion — like a crowd cheering when the bad guy gets caught. But then the roar died away, and I heard… not words, exactly. More like the thought before the words."

"What did it say?"

"It said *you are not him.*"

Everybody looked at Vern. He nodded. "That's right. I heard it, too."

"That doesn't make any sense," said Hunter. "You are not *who*?"

"No idea," I said.

Vern said nothing a-tall.

In fact, nobody said anything for a long while. Cinder took a big swig of pulque and passed the jug to Kinglet. Hunter stood in the doorway, scanning the desert with wary eyes. Wren kept shifting her gaze from Vern to me, then back again. Finally, Cinder broke the silence. "What happened next?"

"Nothing. No more ghost thoughts, no more prickly sensations, and no more malevolent anti-Worms bursting through the pan. Took us hours to get back on course, but here we are."

Hunter said "I get it now: *you are not him.* You both heard that. You know what that means? It means the Great Empty is coming after one of *us.*"

"Piffle," said Wren. But she glanced back at the storerooms as if she wanted to barricade herself in. Or grab her gear and fly.

Cinder said "doesn't matter who It's after — we need to spread the word. Tell the rats to scatter."

Hunter disagreed. "We need to fortify this place. Maybe pile rocks in front of the door."

Kinglet said "to stop the Eater of Worlds? A few rocks won't make any difference."

"Might slow It down some."

"Might trap us in here, too," said Kinglet. "Cinder's right: we need to get the word out."

Cinder said "you boys have any idea what direction It might be heading?"

"Nope."

Vern piped up. "Might learn something if we have a poke around the encounter site."

"Good idea," I said, imagining a retinue of desert rats escorting us halfway back to Youda Tank.

Cinder nodded. "If It's headed for Woolly Mountain, I want to know it."

Cinder had a flock to protect. Probly more than that: she wouldn't have traveled this far away from her spread without leaving somebody behind to watch over the sheep. I wondered who it was. Partner? Family member? Hired hand?

I didn't ask. In the desert, one doesn't pry.

Kinglet said "we'd better get some sleep. Too hot to stir right now. Let the sun come around the other side of noon. Then we'll see what happens."

HEE HAW! HEE HAW! HEE HAW! HEE HAAAAWWWW!

Eater of Worlds! I ran to the doorway in time to see Grudge coming around the side of the building with half a dozen mules in tow. They were not happy about being out and about in the heat of the day.

"Why didn't you leave them where they were!" screamed Wren.

"I lose them, I lose everything."

"Well, they're not coming in here!"

But it was too late. The mules could already smell the relative coolness of the air inside No Aces. They crowded the doorway in their haste to get in.

"Out!" screamed Wren. "Out!"

"They're family," said Grudge.

Kinglet said "that ain't what you call 'em the other six days of the week."

"They'll be safer here than down in the paddock."

"That's debatable," said Cinder. "But if it were me, I might do the same."

"Hyah! Scat!" Wren flailed her arms, to no avail. "Somebody help me keep them out of the pump room!"

INTERLOGUE:
Pursuant to Council Rule 2(b)

THE Old Ones' apprehension grew. The people no longer seemed content to remain in their isolated valley. Sooner or later, they would find a way back into the Garden. The Old Ones could not allow that. But even all-powerful supernatural Beings must follow the rules, and the rules are quite clear on this point: no One can unmake an entire species without its Creator's permission.

So They did the only thing They could do. They called a meeting.

Now, the ways and means of the Old Ones are unknowable, and it's plain hubris to describe a gathering of ancient, immortal supernatural Beings in terms more appropriate to an official gathering of culturally homogenous humans. Plain hubris, that's what it is. Still and all, there's never been a teller in the history of storytelling who didn't engage in a spot of hubris now and then.[29] So here goes:

The Old Ones called a meeting, and you know what that means: Everybody groaned. Most of Them tried to postpone, and half of Them showed up late, and several of Them pretended They didn't receive any of the numerous multi-formatted, high-priority meeting notifications and didn't even show up at all.

---

29 Except for the absurdly-named Hugh Briss, who only ever told self-deprecating stories about jars he couldn't get open and doors he couldn't get closed. There are those who speculate that Hugh's repertoire, taken as a whole, was meant to point to some deep metaphysical revelation hidden behind a Zen koan-like metaphor, to wit: *the door is a jar*. But most commentators are quick to dismiss any deeper-meaning theory by saying "nah, that's just Hugh Briss."

And a very, very small percentage of Those who did turn up were only there for the doughnuts (figuratively speaking, of course).

"*Meeting will come to order,*" said The Spider, who always chaired such meetings.[30]

"*I'll have steak and onions,*" said Mischief. "*To go, please.*"

"*Not that kind of order,*" said The Spider. "*We are here to discuss... checks notes... your most recent failed experiment.*"

"*Define 'failed'.*"

"*We did that last time. Does no One read the meeting minutes? 'Pursuant to Council Rule 2(b), the species of being colloquially referred to as* people *are deemed by a majority of Those present to be ill-conceived, poorly executed, and insufficiently supervised. Said decision not being unanimous, the aforementioned species is hereby relegated to abide in the Valley of Misfits until such time as'... well... forever, really.*"

"*It does not say forever. You added that last part just now.*"

"*So You do read the minutes. Good. Then You know We agreed to keep them there until such a time as We see fit.*"

"*I vote We set them free.*"

"*You dreamed them up. You don't get a vote.*"

"*Oh, come on. They're fun! They're unpredictable. They make life interesting.*"

"*You know the rules. Once an experiment has been relegated, the Creator may not release them back into the Garden. Only another member of the Council may do that.*"

Here, a new "voice" joined the conversation. It belonged to a Being currently taking the form of an unblinking falcon. "*This is old business,*" said The Falcon. "*The issue is not whether to release*

---

30 The Spider, like Mischief, has many names. Her domain is often described as the so-called "web of life," but it's best not to get carried away with the whole spider-and-web analogy. She was not there to trap prey — Her function at these gatherings was to hold things together and to bind Everybody to a common cause. And obviously, She didn't actually *say* "meeting will come to order," on account of that's not how the Old Ones communicate. What She did was, She broadcast Her thought in such a way as to be understood by Those present. But you knew that already, so let's move on.

them. The point is, they are dangerously close to getting loose by their own efforts."

"Good for them!" said Mischief. "You gotta love their sense of adventure."

"If they enter the Garden on their own, it will be their undoing," said The Spider. "Your experiment will be deemed out of bounds, and Your people will be unmade."

"Yes, well. I'd best not let that happen then, eh?"

"And how do You propose to prevent it?"

"Ah. I'm glad You asked," said Mischief. "Let Me tell You about a little side project I've been working on..."

CHAPTER 26:
The Mark of the Tinderfoot

NOBODY got much sleep that day. The mules were excited and eager to explore their new surroundings. Grudge had his hands full keeping them out of the storerooms. He and Cinder rigged a picket line between two tables and tied them to it. They complained and did their best to shake off their halters. But eventually, they settled down and made themselves at home by filling the air with a sweaty, flatulent, mule-breathed bouquet of aromas.

The rats spent half the afternoon arguing about what to do with the mules. Grudge wanted to take them along on our search for Great Empty tracks. Wren and Kinglet objected, saying it was a recon mission, not a milk run. Cinder said yes, but what happens after we find the trail? Do we waste time coming all the way back here, or do we scatter and warn the others? Hunter said just finding the trail wasn't enough — that we had to follow it, for as long as it takes. Grudge said all the more reason to bring the mules, and around and around they went.

I fell asleep in the pump room.

Any other day, that would have been an inexcusable breach of No Aces etiquette — too much akin to staking out a personal claim on the water source. You're supposed to pump what you need and get out of the way. No aces, remember? But it was the coolest room in town, and the air was clean and fresh, and the debate going on in the common room sounded as far away as a dream. I only meant to rest my eyes for a minute…

Woke up to a mule braying in my ear.

Not really, but that's what it sounded like. I finished filling my water bottles and crawled sheepishly back into the common room. Kinglet gave me a look, but nobody said anything.

Vern didn't even try to sleep Town Side. He's not used to all that commotion. He found a sliver of shade further down the escarpment and tucked himself into it as best he could.

It was one of those days, you could almost hear the ground popping and crackling from the sun's heat. Late afternoon didn't bring any relief — but by then, most of us couldn't stand the fetid air inside No Aces any longer. Vern, Kinglet, Wren, Hunter and I loaded up with water and pushed ahead in search of Great Empty sign. Grudge and Cinder followed behind with the mules.

Hunter raced ahead, eager to show off his tracking skills. He followed our back trail, chuckling to himself from time to time about how easy we'd made it. Vern let him build up a sizable lead, then called him back. He said "it's this way."

Hunter stood like a dog caught between a squirrel and the dinner bell. "The tracks go this way."

"We didn't come by the most direct route. Remember? The Great Empty forced us off course. We can save a few steps by shaving the corner."

Hunter looked doubtful. "Better to follow the tracks. We take the direct route, we might miss the exact spot where the Great Empty broke off pursuit."

"Suit yourself," said Vern. And without another word, he lit out straight across the pan.

I followed Vern. So did everybody else. When the cost of every step is another drop of sweat, it's hard to turn your back on a shortcut.

Three hours later, we were crossing the broken, gouged, and gully-scarred mesa just east of Midnight Canyon. The sun had gone to ground. The twilight was giving me the jitters. I swiveled my head from side to side, searching for any sign of a looming, malevolent Void. The doubts piled up in the back of my mind like scree: *is this really such a good idea? What if The Worm is still skulking about? Shouldn't we be giving Its last known location a wide berth?*

That's when Vern stopped short. I nearly walked into him. He threw his arms out wide to keep me from scattering the five stones arranged on the ground in a familiar pattern:

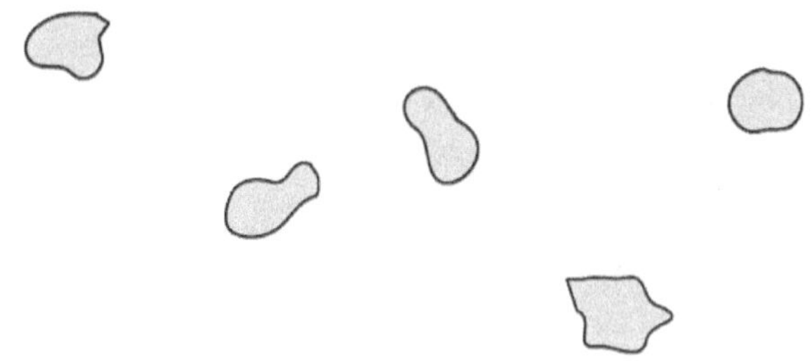

"Huh. Fancy that," I said.

"He was here," said Vern. "Yesterday, when you and I were leaving Youda Tank. We missed him by a few hours."

Hunter trotted over. He'd been scouting our flanks. He said "whatcha got?"

"Have you ever seen this sign before?"

Hunter stared blankly at the ground. "What sign?"

"The rock pattern," said Vern.

"Which rocks?"

He had a point. The mesa top was hard sandstone, swept clean of loose dirt and dust by the wind — but rocks and pebbles were scattered all over the place. Amid such a landscape, the sign of Pedestrio doesn't stand out all that much — unless you've seen it before.

Kinglet and Wren caught up. Kinglet recognized the pattern at a glance. "That's the mark of the Tinderfoot."

Vern's eyebrows shot up. "*Tenderfoot?*"

"No, Tinderfoot. I call him that on account of I've seen him walking barefoot across the pan in high summer. Surprised his feet didn't burst into flames."

"You've seen him?"

"Couple of times. From a distance."

"More than meets the eye with that one," said Wren.

"When?" Vern demanded. "Where?"

"Easy, Vern," I said. His voice had a hard edge to it. That spooked me. We'd spent a gallon of sweat to get this far, but it was worth it: we were ten miles closer to spring rains and leafy greenery. Last thing we needed was for Vern to go bounding off into the desert on a wild Pedestrio chase.

Hunter said "hey, are we gonna track down the Great Empty, or not? We're losing daylight."

"You wanted to know who It's after," Vern said sharply. "Now you know."

"We don't know squat," answered Hunter. "You ain't even showed us your backtrail yet. How do we know you ain't making the whole thing up?"

Vern ignored him. He bent down to study the pattern more closely. The awkward silence didn't last long. Kinglet said in a calm, quiet voice, he said "you're telling us the Great Empty is after Tinderfoot?"

Vern nodded.

"What's your evidence?"

"It was looking for *someone,*" said Vern. "No sign that anyone else has been out here, apart from this mark. And it's less than a day old."

"Where's the Great Empty's trail?"

"Down in yonder canyon."

"You see any sign of Tinderfoot down there?"

"Not that I noticed. I think It got here too late. The man you call Tinderfoot was already gone, so It sniffed out Abner and me. I reckon we were the only two people nearby."

"Reasonable assumption," said Kinglet reasonably. "Tell you what: let's see if we can find the Great Empty's trail while there's still some daylight left. Might learn a bit more from that."

I reckon Kinglet could have talked a winter wind into staying home by the fire and not coming out again till summer, so long as he showed a willingness to listen to what it had to say. Vern nodded once, stood up, and stomped off in the direction of the canyon rim.

CHAPTER 27:
The Sociable Type

THE crescent moon kept watch as the light of day faded. Wasn't dark enough yet for any stars to peek through, but shadows were gathering. I searched every one of them for seething patches of emptiness. Terrifying thoughts scudded through my head as we found a passable route and scrambled down into the canyon. *What if The Worm lives down there? Could we be walking right into Its lair?*

"There they are," said Wren.

I looked up. Grudge and Cinder had found an easier mule route into the canyon. They reached the encounter site about the same time we did. Cinder gestured at the furrowed track near the base of the canyon wall. It was several inches deep — negative space or not, The Worm definitely had mass. "That it?"

Vern nodded. "This is where It cut us off the first time."

"Mighty big track," said Grudge. "Gotta be a yard across."

"It bunched up a bit when It got near the wall. The track gets narrower over that way."

We followed The Worm's backtrail. Sure enough, the track thinned to about the width of a large, well-fed snake. Kinglet said "you sure you didn't get accosted by an anaconda?"

Wren said "anaconda's a jungle snake, you old fool."

Kinglet studied the ground in an effort to hide the twinkle in his eye.

Hunter said "maybe it got lost."

I brightened up. Just for a second, I felt like I was back at Elmer's Café again. "If It's this wide," I said "imagine how long It is. Maybe we only saw the head, and the tail is still down there in the jungle."

Wren muttered something about fools. I didn't catch all of it. But it went something like this: *some 'at's old fools, and some 'at's young fools, and some 'at's continuous.*

"It's not a snake," said Vern. "A snake would exhibit a completely different movement pattern."

Grudge said "the way I heard it, the Great Empty is supposed to be a shapeless Blob."

I said "that's what It looked like when we first saw It. Like a hole in the world, only the hole didn't have any edges. You know, like the hole kept widening itself, like the edges were being eaten away."

"Eater of Worlds," muttered Wren.

Hunter said "that track wasn't made by a shapeless Blob."

"No, It sort of stretched out when It started chasing us."

"There's your hole in the world," said Vern. He stopped and pointed to a dark stain on the ground. "This is the spot where the Great Empty dry-gulched us."

"Looks more like a hole in the pan," said Kinglet. "Patched with clay."

Vern crouched down and studied the ground. Kinglet was right — all around, the canyon floor was either hard rock or dry sand, but this patch looked like somebody had rolled around on a mountain of loam. Vern ran a fingertip along the edge of the stain. I winced, half expecting him to get sucked in — or a shadowy Monster to rise up and devour him. But nothing of the sort happened. Instead, he dropped to his knees and crawled forward, testing the ground in front of him with his hands. His knees sank in deeper and deeper with every advance.

Near the center of the patch, he stopped crawling and began to dig.

"I think it's a tunnel," he said. "The Great Empty came to the surface here. Then It settled down to wait."

The sky was getting dark. The heat of the day still lingered, and yet I felt a chill nonetheless. I said "Vern, stop digging!"

He looked up. "Why?"

"It's a trap, that's why! You're gonna fall right into Its lair!"

Vern sat back on his heels. "This is cast," he said.

"Fine," I said. "Whatever. You're gonna get *cast* right into Its lair."

"No, I mean castings. Dissolved or digested rock and soil and vegetation. They'd be piled as high as an anthill, if the Great Empty hadn't smooshed them all around."

Wren squatted down and rubbed a pinch of patch between her fingers. "That's good soil, that is. The Eater of Worlds must have devoured half of Arcadia to dump a load this rich."

Kinglet said "from now on, every time I see a desert rose in bloom, I'll wonder if it's sitting atop an old giant Worm hole."

Vern stood up. "There'll be another track a ways down canyon that'll take us to the opposite wall. If we climb up to the rim, I can show you where the Great Empty chased us, and where It broke off the chase. We won't get there before dark, though. So if you don't mind, can you tell me a bit more about Tinderfoot?"

Good thinking, Vern, I thought. *Let's get what we came for and get out of here.*

Kinglet explained to Grudge and Cinder. "We found the mark of the Tinderfoot up on the mesa. Vern thinks that's who the Great Empty was after."

Cinder's eyebrows bunched up like scared caterpillars. "*Tinderfoot?* What for? He barely leaves a footprint."

"Agreed," said Grudge. "The Earth spirits don't show Themselves to those of us who live small."

Wren curled her lip and tossed her head at Grudge's string of mules. "You call that living small?"

"All I'm saying is, you'd have to put a mighty big stamp on the world to rate a visit from the Great Empty."

Vern said to Cinder, he said "you've seen him too?"

"I have," she said. "Early one morning, on Woolly Mountain. Wasn't quite light yet, and all I saw was a shadow outlined against the sky. But there was no reason for anybody to be up that high, so I set out to investigate. 'Course, he was long gone by the time I got there."

"Did he leave anything behind?"

"Not so much as a buried char. I'll say this for Tinderfoot: he keeps a clean camp."

"No, I mean, how did you know it was Tinderfoot? Did he leave his mark behind?"

"If he did, I never found it — and I searched all over the summit."

I said to Vern, I said "maybe he only does it in the evening." But Vern ignored me. He had something on his mind.

Cinder said "you're right, of course — I don't know for a fact that it was Tinderfoot. Howbeit, all the stock was accounted for, and nobody came a-calling, so I've got no answer as to who else it could have been."

Cinder's the rare desert rat who welcomes visitors. They come to trade for mutton or wool or pulque. On occasion, she'll drive the odd rustler out of her territory, but most of that ilk has learned to stay away by now.

Kinglet said "first time I saw Tinderfoot, I thought he was drinking sand. He kept reaching down between two boulders, then touching his hand to his mouth. Turned out he'd found himself an ace."

"A spring?" I said.

"More like a seep," said Kinglet. "Pretty well hidden. Hard to reach, even when you know it's there. But it's a real lifesaver — the only perennial ace in the whole Rhea Range."

"Where did he go after that?"

"Disappeared behind a butte. I thought he might have a bivvy nearby, so I settled in to say howdy. He never came back, though."

Now, that's about as neighborly as a lot of folks want you to get in these parts. Best not to go looking for them, on account of they might take exception to being found. But you might hang around the water hole for a spell. If they want to talk, they'll show. If not… well, they're likely to send you a clear message, one way or t'other.

Kinglet wasn't done, though. "A few days later, I climbed up that butte. Wasn't easy. Even tougher coming down. But the top of that butte is where I found the mark of the Tinderfoot. First time I ever saw it. Seen it a bunch of times since."

Vern rubbed the back of his neck and scowled. He kept taking shallow breaths, then letting them out slowly. His jaw worked as if he were teetering on the verge of saying something.

I said "what about you, Grudge? You ever seen Tinderfoot?"

"Sure enough," he said. "I've seen him a bunch of times — mostly from a distance. I like to point him out to clients — especially the camel hunters. Gives 'em a tale they can tell back Town Side: poor old Tinderfoot, cursed to wander the desert without any shoes on — "

Vern exploded. "Why am I the only one who's never seen this guy?!"

And there it was: the bug in his porridge. The nettle under his skin.

Nobody spends more time out-of-doors than Vern. Nobody covers more ground, excepting Pedestrio himself. All those years, wandering the length and breadth of Wild Side, telling himself stories about a legendary rambler who probly wasn't even real, only to find out his imaginary hero is a familiar sight to everybody but him. That's gotta sting.

I said "I've never seen him."

"Who was it sitting on the Bored Rock, Abner?"

"That wasn't — "

"You know it was. Of *course* it was."

"I've never seen him, either," said Hunter.

Vern just gave him a look. There wasn't enough venom in it to make it a contemptuous look, nor enough air to make it dismissive. If such a look could be put into words, it might say something like: *you're out here, now. You're one of us… now. But you ain't been out here that long, and you've got a ways to go. Put a few more years on your bones. Then tell me you've never spotted old Tinderfoot out there on the horizon.*

I never heard Vern whine before, and I've never heard it since. It sounded foreign, coming from Vern. He, of all people, knows the world is not out to get anybody. The world just does what it does, whether you happen to be standing in its way or not. But everybody's got a right to complain about The Unfairness Of It All at least once in their lives, so I gave Vern an awkward pat on the shoulder. He shrugged it off.

"I've put in my time," he said. "I've seen all manner of wildlife, including some that nobody knew existed. I followed the great-horned wildegoose on its annual migration from Lower Sagbelly all the way to Rednose, up in the Yukold Territory. Why have I never caught sight of this one man who seems to turn up everywhere I'm not?"

The silence went on so long, it could have retired and moved to the country. Finally, Grudge scratched the back of his head. "No offense, Vern. But you ain't exactly the sociable type."

Vern blustered, but Grudge cut him off. "Now hold on! It's no slight on your character, and you won't find a rat anywhere in the world who doesn't shy away from people from time to time. But you go out of your way to avoid contact, and that's the only reason you're a stranger to Tinderfoot."

"I don't avoid contact."

"I've *seen* you, Vern. I've seen you crisscrossing the desert on business of your own, and more often than not, you hide whenever you see me coming. Always, if I'm leading a group. Half the time, I'll say 'hey, look everyone! There goes old Tinderfoot, sure enough!' But it's really you, ducking out of sight before anybody can take a decent gander. Now, we all know you, Vern. You drop by No Aces three or four times a year, and you're always welcome. You're good people, and we appreciate your society — so far as it goes. But I reckon if you ever saw Tinderfoot out here in the Wild, like as not you'd turn tail and head in the other direction. What do *you* reckon?"

Vern looked like he wanted to crawl into a thinkhole. I didn't blame him. When a desert rat calls you out for being too much of a hermit, that's gotta dissonate your cognitivity.

"I would have noticed," he insisted. "Pedestrio doesn't move like other people. I would have noticed he was different."

Cinder, in her soothing, melodic voice, said "if Tinderfoot were a speckled skink, you'd notice everything about him. You're a fine observer of nature, Vern. But honestly, how long would you keep watch on a man you didn't recognize?"

"Long enough," he said stubbornly.

Kinglet decided it was time for a strategic changing of the subject. He said "even if Tinderfoot *is* the target, we still need to put the word out. People need to know the Great Empty is abroad again. I say we follow the track as far as it goes, find out everything we can, then split up. Between us, we can carry the message all the way to the Verges."

I said "that sounds like a plan. Vern and I can warn the Arcadians on our way back to town."

Everybody turned and stared at me. I stared back.

"We sort of thought you'd stick around," said Grudge. "Some of the rats are pretty isolated — it's gonna take all hands to reach everybody."

"All the more reason to go Town Side," I said. "Plenty of hands there."

"Let 'em go," said Hunter. "We can take care of our own."

"I'll stay," said Vern. "I want to help."

INTERLOGUE:
The Beguiling Art of Figmentalism

"E*NLIGHTEN Us*," said The Spider.

Mischief looked around. She did this merely for dramatic effect — Her senses already told Her the Earth spirit for whom She was looking wasn't there.

"*Where is The Bear? She should be here for this.*"

"*Then go and get Her,*" said The Spider.

Mischief grinned and performed a slight bow. The Spider was making a joke, you see: only a Fool would ever deliberately set out to wake The Bear.

"*Point to you,*" said Mischief. "*The Bear's presence is not required, so long as Her contribution is acknowledged.*"

"*What contribution?*"

"*Oh, a most ingenious one! You see, The Bear has invented the beguiling art of figmentalism.*"

And it was true: while the other Old Ones dreamed dreams that became true and real and alive, The Bear had somehow learned to dream in abstract concepts that never took any shape or form in the physical world, but lived only in the imagination. These visions had lately been seeping into the minds of some of the larger-brained animals while they slept.

Now, ordinarily this sort of development would have caused a turf war (so to speak) between The Bear and the Old Ones who held dominion over those large-brained animals. But of all the Earth and Sky spirits, The Bear was arguably the most powerful — even if She did spend most of Her time slumbering away.

She also had a reputation for being especially cranky if awakened unnecessarily. It was said that The Bear once fell asleep inside a volcano, and when it erupted, She slapped down so hard on the surging magma that it blew out the other side of the world and shot off into space. It's still out there, afraid to come home. You can see it, most nights.

Now, The Moon will tell you a different story as to how She found Her place in the sky — but the long and short of it is, no One cared to challenge The Bear over trivial matters.

"And how will a few insubstantial visions prevent people from entering the Garden?" asked The Spider.

"They won't," said Mischief. *"They're too light and breezy. They lack emotional impact. What We need is a school of figmentalism that triggers a lower life form's deepest fears. Let Me show You what I mean…"*

Mischief closed Her eyes, and a flash wave of surprise and alarm swept through the Gathering. Outwardly, nothing had changed. But for one terrifying moment, a frightfully realistic vision ripped through the Old Ones' senses: teeth and claws and palpable rage.

You understand, the Old Ones are not accustomed to fear. After all, They are immortal — and while some of Them understand that certain lower life forms do experience the occasional moment of dread, They still don't get it. In Their Garden, the Old Ones have made a place for all living things — what is there to be afraid of?

To be sure, the Garden is not without its garden-variety hazards and worries — but there are no bloodthirsty monsters hanging about. There are no wantonly destructive forces careening across the landscape. There are no things that go bump in the night. Or, to be more precise, there are all of those things: there are lions and wolves and sharks and vicious wild chooks; there are violent thunderstorms, and raging hurricanes, and whip-tailed tornados; and there are lots and lots of things that go bump in the night. But none of these things have what might be called evil intent — they are not out to "get" anyone. They simply act according to their nature. And they certainly pose no threat to the continuing health and well-being of the Old Ones.

Therefore, it is safe to say that Mischief's little demonstration had a profound impact on the Earth spirits present.[31] For one brief moment in Their fantastically long lives, They understood what it means to be terrified. And after The Falcon flew off to check on The Bear — and returned to report that She really was still asleep — and after the rest of the Old Ones had spent an eon or two chasing Mischief through the Garden with malice in Their hearts, They settled down and admitted that Mischief's plan just might work.

So Mischief invented nightmares. She invented the most horrifying visions, and She set them loose in the valley — and the people dreamed of terrible things. They dreamed of deadly creatures lurking in the mountains, waiting to tear the limbs off unsuspecting travelers. They dreamed of uninhabitable valleys, where the bird droppings were poisonous and the trees spit pitch that tasted even worse than the pitch they spat back home in Paradise. They dreamed of falling into bottomless voids, and being run over by tumblerocks that didn't just roll away afterward, but bounced up and down on their poor, broken bodies, until their bones were ground into a fine powder. They dreamed of unspeakable demons — prowling unseen through the dark, ugly regions beyond the mountains — and they trembled in their sleep.

But then they woke up, and looked around, and said to themselves "you know, this life is not so bad. This valley is actually

---

31 The Sky spirits, on the other hand, found the whole thing rather amusing. Only The Moon showed any sign of distress — but the Wishing Star winked at Her as if to say "*it's all right. You're safe. The Bear cannot reach Us up here, You know.*"

quite safe and comfortable. I mean, it could be worse." And so the people remained in Paradise, and counted themselves lucky to be there.

They might still be there today, if only the Old One who is variously called Midnight, or the Great Empty, or the Eater of Worlds, or simply The Worm had bothered to keep Itself informed of Council decisions.

CHAPTER 28:
More Ways to Kill You Than the Sky's Got Blue

Y*ou rat!* I thought. *You want to stay?! How long have you been planning this?*

Out loud, I said "that wasn't the deal, Vern. Two days. Remember? Two days in, two days out."

He said "it's our civic duty, Abner."

I laughed. Nobody else did. "Our civic duty was to warn all the good folks at No Aces. We did that. Now we get to go home."

"And you call yourself a waggie," said Wren. She didn't mean it as a compliment.[32]

"Actually, I don't. I'm a storyteller, not a gossip."

Vern's face was in shadow, but I could tell by the way he stood that I was embarrassing him in front of his friends. "The story's not over yet, Abner. Don't you want to know what happens? Don't you want to know why the Great Empty is after Pedestrio?"

"If the answer's gonna kill me, I'd just as soon read about it in a nice, air-conditioned library."

"What if it's not in any of the books?"

"What if it's not out *there*, Vern? What if the *real* key is somewhere in Faroffistan, only we never find it, on account of the desert's got more ways to kill you than the sky's got blue?"

---

32 A swagman, or swaggie, is an itinerant laborer who travels from place to place in search of a day's work. By contrast, a waggie is more of a wandering fool whose only stock-in-trade is his wagging tongue. Waggies are generally considered to occupy a lower rung on the social ladder than swaggies, as they contribute so very little to the commonweal. However, in certain remote areas, waggies are the only source of news from the outside world.

"What if the Great Empty means to destroy Pedestrio? What if nobody warns him? What if a million years of experience and knowledge is wiped out, all because we turned back now?"

Well.

I didn't have anything to say to that. Vern had his mind made up. He'd roam the Great Empty Desert from now to nevermind if he thought it would bring him closer to Pedestrio. He'd ride the Eater of Worlds without a saddle if he thought he could steer It away from his hero. Sure, it burned knowing he'd walk away from our deal — but if I had Vern's terrible affliction, maybe I'd be stuck out here, too. All I could do now is hope his Undivided Attention Syndrome didn't turn fatal.

"Okay," I said. "Fair enough. See you 'round, Vern. Folks…"

I reached up to give them all a tip of the hat — then remembered I wasn't wearing one. *Have to rectify that, soon as I get Town Side. Have to pick up a few coins first. But that shouldn't be a problem — all I need is a tale to tell. Too bad the legend of Pedestrio fizzled out the way it did. I could have told that one all summer long, if it only had a decent ending.*

As I headed down canyon, my brain already sifting through a surplus of worn-out yarns, I heard Hunter asking "who's Pedestrio?"

Things move around at night. You ever notice that? Landmarks wander off, assuming they won't be needed again till morning. Trees and bushes congregate in the middle of the trail to discuss the latest news. The same rock that tripped you a hundred paces back somehow appears once again directly in your path.

I still don't know how it happened, but within an hour of leaving Vern and the desert rats, I was forced to conclude the canyon I was hiking down wasn't the same one I started in. For one thing, it was a lot narrower than it should have been. The walls were steeper and higher. I couldn't see enough stars to tell for sure, but I suspected it was leading me in the wrong direction. *Gotta get up to the rim,* I thought. *Gotta get reoriented.*

But the canyon walls were smooth as slate and worse than vertical — they leaned in so much, they near about came together at the top. The passage got even narrower as I slogged down canyon, till finally I couldn't go any farther without turning sideways.

"Must have got off into a side canyon," I muttered, turning back. Sure enough, after retracing my steps for a good half-mile or so, the side canyon spilled out into a much larger canyon — only this one didn't look familiar, either. I found a steep bank of shale reaching up almost to the rim, and I scrambled up. But the rim dropped off almost immediately into a parallel canyon, and not knowing where that one went, either, I slid back down into the devil I knew and looked for a way up the opposite side.

By moondown, I was completely lost. Seemed like one canyon led to another — and when I did reach the high ground, I couldn't make out anything on the horizon that I could use to find my way. The desert sounded unnaturally quiet — even the wind stopped whispering. Shadows moved — then snapped back to their original positions when I looked their way.

My head felt dizzy and my legs felt like rubber as I plunked myself down on a weathered boulder and thought.

Youda Tank was a small target, which I now had almost no chance of finding except by accident. Maybe the landscape would look more familiar come daylight, and maybe not. I could try to get close… or I could forget about Youda Tank and head straight west. No question I'd run out of water long before I reached Arcadia, but as long as I stayed more or less on course, there was no way I could miss it. Trouble was, canyon country is tricky terrain for that kind of straight-line navigation. More than likely I'd wear myself out with all the up-and-downing.

Truth is, I might not make it.

My feet scuffed the ground as if to wipe away that last thought. "Okay, then," I told myself in a loud, confident voice. "West it is."

I stood up and stretched until my backbone cracked. Then I shouldered my rucksack and, checking the stars, I lit out cross-country. I got all of three steps — then jumped out of my shoes as a bugle sounded directly behind me.

You ever seen a blue-footed betchacant? They're actually among the fastest woodland creatures on the planet. They run so fast, they leave rooster tails of dirt and rocks and duff in their wake.[33] They're bigger than foxes, but smaller than coyotes. They have no tails. What they've got instead is a trumpet-like protuberance growing out of their backsides. They love being chased, and they especially delight in tooting out rude, derisive, mocking fanfares as they skedaddle away from their pursuers.[34] But I'd never seen one outside the forest, and as far as I knew, they were daytime creatures. So… why was this one skulking around the desert in the dead of night? And more importantly, how did she come to be in possession of my saggy old bush hat?

The betchacant tooted a raspberry at me and took off. All doubts and concerns were driven from my mind as the old predator instinct kicked in. Never mind the whys and wherefores — that varmint had my hat! It was stuck to her rump — the brim pulled down low, so that from the back, she looked like the world's ugliest bugler.

---

33 Actually, blue-footed betchacants are a step or two slower than red-footed betchacants. But the blue-footed ones are far more common, owing to the fact that red-footed betchacants have a tendency to run so fast, their own feet burst into flames.

34 It is a little-known fact that the sport of foxhunting originally derived from early misguided efforts to make a sport out of hunting betchacants. Many an old, epic saga has told of kings and queens who set their sights on bagging a betchacant, and how the chase would often go on for many years. However, since no one in the history of betchacant hunting ever actually caught one, the sport grew out of favor as queens and kings began pursuing foxes instead. Of course, after suffering such relentless taunting from the betchacant's insolent backside, one could hardly blame the foxhunters for wanting to turn the tables — which is why a much more dignified fanfare traditionally announces the start of every modern foxhunt.

She did that on purpose. She knows whose hat it is. She's goading me.

I didn't care. The Great Empty Desert might kill me yet — but if I could get within a stone's throw of that vulgar little brute, at least I might die with my hat on.

The betchacant raced across the mesa. I lumbered after it. The betchacant tooted in delight. Poor, lost critter probly hadn't had a good run in weeks.

And I wasn't fit to give it one. After half a night of stumbling through the canyons, I could barely walk a straight line. My toes kept catching the odd snag, very nearly sending me sprawling. Every time, the betchacant would bugle a cascade of notes that sounded like laughter.

I threw a rock at her. "You think this is funny? That's my hat, you tuneless terpsibore!"

The rock missed. The betchacant let me get close, then scooted out of reach. I picked up another rock. She let fly with an ascending series of comical whizzers as she disappeared behind a jumble of stone. I couldn't see her, but I threw the rock anyway. From behind the pile, a pair of notes blooped out like a small child saying "uh oh!"

"That's right! Run, you slow-footed spitblower! If I ever see you again, I'll shove a beehive up your horn!"

I turned my back on the blighter and stalked off. But I didn't get more than three paces when there she was again — standing in front of me with her back turned. Her rump swayed from side to side as she bugled away like an elephator.[35]

---

35 The elephator is closely related to the elephant, except it's got multi-jointed legs like a spider. This means it can elephate — sorry: *elevate* — its body from near ground level all the way up to forest canopy level. Pachydermologists believe the elephator's legs evolved in this way so as to compensate for its severely truncated trunk. Why the species didn't simply grow a longer trunk is a question that lacks a satisfactory answer — although, it must be said, the elephator's abbreviated proboscis is rather more versatile than a standard elephant's trunk, musically speaking. Elephators are fond of organizing themselves into trios and quartets and blowing out improvisational elephator music while their bodies swing back and forth below their knees like metronomes.

That did it. I lunged at her. She darted away. I lurched after her. I was too tired to think about it — too tired to consider the implications of what I was doing.

One doesn't waste energy in the desert. One doesn't go charging after uncatchable creatures in the dead of night, without so much as a glance at the Guide Star.

I was reckless. I had no idea where I was, nor where to find water. In short, I had no reason to expect I would get out of that chase alive.

So imagine my surprise when dawn finally came, and I found myself standing at the edge of a cliff — staring down at the sturdy roof of No Aces.

CHAPTER 29:
A Second Chance

LOCATING a safe route down the escarpment took ages. It was midmorning by the time I found a notch I could clamber down. Even then, I had to double back along the cliff base for at least an hour before I got to No Aces. By that time, the temperature was fast approaching the boiling point of sweat, and all my canteens were about as dry as Bordman's *Necrology*.[36]

No complaints, though. I made it; that's all that matters. Thank Blue.

I expected to find the trading post empty, on account of there weren't any mules loitering about — but Vern's voice called out from the gloom the moment I staggered through the open doorway.

"Welcome back, Abner."

"Vern? What are you still doing here? I thought you were gonna help spread the word."

"We are. But by the time we got back here, half the night was gone, so Wren and I decided to wait till this evening. That'll give us more twilight time for traveling."

"And the others?"

"They loaded the mules up with water and headed out last night. Neither of us really felt comfortable traveling with a mule, though."

"Filthy beasts," muttered Wren. "Never needed a mule to get from camp to camp. Ain't gonna start now."

---

36 Yonnus Bordman is generally considered the most tedious author who ever lived. His *Necrology of the Bromides* is so dry that reading it can make your eyes shrivel up like prunes. And yet, teachers keep making us read it on account of it so perfectly encapsulates the Age of Enfuddlement.

"Oh," I said. "Speaking of water, do you mind if I top up? I'm a little low."

Vern almost smiled. "Help yourself."

He didn't ask why I came back, so I didn't tell him. I filled my water bottles, then drank up half their contents and filled them again. Vern and Wren were grinding mesquite seeds into powder when I reentered the common room.

"So, how far away is your first port of call?"

"'Bout 15 miles east," said Vern. "Place called Camp Fire."

"I don't know that one."

"It comes and goes. The ace isn't reliable, but a few nomads'll pop in whenever there's water."

"What if it's dry?"

Wren cut in. "Hardlot is only a few miles further on. One or t'other'll have water."

I said "you reckon the nomads'll carry the news from there?"

Vern gave me the kind of look you give a new rucksack when you're trying to forecast how long it'll hold up. "They might branch out. A lot of camps are off the beaten track. As for Wren and me, we're going all the way to Dunghovel."

"Dunghovel! That's dead center."

Vern shrugged. "Cinder's taking the Western Verge, after she checks in at Woolly Mountain. Hunter's got the Spree, up north. Grudge is traveling south to Dangenblast, and Kinglet's covering the Eastern Verge. That leaves the middle."

"You'll cook," I said. "You'll be fried out there."

"It won't be so bad. Wren takes the Dunghovel route all the time. Part of her medical rounds."

Wren slid the pestle and a pile of seeds across the table — an invitation for me to start doing my share of the work. "Grind these," she said gruffly. "I've got a brew to make."

She tottered off to one of the storerooms. Vern shot me a sidelong glance. "You coming with us?"

I thought about it. The odds of finding my own way back Town Side were probly pretty good, last night's adventures notwithstanding. I could rest up today and make a fresh start in the evening. There was a stack of old bladders and bota bags in the pump room. If I loaded up on water, I could bypass Youda Tank… as long as I didn't get turned around again, I shouldn't have any trouble reaching Arcadia.

But that betchacant led me back here for a reason.

I know, I know — she didn't *lead* me. She was only a stupid animal, doing what stupid animals do. There's nothing mystical about that. It's ridiculous to imagine the betchacant had my best interest at heart when her only goal was to harass and torment me all night long. If the chase just *happened* to lead to an ace, well… that's pure chance. Still… only a fool turns his back on a second chance.

"Yeah, I might tag along, if you don't mind. Never been to Dunghovel before. Who knows? Might be a tale out there, waiting to be told."

So the three of us pulled stakes for Dunghovel early that evening. Vern led the way. He set a fast pace — provoking Wren to snap at him once or twice. Wren herself had no intention of moving any faster than a lazy summer afternoon.

I stuck with Wren. I'd had enough of haring through the desert at night. By way of making conversation, I said "so, how long have you known Vern?"

It was easy to see she respected him. Her sharp edges grew considerably duller whenever they put their heads together. Standing on the skirt of that observation, it wasn't too far to leap to the conclusion their paths had crossed before.

"Years, I reckon."

"You two meet at No Aces?" That would make sense — a permanent camp like No Aces would be a regular stop on her rounds, and Vern drops by pretty often, according to Grudge.

"Nope."

"Where, then?"

"You ask a lot of questions, boy."

"Just passing the time," I said. "I could tell you a story, if you druther. Vern ever tell you about the time we almost got blasted by a wolverskunk?"

"I surprised him," she said. "He was harvesting quickpurge root out by Retcher's Gorge. Down on his knees, digging in the dirt."

"You snuck up on him, huh?"

"I don't sneak, boy," she snapped. "But he wasn't looking and he wasn't listening, so focused was he on his task."

"Yeah, he gets that way," I said. "He's got Undivided Attention Syndrome."

But Wren wasn't interested in my diagnosis. The way she plowed ahead as if I hadn't said anything a-tall gave me cause to wonder if she might have caught a touch of the syndrome, herself.

"I come up behind him," she said, "all puffed up to give him what-have-you for prospecting in my medicine patch — till I saw what he was doing. Not many of us know where to find quick-purge root, nor even less how to use it. 'Course, I yelled at him anyway. But the man knows his herbs — I found that out right quick. Many a patch he's told me about that I didn't know before, and many a time he's fetched me a supply of touch-me-nevers, knowing I'm too old and too crotchety to climb up and get 'em myself."[37]

I said "has he ever tried to avoid you like he does Grudge?"

---

37 Touch-me-nevers are rare and delicate epiphytes that only grow atop the very tallest sequoia cacti. It is possible to climb the barbs of a sequoia cactus the same way you climb the branches of a tree — but you have to grip them uncomfortably close to the trunk, where the barbs are thick and strong. Problem is, close to the trunk is where all the glō-kids like to hang out. Glō-kids are sort of the desert version of dryads, only they're a lot smaller and instead of being bound to a particular oak or laurel or walnut tree, their entire lives are spent in service to a single sequoia cactus. If the glō-kids think you're doing harm to their cactus, they'll swarm out and stick your hands full of tiny barbed spears. They particularly don't like it when you try to pick the touch-me-nevers from their own private rooftop garden without permission. On occasion, however, the glō-kids will strike a bargain with an herb collector who demonstrates a sufficient level of respect and has something useful to trade.

"'Course not. And I don't blame him for dodging that fool Grudge, either. Them smelly old mules are enough to keep anybody away, let alone the wets."

"The wets?"

"The greenhorns. The wet-behind-the-ears. Grudge's *clients.*" She spat out the word like poison. "Ain't got sense enough to go to ground with the sun beating down — then that sweaty mule-herd expects me to salve their burns and pour tonic down their gullets."

"You think Tinderfoot holes up at midday?"

"No."

"You think he ever gets sunburned, or heatstroke?"

"You ask a lot of questions."

"I'm just curious what you know about Tinderfoot, is all."

"Nothing. Seen him once or twice, that's all. Heard some talk. But I do my rounds, and I stick to the usual tracks. I don't go freebooting across the desert like some folks. 'Less it's to gather medicines or some such."

"That's a very sensible approach," I said agreeably.

Wren gave me a sidelong glance, then muttered something that sounded like: *and some 'at's continuous.* I didn't get more than three words out of her the whole rest of the journey.

INTERLOGUE:

A Secret Compartment in a Forgotten Desk in a Locked Cabinet without a Keyhole

---

For a long time, Mischief's plan worked. She built a vast arsenal of hideous phantasms, trembling torments, and panic-inducing visions — and She sent these dreaded apparitions into the valley with soul-crushing frequency. Both day and night, Mischief's diabolical creations stampeded through bewildered minds, even overwhelming the senses of those who could not sleep.

The visions were not real. But they *seemed* terrifyingly realistic. And the Paradisians cowered in their beds — no longer daring to think about finding a way into the Garden.

The scheme was nearly flawless. If only The Worm had bothered to read the memo…

The Worm had dominion over much of the subterranean landscape. The Worm was responsible for cultivating the soil and for keeping the underground ways navigable. It chewed through solid rock, opening seams and widening fissures. It created drainage channels for the standing water left behind by summer squalls. When trees and bushes reached down with their taproots, sending them deeper and deeper into the earth, seeking out the strongest anchorages and the richest nutrient stores, The Worm prepared the way.

Of course, that meant sacrificing some vegetation in order to serve the greater good. It meant displacing the occasional burrowing creature. From time to time, The Worm found it necessary to destabilize an entire hillside, causing great harm to the critters downslope. Still, it must be said that the Garden could not have survived without The Worm's tireless efforts.

But The Worm was a solitary Being. It refused to attend Council meetings — and so, It was not aware of Mischief's machinations. Indeed, It was only dimly aware of the existence of Paradise, because Paradise was not part of the Garden. The Tallest Mountains in the World naturally extended for many miles underground, creating a barrier that The Worm had no reason to penetrate.

Paradise remained hidden, like a secret compartment in a forgotten desk in a locked closet without a keyhole. The Worm had never tasted the valley's soil — that is, until the day a minor tremor broke the roots of the mountains. The earthquake — though barely strong enough to be felt — created a fault line that stretched underground from Garden to valley.

The Worm decided to investigate. It burrowed through the fissure, leaving behind a tunnel just wide enough for a man to squeeze through. Then It broke for the surface, curious as to what It might find.

It emerged in the midst of a maelstrom of menacing visions that stalked Paradise from one end to the other.

Suffice to say, The Worm was not prepared for the onslaught.

CHAPTER 30:
Dunghovel

WE had good light to travel by on our way out to Dunghovel. The waxing gibbous moon illuminated the evening sky for a week leading up to the full flower moon. Then the evenings grew dark, but the waning gibbous consented to light the way till dawn. Good thing, too — the desert by day was getting hotter than a forest fire.

'Course, it wasn't a continuous trek. I mean, we took the news to as many camps and freeholds as would let us in. Most of them did without hesitation, soon as they saw Wren. Then, while she tended to those who needed physicking, Vern and I would tell the tale to anybody who would listen. Funny how quickly news travels, though — more than once, I launched into a dramatic account of our narrow escape and the results of our subsequent fact-finding mission, only to be told they'd already heard it from somebody who heard it from somebody who got the news from Hunter or Cinder or somebody else who got it from Kinglet. Still, folks were mostly appreciative and thanked us for our efforts.

Desert rats are sometimes unfairly cast as being uniformly misanthropic and hostile to outsiders. But that's not the way of it. Fact is, we were treated like everything from old friends to visiting royalty all the way to Dunghovel. Howbeit, nobody could add much to the legend of Pedestrio, nor tell us more than we already knew about the Eater of Worlds.

Wren hinted that we might find some answers at the conclusion of our journey, but she refused to elaborate.

Dunghovel is a trash heap in the middle of the Great Empty Desert. People have been living there off and on for a million years, which makes it just about the oldest settlement in those parts. The place is a mountain of old bones, refuse, and bits of broken tools. At the midden's core is Dunghovel's ace-in-the-hole: a shallow oasis, fed by an underground spring.

Word is, the water used to be pretty good, and plentiful enough to sustain a thriving community. But the water turned sour after a thousand years, as the garbage piled up. So the residents packed up and moved on, leaving Dunghovel to the next generation of nomads, who threw their own garbage onto the pile, and on and on throughout history. Today, Dunghovel has a population of almost one — a madcap who goes by the name of Sputter.

Wren said he was "touched" — saying it like there was all the difference in the world between being a madcap and being touched, and snapping at me whenever I asked her to explain the difference.

Anyhow, seventeen days after leaving No Aces, we arrived on the outskirts of the ancient metropolis at first light. Wren stopped us well short of the mound and called out "hey, Sputter! Yoo! Hoo!"

Wren put her own flourish on the traditional "yoo-hoo" greeting. She gave it a high-pitched bark, emphasizing each syllable equally. Sounded more like she was calling hogs than attracting the attention of a fellow human.

I saw movement at the top of the heap. Somebody was watching us.

Wren said "it's Wren, Sputter! It's Wren! I brought your medicine!"

We waited. It didn't take long. Sputter lacked the patience required to play the desert equivalent of that popular Town Side game of Draw-the-Shades-and-See-If-They-Leave. He scrambled up and over the wall of trash like a trapdoor spider coming out of its hole. Then he sprinted over, waving his arms wildly and screaming. "Hyah! Hyah!"

We stood our ground. Sputter halted in front of Wren and jumped up and down a few times, waving his arms. She punched him in the sternum, making him stumble backward. He wasn't much more than rags and bone, Sputter. If the wind ever picked up, there wouldn't be enough of him to pin his feet to the ground.

"Don't you go scatting me, you danged fool!" she scolded. "I've got your medicine!"

She must have passed some kind of test, on account of Sputter left her alone and fronted me — waving his arms and jumping up and down and shaking his mangy head. "Hyah! Go away! Scat! Git!"

"Just stand fast, waggie," muttered Wren. "He won't hurt you, 'less it's by accident."

I wound up to say "I'm not a waggie!" but she shooshed me before I could get the words out.

Presently, Sputter moved on to Vern — standing almost nose-to-nose with him. "Hyah! Scat! Git out!"

Vern just stood there. Vern could be a Draw-the-Shades champion, if only he had a house with a window. And a shade, of course.

Now, by this point, you might have concluded that Sputter was more than a mite "touched." Then again, you might not have. All depends on your tolerance for outlandish behavior. As for me, I didn't see it yet. I mean, shucks, I've done a fair amount of soloing out here on Wild Side, and many's the time I've jumped up and down and waved my arms at some nosy beast who's intruding upon my solitude. I've screamed at everything from bluebugs to brown bears to buzz off and leave me alone. Seems to me, it ain't that much of a stretch to extend that courtesy to a nosy pack of humans.

As to what happened next, though… well, I've just never seen the like.

Sputter got tired of yelling at Vern, but he didn't give up just yet. Instead, he backed off a couple, three, four paces. Then he started walking around us in a circle, as fast as he could walk. And as he walked, faster and faster, he chanted these words over and over again:

> *Circle of doubt! Scream and shout!*
> *Stumble, tumble, in or out!*
> *Circle of doubt! Scream and shout!*
> *Stumble, tumble, in or out!*
> *Circle of doubt! Scream and shout!*
> *Stumble, tumble, in or out!*

Around and around he went, till I got dizzy looking at him. And every time he passed in front of Wren, she said something to him — not snapping, the way she usually does, but gentle and soothing-like: "It's Wren, Sputter… Sputter, it's Wren… I brought your medicine… Can we go in?… These folks have news, Sputter… Can we go in?… It's about the Eater of Worlds…"

A few times around, and Sputter was so wobbly he couldn't hold his course. But he stumbled and staggered twice more around the circle, and Wren said "It's been seen, Sputter… It's on the move…" and Sputter weaved way off track and stood for a second, trying to catch his balance. Then he took two more steps before his legs gave out, and he fell down right at our feet.

"Lucky break," said Wren. Not to Sputter, mind you. She said it to Vern and me.

"Hmm?"

"That's gyromancy, that is. Lucky he fell on our side of the magic circle. If he'd a fallen away over there, you two would have been banished from Dunghovel forever."

Sputter lay on the ground heaving like he wanted to vomit, only he'd turned his stomach inside out and found nothing to contribute. "Not so lucky for him," I muttered.

"He'll be okay. Gyromancy takes a lot out of you."

"He should switch to tea leaves. More nourishing."

Wren shooshed me and squatted down to give aid and comfort to Sputter. I shot a smirk in Vern's direction. He didn't return it. Instead, he squatted down and said to Sputter, very serious and formal-like, he said "thank you for accepting us into your home. My name is Vern. That one over there is Abner. We bring news…"

Wren waved him silent — not disapproving, just letting Vern know he'd said enough for now.

Sputter rose in stages: first sitting up and holding his head as if trying to keep it steady, then rolling over onto his knees, then one knee and a hand. Finally, he pulled himself to his feet. "The signs augur well for you," he said in a woozy-yet-formal voice. "Welcome to Dunghovel." Then he gave a big, wide, boyish grin. "Come on in!"

And he turned and ran — well, tell you true, it was more of a cross between a lope and a stagger… he turned and laggered back up the mound of debris and into the spider hole.

CHAPTER 31:
Theatre of the Macabre

WE followed Sputter. It wasn't easy. There was no path through the detritus. We stepped carefully across a bunched and wrinkly carpet of rocks, bones, pottery shards, broken tools, and corroded flakes of metal. The mound must have been twenty feet high. Junk of a more recent provenance littered the upper slopes: an old clock, a broken umbrella, miscellaneous bits of hardware, fresh wood shavings, odds and ends of cordage, the blade of a shovel… part of an old tin canteen.

"Why an old clock?" I said to no one in particular. "Who's keeping time out here?"

"Why an old umbrella?" muttered Vern. But Wren turned around and thumped him on the chest.[38] [39] [40] [41]

"Pipe down!" she hissed. "Both of you!"

The smell hit me just as we crested the rim. It wasn't all bad. It smelled of life… and decay. Water… and rot. Rich, humidified air… and marsh gas.

---

38 Why, indeed? It's a good question, and I'm sorry to say there is no satisfactory answer. The umbrella is just there. Why is it there? And who would bring an umbrella out into the middle of a desert where it almost never rains? Those are both mysteries that may never be solved. Of course, how the clock got there is no mystery at all…

39 The clock is not important. It doesn't figure into the story, and will never be mentioned again. I'm just saying it's no mystery how it got there. Some things are obvious, when you think about them.

40 No, nobody put the clock there. It got there all on its own. But honestly, that doesn't matter. Dunghovel is a junkyard; all kinds of weird and unusual things turn up at junkyards, and nobody ever asks how they got there. Why is it such a big deal, anyway? Can't you just let it go?

41 Okay, fine. The clock is there because time flies. I'm sorry, but you asked.

The source of all these contradictory aromas was a mud puddle at the bottom of a small basin. The puddle was covered in green slime, and the banks were brown with dead moss and algae. As an ace-in-the-hole, the puddle looked thoroughly unappetizing—but I was glad to see it, all the same. Water is life, even if you have to chew it.

A man-made stone wall about three Sputters high surrounded the basin. It was like standing at the rim of an extinct volcano, looking down into the crater. I reckoned I could just about throw a stone across to the other side.

The wall had begun as a fortification built around the ace—but as generations of inhabitants tossed their garbage over the wall, it had been necessary to build the wall higher and higher, just to keep the garbage from falling back in. Not all the junk had made it outside, from the looks of it. But the basin was pretty well cleared, apart from a few scattered mounds of debris.

"Come on down!" said Sputter, cheerfully beckoning us from the bottom of a set of breakneck stone stairs built into the wall. "Wanna show you something!"

I said "I thought this used to be a city? Not a building in sight down there."

Wren said "just go on down. Mind your step."

Then she proceeded to waltz down the staircase like she was walking on air.

"You're kidding," I said. The steps weren't much more than protruding stones—too narrow to fit my entire foot, and too worn and rounded to offer much of a tread. "Didn't anybody ever think of putting in handrails?"

"Don't think," said Vern. "Just do it."

And he practically ran down the stairs.

"Easy for you to say," I said.

"Best way is to come down quickly. Forward momentum helps keep you upright."

"Thanks."

The first few steps were easy — I turned my toes inward and went down sideways, holding on to the top of the wall. But as the wall rose above my waist, it forced me to straighten up. By the time I got halfway down, I was holding on by my fingertips. My cheek felt raw from scraping against the rock. My toes cramped up as they felt around for the next step.

"Come on, come on!" said Sputter.

"Slough off," I muttered.

I took a shortcut the last few steps. Vern steadied me as I landed off-balance. "That wasn't so hard, was it?"

"Pfft! Cakewalk all the way," I said.

Getting out would be fun. Maybe we could make a ladder for the return trip.

I looked around. We were standing on a ledge at ground level — the wall being set back a ways from the rim of the basin. Somebody'd been digging down there — that explained the mounds of debris I'd seen from atop the wall.

Probly not The Worm. Unless It's on a mission to turn this basin into a sieve.

"Come on!" Sputter beckoned us from further down the ledge. "In here!"

And he promptly vanished into the wall.

Vern turned and examined the stone with renewed interest. "A secret passage. Built into the wall itself."

"Not exactly secret," said Wren. "Used to be the prime living quarters, up till a few years ago. Mind your head and your elbows."

She led the way through a low arched opening and into a narrow passageway that followed the curve of the wall in both directions. We took the right-hand passage. After a dozen paces, it opened up to reveal a cluttered chamber — lit from the basin side by a couple of chinks in the wall where the rocks had fallen out. Or who knows — maybe they were pushed out. In a place like Dunghovel, sometimes it's tough to tell the difference between happenstance and intentionality.

Sputter was practically jumping up and down at the far end of the chamber. In the middle…

Well. In the middle stood a pit filled with the ghastliest arrangement of skeletons and skeleton parts I've seen this side of Neverwhere. The bones had been scoured with red dirt, giving them a raw, bloody appearance. The jaws were wide open. The brows were mottled in a way that suggested sweat, and the cheeks were streaked with what could have been tears. Together, they presented the image of a desperate, howling pack of revenants clambering over each other in their haste to escape the pit.

The weak light threw the pit into shadow; it could have been a bottomless hole, for all I could tell.

Sputter waved manically, urging us to behold, admire, and move on. "It's the beginning, you see! The beginning! Come on, follow me! This way, this way!"

"Go on," said Wren. "He won't stop till you've seen the whole tale."

"What tale?"

"Go along," she said. "Only way out is through."

Twenty paces on, we came to another chamber. The scene here was just as haunting, though I don't reckon it was intended to be. It's just uncommonly hard to make a diorama out of human skeletons that doesn't raise the hairs on the back of your neck.

There was a painting of a tree on the back wall. An actual, three-dimensional skeleton stood in front of it with its head tilted back, staring up at the foliage spreading across the ceiling. I don't know how Sputter got the bones to stand upright. He must have nailed them to the floor and fused all the joints somehow.

A second skeleton crouched behind a boulder and stared at a mural that featured a couple of saber-toothed bunnies cavorting in a field of flowers. A third bony figure was on its knees — one hand resting on the ground, the other scratching a furrow into the chamber floor with a sharp stone. Planting seeds, I spose. Or digging for grubs.

All the skeletons were small enough to be child-sized, which made the tree seem taller and the whole painted tableau seem larger, but creeped me out all the same. I felt like I'd walked into some kind of weird, postapocalyptic landscape where the last survivor had gone mad and stolen all the bones from a nearby children's hospital.

"Poor kids," I said.

"New world!" said Sputter. "Big world, better world. Lots to see, lots to do. Come on, come on!" And he disappeared again down the stone passageway.

The next chamber was a charred wreck. Boulders had been torn from the walls and ceiling. The chamber floor was pocked with deep divots in some places and piled with dirt and scree in others. Everything was black with soot, as if somebody had packed the chamber with kindling and lit the whole place on fire. The air still smelled like charcoal. Sputter was nowhere to be seen. Vern started into the room, but Wren caught him by the collar. From a hidden ledge above our heads, Sputter threw a burning knot of creosote. It hit the ground in front of us and exploded in a shower of sparks.

"Boom!" Sputter laughed as he jumped down off the ledge and scampered through the chamber. "Ha ha! Come on, come on! Follow me!" He disappeared down the next tunnel, still shouting "boom!" and laughing to himself.

"That's his favorite part," said Wren. "Go on, then. The pass is clear."

"What is this?" I said. "What's going on?"

Now, you understand, we'd been traveling all night. I was tired, and thirsty, and nobody told me anything about Sputter chucking creosote bombs at our heads. So you can imagine, right about then I'd a notion to start throwing things back. But Vern, he didn't seem the least bit perturbed. "I think I know," he said.

Wren said "it's the origin tale, according to Sputter. How the first humans passed from the underworld into this world, and how the Great Empty Desert was formed."

"Scorched earth," said Vern. "Mountains leveled and oceans vaporized. Possibly an exploding supervolcano."

Wren shook her head. "The way he tells it, the Sky spirits became angry at the appearance of humans. They tried to drive them back underground by raining down fireballs." She mimed a little mini-explosion with her hands. "Boom!"

Vern scratched his head doubtfully. "Yeah, that… that could explain it, too…"

Sputter darted back into the chamber and beckoned us impatiently. "This way, this way! Come on, come on!" He vanished again.

I bent down to pick up a soot-blackened rock, but Wren thumped me from behind, knocking me off-balance. "Go along, waggie," she said. "There's hospitality awaiting, but you gotta get through the tale, first."

It took six more chambers to finish the story: how the people refused to crawl back to the underworld, but instead hunkered down and rode out the firestorm. How the devastation got so bad, even the hills and some of the smaller mountains packed up and moved away, but the people hung on. How they gathered at the spring at Dunghovel, protecting and sheltering it, and how it became the site of the first human habitation on this plane of existence. How the people not only survived, but prospered until their children grew so numerous, they began to settle in distant lands. How the Sky spirits eventually eased up on the barrage of fiery sendings, but even today they refuse to heal the burning desert with soothing rains.

The last chamber held the grisliest scene of all: a skeleton of recent vintage sat at a stone table incised with vague pictograms and cryptic symbols. I say "recent vintage" on account of the bones were still partially clad in leathery patches of skin. Wisps of white hair still hung from the scalp. Decayed ropes of sinew still clung to the joints. I reckoned I could smell the faint aroma of decomposing flesh.

"Come on, come on!" said Sputter as he dashed off again.

I could certainly understand the urge not to linger. Several parts of me wanted to follow that urge — trouble was, my various constituencies couldn't agree on whether to bolt, sneak, or pay respects and bow out gracefully.

Being as how a consensus could not be reached, my federated parts and I were left with no choice but to stand rooted to the spot.

"Last known visitor?" I inquired.

"Nope. That's old Sputter," said Wren.

"You mean it's his granddad?"

"Nope. Leastwise, I don't believe so. Old Sputter was the madcap who lived here before. Fancied himself a wizard." Wren's lips parted in a sneer that traveled all the way up her face and made her eyes roll. "Old fool was no more of a wizard than I am."

" 'Course not," I said. "Big difference between a wizard and a hedge witch."

"Ain't that, either," she snapped. "Don't know a lick of magic, and neither did he. But that didn't stop him from wasting a lifetime studying how to rain fireballs down from the sky."

"Fireballs again," said Vern.

"Yep. You ask me, the old man was crazy, and some of it rubbed off on young Sputter. Taught him that gyromancy trick, as well. But at least the young'un's got sense enough not to call himself a wizard."

"What *does* he call himself?" I said — meaning, what's his profession? How does he make a living? But Wren took the question differently.

"He doesn't."

"Doesn't what?"

"Doesn't call himself anything. I don't know as I ever even knew the name he came here with. But he sure took a shine to Sputter, so when the old fool died, it just seemed natural to call the young'un by the same name."

"I mean, why did he come here, and what's he still doing here?"

"Why, I thought that was plain: he's looking for the origins of humankind. Everything you've seen in these chambers, it ain't just a campfire yarn to him. He believes every part of it. Swears the portal to the underworld's around here somewheres, and he'll keep looking till he finds it."

I said to Vern, I said "in the meantime, he keeps himself busy doing set design for the local Theatre of the Macabre."

Wren gave me a backhanded whack. "Don't you go making light of another man's work, ya half-wet! He may not be a waggie like you, but he found himself a story here in these ruins, and he told it as best he knew how."

"Where does he live?" said Vern. "Seems to me we're almost right back where we started, and I haven't seen a chamber that looks slept in."

Wren cracked a sly grin. "You'd be right about that. But you ain't seen the diggings yet."

INTERLOGUE:
A Dream of Gardens and Growing Things

THE nightmares pounded against The Worm's senses. They howled and shrieked and scratched and bit and burned like salt and smelled of molten lava. These were not orderly, filing-cabinet visions of the world — they were dark and disturbing and momentarily terrifying.

In time, The Worm would understand that the apparitions were not real. The Worm was not in danger — It could safely file the dreams away in Its vast archive of personal knowledge and experience, and never give them a second thought. But for one fleeting instant upon reaching the surface, the visions planted a tiny seed of uncertainty in Its mind, and The Worm panicked.

It thought: *perhaps they can hurt Me. Perhaps they can even kill Me. Perhaps I am not immortal, after all.*

The Old Ones do not have such thoughts. They do not suffer from anxiety or self-doubt. They are secure in the knowledge that Their power is absolute, and Their time on this mortal coil is very nearly infinite.

But fear breeds doubt. And for perhaps the first time in Its long life, The Worm was afraid.

The Worm acted quickly to dispel the danger. It did this by dreaming a dream — an Old One's dream — a surface dream of Gardens, and growing things, and waterfalls, and scented breezes. And in a flash, the little valley of Paradise transformed into a lush and beautiful wonderland, full of beetles and butterflies and bunny toads. The nightmares ceased, and The Worm knew that the world was right again.

And the dream also contained something else: it contained a comforting reaffirmation of The Worm's immortality. It contained a soothing reassurance that nothing in this world could harm The Worm — nothing, that is, apart from the touch of another Old One.

So The Worm dreamed, and the dream came to life. But only for a moment: a moment is all it took for The Worm to realize what had happened. A moment is all it took for The Worm to recognize that the little isolated valley was not the domain of any single Old One. In fact, the valley was off limits to All.

The Worm had missed that meeting. It had missed most of the meetings. But sometimes, after the really important meetings, a memo of sorts would be distributed. And so it was in this case: The Worm recalled having received such a message, long and long ago. The message said simply: do not enter this valley, for it is The Place Where We Shall Put All the Dreams That Don't Quite Work Out.

The moment The Worm recalled that message, It realized that It was in Big Trouble.

Quicker than a hummingbird's blink, The Worm undreamed Its dream. The valley was restored to its original state. The spitting trees hawked and spewed. The tumblerocks blazed new paths of wreckage through the rubble. The fearsome apparitions contin-ued their unyielding torment, and the people thanked their most benevolent Supreme Beings that things hadn't gotten any worse.

Then The Worm ducked back underground and made Its way back out of the valley, never bothering to look back.

But a part of the dream did not get erased. A part of the dream would remain true forever. It was the part about immortality. The Worm did not bother to undream that part, because it could not possibly make any difference: immortality had always been The Worm's destiny. Undreaming it would not change anything.

So The Worm thought. But It was mistaken.

CHAPTER 32:
A Pig-holler Degree in Ancient History

SPUTTER was waiting for us outside. The minute we stuck our heads out of the entryway, he galloped off down the basin, around the ace, and halfway up the other side. Then he climbed a hill of rock and dirt and turned back to wave us on.

"Over here, come on!" he called. "Don't drink the water! It'll kill ya!"

"I wish he wouldn't say that," I groused. "I'm so dry, I've got quills of salt sprouting out of my pores."

"Quit your bellyachin'," said Wren. "There's water aplenty — just not from the pond."

The basin itself was littered with artifacts — stone metates and flaked blades and bits of clay and bone, all sifted into a soft, dusty topsoil that gave me the impression I was sinking ankle-deep in a bowl of desiccated coprolites. We giant-stepped down the slope, skirted the foul-smelling puddle at the bottom, and trudged up to the mound that Sputter was playing king of.

Sure enough, behind the mound was a mine shaft with a really steep downward grade. The walls and ceiling weren't nearly reinforced enough to suit me — but after a few feet it didn't matter, on account of I couldn't see a blasted thing. We followed Sputter, crawling on hands and knees — first Wren, then Vern, and me last. Then the grade leveled out and I felt Vern standing up, so I stood up and grabbed hold of his trilliard vest, and he started walking so I started walking, and truth be told, I couldn't tell you if the tunnel turned left or right or opened up into a vast underground cavern. I had to recite the first few rhymes of "The Sun Quest of Bright Flowing Water" just to keep from panicking.

Vern said "Abner, open your eyes."

"They are open."

"No, they're not."

"Are you sure?"

"Positive."

"How can you be sure, when it's so dark even I can't tell?"

"Because I'm standing right in front of you, and I can see your eyelids are shut."

"Oh." I opened my eyes. Vern wasn't even looking at me. But Sputter was. He loomed in front of me with a big old, lookee-here grin on his face — the kind you flash at the prize-winning fish you just caught.

" 'Toady Batcher, lizard catcher,' " he chortled. "That's good! That's good! 'Bring it down to show the Crown.' Ha ha!"

"I think he likes your poem," said Vern.

"I'm glad to hear it. My pleasure, as always." I stepped back and aimed an exaggerated bow in Sputter's direction. By the time I reestablished verticality, he'd wandered off. Audiences are mercurial that way, sometimes. But I didn't mind, on account of it gave me a chance to look around.

We had tunneled our way into a half-moon shaped cave lit by a single flame. Ancient petroglyphs carved into the rounded limestone walls danced in the flickering light. "Where are we?" I said.

"Back in time!" said Sputter. "Sputter found it. Million years old!"

Wren explained. "This is where the first people lived — before landslides and weathering covered the mouth of the cave and turned the sinkhole into a bowl."

Vern nodded. "So these glyphs must have been buried for thousands of years. Quite a find."

Sputter beamed. He started pointing out some of his favorite designs — misshapen beasts and humanoid figures with three toes and one eye. I looked around the chamber some more.

The room smelled like frying bacon. Or grilled duck. Or something in between. The source of the aroma was the same as the light source: a primitive oil lamp made from an old tin can. It sat on a stone boulder in the middle of the chamber. Sputter must have lit the thing as soon as we arrived. I wondered where he got the animal fat — the local critters weren't even big enough to make a meal, let alone a pint of lamp oil.

Unless he boiled down old Sputter...

I gave my head a vigorous shake to clear the unwelcome thought from my mind. As an added distraction, I studied the can. It couldn't have been more than fifty years old. "Not much of an artifact," I muttered.

Wren said "old Sputter ransacked the place when he found it. He didn't care about the history. Dang fool got some wrong-headed notion about how these people set off a fireball, and that's what buried them alive. Tore the cave apart, trying to figure out how they did it."

I watched Sputter animatedly telling Vern about the significance of a series of concentric circles. "That's the sun!" he said, flinging his arms wide. "Fire in the sky! Guardian of the Gateway! Boom!"

I said to Wren, I said "young Sputter seems awfully knowledgeable about all these markings."

"Well, he ought to know. Got himself a Pig-holler Degree in ancient history before he showed up at Dunghovel with all his fancy notions about finding the Gateway to the underworld."[42]

"You put any stock in those notions?"

"Ain't my concern," said Wren. "Might be we all crawled out of a hole a million years ago. Then again, it might not be. World

---

42 In certain cultures, a Pig-holler Degree (or PhD) represents the highest level of scholarly achievement. Some folks begin studying for their Pig-holler Degree as soon as they've earned their Back-a-Lorry-Up, while others choose to become a Master of Signs first. Either way, the old saying still holds true: "you show me someone who's earned herself a Pig-holler Degree, and I'll show you a person who is really dedicated to her calling."

keeps turning, did or didn't. Now, you might want to hush up a moment, being as how this is what you came all this way for."

Sputter had picked up a piece of charcoal and was using it to fill in a squiggly line — darkening the groove and making it easier to see.

"Demon from the underworld," he said. "Chasing the first people. You see? These are the people." He looked at Vern while tapping his charcoal against a stick figure in midstride — the way a mad professor drives his point home with a piece of chalk on a blackboard.

Vern stared at the figures. "It's The Worm," he said. "And Pedestrio."

Sputter shook his head. "Not a worm. A demon. It followed the first people through the Gateway."

"Are you saying the Eater of Worlds is a demon?"

Sputter looked surprised. Then he burst out laughing. "EATER OF WORLDS! Ha ha!"

Vern didn't know what to make of that. He nodded slowly. "Yeah, the Eater of Worlds. Also known as the Great Empty, or The Worm."

Sputter laughed all the way down to his belly. "Yeah! Ha ha! EATER OF WORLDS! GREAT EMPTY MONSTER, ha ha ha!"

Vern frowned. This wasn't going the way he expected it to. Not at all. He looked unsure what to do or say next.

Wren stepped in to save him. She said to Sputter, she said "don't you go disrespecting your guests, boy! These gentlemen have *seen* the Great Empty! That's what they came to tell you."

Sputter did his best to pull himself upright and tuck the laughter back behind his teeth. "Begging your pardon," he said.

Vern looked at me. I looked at Sputter, who was looking at his toes and trying not to grin. I said "I take it you don't believe in a supernatural Being that made the Great Empty Desert."

Sputter shook his head.

"But you do believe in worm-shaped demons from the underworld?"

Sputter nodded — still looking down, but with a glance at Wren as if to say *hey, I'm trying really hard not to be rude, but these guys... where did you get these guys?*

I said "okay, I give up. How is it you believe in one and not the other?"

Sputter took a deep breath and let it out slowly. Then he drew a second breath. Finally, he raised his head and looked at me. His eyes still glittered with amusement, but he did manage to clear the smirk off his lips. "One's ancient history," he said. "The other's a made-up story."

"Which is which?" I muttered.

"The demons were driven back to the underworld," he explained patiently — half sounding like a real professor instead of a touched madcap. "They tried to catch the people, but the sky fire drove them back."

Vern said "maybe It's not a demon, then. Maybe the Great Empty is an Earth spirit."

"No such thing."

I said "then who rained down all those fireballs?"

"That's ancient history," he said.

I said "you hear that, Vern? We got chased halfway across the Western Verge by ancient history."

Vern wore a look on his face like he was only a short reach away from a well-deserved cookie, only somebody kept moving the jar. He pursed his lips in frustration and reached out one last time. "Have you ever heard of a man named Pedestrio? Or Tinderfoot?"

"Nawp."

"Ever seen anybody out here walking barefoot?"

"Huh uh."

Wasted trip, then. But Vern took it well. He turned back to the cave wall and stared at the petroglyphs like he meant to burn them into his memory. "Thank you for showing us all this," he said to Sputter. "It's really been a fascinating lesson in early human history."

It was absolutely the right thing to say. Sputter beamed. Wren nodded in approval. But before Sputter could launch into another deep lecture on the significance of a carving that looked like an armadillo with two heads, she snapped "right! That's enough for now, professor. You got victuals enough for the lot of us?"

Sputter's living quarters were back up on the rim. Turned out there was another room inside the wall that we hadn't seen — a small, isolated chamber tucked in under the steps we'd come down. I expected a packrat's paradise, but it was more like a studio apartment — kept neat and tidy by necessity, on account of there wasn't room enough to spread out.

'Course, he didn't have to confine himself to this one room. He could have tossed old Sputter's bones over the wall and built himself a palace, with separate chambers for eating, sleeping, working, and the leisure-time construction of miniature fireballs. But that would have meant sacrificing the space he'd already allocated to his gruesome historical dioramas. Say this about Sputter: he kept his priorities straight.

The day was already heating up, but the wall would shade us for another few hours yet. We sat with our backs to the stones and dined on grilled cactus mittens. It was more of a snack than a feast — food is scarce in the heart of the Great Empty Desert, though the bounty would improve once the rains came. Turned out Sputter's water supply didn't come from the mudhole, but from an underground spring he'd discovered during one of his excavations. The same spring probly fed the mudhole, but the water was cleaner when pulled from upstream. Even so, we strained and boiled it before drinking — no telling what toxins might still be leaching out of the trash heaps.

"So, what now?" I said, cleaning my teeth with a grimy finger. "Back the way we came?"

Vern said "let's not cover the same ground. We'll learn more by taking a different route."

"I don't know what more there is to learn, Vern. Seems a mighty slim chance we'll run into Pedestrio out here — especially when we go to ground most of the day."

Sputter piped up so suddenly, I think he took his own self by surprise. "Help me look for the Gateway. The origin point of the first people. It can't be far."

Vern looked tempted. But Wren shut him down. She said to Sputter, she said "now, you know the rains are a month away yet, and you've been neglecting your stores. We'd be eating our shoes in a week's time, if we stayed on."

"Not to mention I can't go another month in the desert without a hat," I said, running a hand across the top of my scalp. "Feels like my head is melting. Can anybody see any brains dripping down?"

Vern ignored me, as usual. "Next time I pass this way, if you're still looking for help, I'll stop and lend a hand."

Sputter grinned a big, wide, open-mouthed grin — showing us a mouthful of masticated cactus in the process. It wasn't a pretty sight. And yet, I couldn't look away.

Wren said "close your trap, boy. You're catching flies."

Sputter swallowed. "Protein! Ha ha!"

Wren rolled her eyes.

Vern said "how do you reckon you'll find it?"

Sputter took a swig of water and rolled it slowly around in his mouth, like a wave sloshing around in a sea cave. Then he shrugged. "Water would know."

Vern nodded as if the response made perfect sense, and there wasn't anything more to say about it.

I said "what does that mean?"

"The bedrock here is limestone. I think he means if there were a Gateway to the underworld in these parts, water would expose it, sooner or later. But you'd need a whole lot of water in just the right place."

Sputter pursed his lips and nodded in grim agreement. "Trees would know, too."

Again, I looked to Vern for a translation. He said "the roots of trees can spread out over great distances. That's also one of the ways they talk to each other, is through their root networks. Most trees probably know as much about what's going on below ground as above."

I said "great! So all Sputter needs to do is to set himself down in front of a cactus tree and figure out how to say howdy."

Vern smiled indulgently. "Might be a short conversation."

"Why is that?"

"Let's just say cacti have prickly personalities."

"No more so than most desert rats, I reckon," said Wren. "Leastwise, till you get to know them."

Vern said "'course, if you could do it — if you could talk to trees — imagine what you could learn. You'd be like Pedestrio. Or the W—"

I've never seen Vern's Undivided Attention Syndrome come over him so fast. He broke off talking in the middle of a word, and he did it so quick and clean, you could have run your fingers up and down the edge of that word and never got so much as a splinter. I took to reading the shape of his lips in order to guess how the word might have turned out, had it been allowed to make its way out into the world.

"You think The Worm talks to trees?"

"Hmm? No. What?"

No use. I turned to Wren. "He's lost again. You got any tonic to bring a man out of his own thoughts?"

"Leave him be," she said. "Time we get situated for the day, anyway. Mind if we hole up in the museum, Sputter? We won't trouble the exhibits…"

CHAPTER 33:

Flogberries and Boiled Thattle Leaves

I WOKE up to find Vern pacing back and forth across my bedchamber. I'd fallen asleep in the Forest & Meadow room, under the painted tree. Had a nightmare that the tree was chasing me across a desolate valley, spitting pitch at the back of my head. Instinctively, I felt around for sticky wads of resin, but all I came up with was an overabundance of greasy hair, clumped and crusted with dried sweat.

"You're pacing," I said.

"You're awake," he said.

"Am I?"

"Looks that way. You feel like taking a trek up to Greenhaven?"

"No. Why?"

"To see Holly Green."

"What I feel like is a long soak in a hot shower, followed by a dumpster and a bottomless cup of coffee."

"I don't think Sputter's got any coffee, much less a hot shower."

"Fine. Take me back to town, then." At that moment, I'd have traded all my teeth for a decent breakfast down at Elmer's Café. 'Course, I'd have to borrow them back for the chewing. Probly have to agree to return them clean, but I'd wade that ford when I came to it.

"He does have a present for you, though."

"Who does?"

"Sputter. He made it while you were sleeping."

"What kind of present?"

"Come on out to the ledge and find out."

Around the other side of the basin, the wall and ground were soaked in golden sunlight — could be a dust storm out west somewhere. The basin itself seemed hazy, as the muddy pool evaporated and the ground gave up the day's heat. Sputter sat on the edge of the ledge with his feet draped over the side. Wren knelt behind him and rubbed some kind of ointment into his hair.

I muttered side-mouth to Vern, I said "is that Sputter's medicine?"

Vern's head dipped in a slight nod.

"That's it? Just a scalp massage? No pills or anything?"

"That's it."

I didn't get it. Whether you made Sputter out as a deranged madcap or only just one of the "touched," I didn't see how any kind of external ointment could possibly seep through and calm his addled brain. "You think it helps?"

Vern shrugged. "Don't know. I've never had dandruff."

"Oh. I thought… never mind."

"He's awake!" Sputter spotted me, jumped up, and ran into his apartment. He came out holding what I thought was a kite made out of some dirty old red-and-yellow canvas.

"Made it for you!" He pushed it into my hands.

"What is it?"

"It's a hat!"

"It is?" I looked it over doubtfully. "Looks like the canopy from that broken umbrella we saw yesterday."

"You mean this morning," said Vern. "Look: Sputter added a chin strap."

"Try it on," said Wren.

There was no form to it. There was no brim. It looked more like a floppy, pie-colored headdress than a hat. I draped it over my head and fitted the strap under my chin, holding the front bit up to keep it from flopping down over my eyes. "How does it look?"

"Looks don't matter," said Vern.

Wren said "anyway, it'll keep the sun off."

"Rain, too," said Sputter.

"And you'll be seen from miles away," said Vern.

I said "what about from the back?"

Vern said "it looks fine, Abner."

"You don't think it makes me look like a deflated beach ball?"

Sputter laughed. I took it off and handed it to Vern. "You try it on."

He backed away. "I don't need a new hat."

Wren gave me a look that was half scold, half scorn. " 'Round these parts, it's customary to say thank you when someone gives you a gift."

"Oh. Right." I turned to Sputter. "Thank you kindly, sir. Very generous and very thoughtful of you. I surely do appreciate it."

Sputter beamed. "Want some dinner?"

Sputter had apparently felt stung by Wren's eating-our-own-shoes comment. He must have been up all day, foraging. We sat in the gathering twilight and tucked in to a salad made of lizard tails, flogberries,[43] and boiled thattle leaves.[44] The quantity wasn't copious, but the quality was best-you-can-get.

---

43 Flogberry bushes are the stuff of legend — meaning they may or may not exist. The only way to find out is to try growing one. You see, they only sprout after you give the desert floor a good whipping. It has to be done vigorously, for a painfully long period of time, while the sun is highest in the sky. If you do it right, your flogberry bush will shoot out of the ground and blossom in a matter of hours. By sundown, you'll be feasting on ripe, juicy flogberries. Any desert rat will tell you that the harvest is worth the effort. Just... be advised, is all: if a rat hands you a rope or a switch and sends you out into the blazing sun for an hour's hard labor, he or she might just be pulling your leg.

44 Thattle plants are often compared to — and mistaken for — one of the many species of prickly perennials found in the thistle family. Unlike thistles, however, thattles only grow in exceptionally arid environments. The leaves are quite tasty if prepared correctly. More importantly, thattle leaves attract moisture. They seem to suck it out of the air, often coating the plants with a fine layer of early morning dew. First words out of many a thirsty nomad's lips at the start of a new day is this: *thattle dew, my friends. Thattle dew.*

"Excellent meal," said Wren. "Well done. I dare say this'll hold me till I fetch up at Mongrel's Hole tomorrow. How 'bout you boys? Which way you headed?"

"North," said Vern.

"West," I said, glaring at Vern. "Back to town, before my bones turn to charcoal."

"The Northern Trace is the quickest way out of the desert," said Vern.

"You're joking," I said.

"It's true."

"The Northern Trace leads straight through the Mountains of Dett!"

Vern cocked his head and showed me his palms, as if to say, *yeah. So?* "It's the quickest way out. And then, if you still want to head back to town, you can float down Rattlin Creek all the way to Fathom River. Faster than going back the way we came."

Tell you true, I druther walk across the boiling mudfields of Mistep Perish than spend even a single day in Dett. Getting there is easy. Trouble is, you may never get back out again. I said to Vern, I said "have you ever been in Dett?"

"It's really not that bad," he said. "I hear the locals are actually pretty friendly."

Sputter tried again. "You could stay here…"

Wren said "don't be a fool, boy. Last thing you need is a waggie taking up permanent residence. You'll attract all manner of folk. You and old Sputter done a right good job cleaning up inside the wall, but Dunghovel don't need no more slovens."

"Fine," I said, thinking about all the ways a solo traveler can die in the desert. "The Northern Trace it is."

Umbrellas aren't made to be worn.

Some say wool isn't made to be worn, either — it's too scratchy, they say. It irritates the skin, they say. The slightest movement in a wool sweater is an invitation to march an army of ants across your bare arms and neck and shoulders. Mind you, *I* don't say that. I love wool sweaters. I'm just saying, some people don't like to wear wool.

Some people probly don't mind wearing sandpaper. Some people think carpets make dandy trousers. Me, I reckon sandpaper is best left in the toolbox. Carpet is best left on the floor. And red-and-yellow canvas umbrellas ought never to be made into hats.

The coarse fabric chafed my forehead. It wasn't breathable. I felt like my scalp was locked in a pressure cooker full of boiling sweat. And the chin strap left a hand's width of daylight between the strap and my jaw. Naturally, it wasn't adjustable. Vern offered to make a cinch for it, but I told him not to bother. Instead, I wore my new hat as little as possible — never at night, and by day only when the sun got high enough to strike a glancing blow.

On the morning of the fifth day, we crossed a sandy riverbed called Never Wash and entered the badlands known as the Spree.

Now, of all the myriad ways to get into Dett, the Spree is arguably the most perilous. It's a broken country full of ghosts.

Okay, not really. In the three days it took to cross the Spree, I never did see a single ghost — but neither could I shake the feeling that *something* must be lurking out there: a furtive movement atop a butte… a mournful sigh from behind the rocks… a skulking presence just up yonder, disappearing 'round the next bend. The Spree is a land of hoodoos, toadstools, and serpentine canyons that lead nowhere and offer no way out. It's a place built to make you wish you'd never been — and yearn to escape before you're completely spent.

"I hope you know what we're doing," I said to Vern as we hiked up the Grand Bourse.

"Too late to turn back now."

The Grand Bourse is a valley set between a series of boxy-looking buttes. Tall spires of rock stand in front of the buttes like moneychangers loafing outside their stalls, imploring all passersby to come inside and exchange their currency for scrip. I cast a wary eye at a nearby toadstool — a limestone column with a huge boulder perched on top like a giant misshapen head. The boulder had a predatory look on its face. I said "you understand how that answer doesn't inspire a whole lot of confidence, don't you?"

"Relax," he said. "We'll be in Dett before you know it."

"That's sort of what I'm afraid of."

"Hmm?"

"Nothing. Tell me again why we need to pay a visit to Holly Green, all on a sudden."

"She knows the Wodewosen."

"So she does." The Wodewosen are forest people — seldom seen by anyone from outside their own clan. Rumor has it, Holly is married to a Wodewose. "Why is that important?"

"Remember what Sputter said? The trees would know. And they'd pass the word through their networks. They'd know anything that goes on above ground or below — especially anything that affects their livelihood."

"Did that hoodoo just move?"

Vern ignored me. "Like The Worm, for example. The Worm has complete power over the underground climate, so to speak. It can improve the soil, or undercut it so the next hard rain washes it all away. So it stands to reason, the trees probably keep track of The Worm's whereabouts the same as we humans track the weather. They might even know where Pedestrio is, though he's a mite harder to track."

"They're supposed to be alive," I said. "These hoodoos, I mean. They're supposed to be an ancient race of giants. Dishonest giants. Mean merchants and shifty traders who cheated and robbed every traveler who ever set foot in this valley. Then one day the giants tried to rob a powerful sorcerer. With nimble fingers, they lifted the gold from his purse and replaced it with stone. 'Course, you can guess what happened after the sorcerer discovered their perfidy."

"So that's the daisy chain," said Vern. "The trees talk to each other. The Wodewosen talk to the trees. And Holly talks to the Wodewosen."

"They got turned to stone," I said. "The giants, I mean. As a punishment for what they did. So they're still alive — they're just made of stone, is all."

"Hmm?"

"I said they got turned to stone."

"What are you talking about?"

"Nothing. What are you talking about?"

"Daisy chains."

"Oh." I thought about that. In the end, I concluded it would be rude to tell him he wasn't making any sense. So I waited for a sizable parade of minutes to go marching by, and then I tried again. "So, Vern… why are we headed north?"

If anything, the badlands are even trickier to navigate than the desert. In the desert, you can spend hours hiking across a mesa with the whole sky above your head and a clear view of where you're going. Maybe then you hit a canyon, and you've got to find a way to get across the canyon and onto the next mesa. But in the badlands, it's all canyon. You spend all your energy climbing up a striated ridge, only to find there's nowhere to go from there — the ridge drops away again, almost without pause. You can look around while you're up there, and maybe try to map a route through the maze… but it won't do you any good. Things always look different inside the maze than they do from atop one of the walls.

The good news is, we encountered more shade in the Spree than we'd found anywhere this side of the Wandering Hills. The scorching heat of the desert gradually diminished as we gained elevation, so we began the transition from night hiking to daytime travel — albeit with a lengthy siesta to get us through the afternoon. With the solstice approaching, there were too many hours in the day to spend them all hiding from the sun.

The giant hoodoos loomed over us, radiating greed and malice. The one thing they wanted, more than breath itself, was to turn us upside down and shake us by the ankles till our pockets turned inside out. We treaded cautiously, never letting our guards down, just in case they somehow broke free. Still and all, they bore the brunt of the sun for most of the day, and for that, we were grateful.

We climbed to the top of Free Pass on the day of the new moon. I wasn't sure if that was a good omen or a bad one. "So this is what Dett looks like," I said. "I was hoping there'd be trees."

"These are just the foothills. Trees are higher up."

Of course they are. I reached for my useless umbrella hat, then thought better of it and pulled my shirt up over my ears. "How far is it to Rattlin Creek?"

"Two or three days?" He made it sound more like a guess than a promise.

"Can't wait." I touched the bruises on my forehead.

"You look like a turtle," he said. "And your nose is peeling again."

"Yeah. I ran out of that ointment Wren gave me." I did my best to walk with my face turned away from the sun.

"Won't be long now. Look, there's a cloud."

I couldn't remember the last time we'd seen a cloud. "Thank Blue. Hope there's more where that came from. No offense, Blue."

Vern was transitioning, too. I mean, he's always been highly observant — but more and more, as we got ourselves reacquainted with the light of day, I'd catch him scanning the horizon or staring off into the middle distance instead of watching where his feet were taking him.

I figured he was determined to catch a glimpse of a certain barefoot traveler. Given the wideness of the world and the narrow swath of one man's passage, I didn't think much of Vern's prospects. I figured he'd a better chance of spotting a spotless leopard than such an elusive quarry as Pedestrio.

'Course, I've been wrong before.

INTERLOGUE:
Trespasser!

————————

Now, it so happened that when The Worm surfaced in Paradise, only one person was near enough to see It. Only one person had chosen to go for a midnight stroll that night. That person was Pedestrio.

Of course, by this time, most of the valley dwellers had grown used to the nightmares. No one can stand such a constant barrage of hauntings and howlings without becoming inured to some extent. After all, no matter what imaginary terrors stalked their subconscious minds, the Paradisians still had to go on living their fruitless lives. They still had to dodge the tumblerocks, avoid the spiny moss, and gather their daily rations of bird droppings. They still had to get from one day to the next, and the only way to do that was to tune out the nightmares and turn themselves over to sleep.

So it was not fear that kept Pedestrio awake that night. It was restlessness. It was, in fact, latent wanderlust.

One can imagine Pedestrio's amazement upon seeing The Worm. He thought perhaps It was a nightmare come to life. He wondered if he could be dreaming — and yet, he knew that he was not.

He stood there, petrified, as the empty Void reared up and swayed back and forth. He watched, fascinated, as It recoiled in terror — for what reason, Pedestrio could not guess.

And then The Worm dreamed.

The power of the dream pulsed through the valley. It bounced off the mountainsides and rippled back over the land, like a thunderclap in a snowstorm. It ripped through Pedestrio's mind like a tsunami of sound and light and color and fragrance and tactile sensation, and for a moment, he saw it all: a planet-sized Garden of rich soil and beautiful flowers and the sweet ambrosia of edible greens.

But the dreams of the Old Ones are not meant to be absorbed at close range by mere mortals. The power of the vision buckled Pedestrio's knees and robbed him of his consciousness.

He awoke some time later, feeling more alive than he had ever felt before. He looked around. The Worm was gone. The dull gray mountains towered over him. High overhead, a raptor took careful aim and deposited a liquescent gift on his left shoulder. A lichen-covered boulder rolled slowly toward him.

The valley was the only home he'd ever known. It wasn't a bad place. He felt relatively safe and reasonably happy within its limited confines. But things were different now. He recalled his vision of a world filled with greenery and breathtaking natural wonders. He had to seek that world out. The nightmares did not frighten him anymore. He had an odd feeling that he was practically indestructible.

In point of fact, he was not indestructible. The Worm's dream had bestowed upon him a fantastically long expected lifespan. He was still human, however. His life could still come to an abrupt end — cut short by accident or grave misfortune. But why worry about that when there were Gardens and greenery and natural wonders to explore?

So Pedestrio followed The Worm out of Paradise. He discovered the tunnel the Old One had left behind, and he followed it for many miles. The tunnel took him far down under the mountains and back up into a beautiful new world.

Pedestrio looked around. No spiny moss stabbed at his feet. No tumbling boulders tried to roll over him. Most of the trees did not spit at him.

He thought he might like this place.

Pedestrio didn't know where he was. He had no comprehension of how incredibly vast and varied the earthly landscapes could be. But he was a pioneer at heart. He had explored every inch of Paradise, tiny as it was. He looked forward to seeing all there was to see.

Then The Worm turned… and saw Pedestrio.[45]

At once, The Worm knew Pedestrio didn't belong in the Garden. At once, The Worm knew Pedestrio must have escaped from Paradise and followed It to this place. But The Worm did not yet know the full extent of the problem. It did not know Pedestrio had been gifted with near immortality, nor that Pedestrio's kin would soon wake to recall dreams of green grass between their toes, nor that those dreams would once again set people on the path to finding their own ways out of the valley.

The Worm did not realize any of that — at least, not right away. In that moment of initial contact, It knew only three things: first, there was an interloper in the Garden. Second, the presence of this scurvy, malnourished lower life form was probably The Worm's fault. And third, The Worm had better do something about it, lest the blame fall heavily upon Its metaphoric shoulders.

So The Worm reared up on Its Great Empty Fundament and bellowed in a silent voice that nevertheless echoed like a thunderclap between Pedestrio's ears.

Trespasser! It roared.

---

45 Or rather, The Worm felt his presence, since worms can't see (and for that matter, neither can empty black Voids).

CHAPTER 34:
Rock Bottom

THE Mountains of Dett are deceptively easy to climb. Matter of fact, the track winds its way so cleverly up the grade, I barely noticed the change in elevation. By late afternoon, I reckoned we must be getting close to the summit.

I gazed back the way we'd come. "That wasn't so bad. I thought these mountains were supposed to be almost vertical."

Vern said "they are."

"Doesn't feel like it."

"It never does. But wait till we hit Rock Bottom."

"What's Rock Bottom?"

"That's the name of the ridge we're headed for."

"Odd name for a mountain ridge."

Vern didn't answer. His eyes were fixed on something upslope. "Who's that?"

I looked up, expecting to see another down-on-his-luck traveler searching in vain for a way out of Dett. You'd think there wouldn't be anyone left in the whole province, what with all the folks wanting to leave.

But this figure didn't trudge along like the rest of them, all slump-shouldered and shuffle-footed. He walked with his head up and his shoulders back, swinging his arms like he didn't have a care in the world. He had a quarter-mile lead on us. And at that distance, I could have been mistaken — but it sure did look like he was barefoot.

One thing about him that couldn't be mistook, though. That thing on his head? Why, that was my crusty old bush hat, is what that was.

"Hey!" I yelled — but Vern was already huffing up the mountain.

I followed close to. The slope fought back, as chunks of rock shifted and rolled beneath our feet. Vern paid them no mind. He drove his legs like the back end of a catawampus — powering uphill in pursuit of his quarry. I struggled to keep pace. We gained ground.

Then the stranger hit the scrub. His bottom half disappeared in a thicket of nogo bushes, and I pushed a little harder, thinking the dense growth would slow him up. Only it didn't. His head and torso floated above the brownery, bobbing along at the same pace as before.

"Crack it!" Vern cursed. He knew we had no chance of slipping through that scrub as fast and easy as Pedestrio. The chaparral clogged the entire valley between two spurs, but the ridgetops were clear. Vern turned and raced for the western spur. "This way!"

The route took us way off course. Vern kept glancing back to check on the stranger's progress. I checked the sky. The wind had blown gently from the west all day; now it whistled down from the north. Up on Rock Bottom, clouds were gathering. I shivered.

"Storm coming," I said.

"He's almost out of the scrub."

We kept climbing. A few minutes later, we cleared the thicket. Vern pointed us back down into the draw, angling to cut the stranger off just below the ridge.

We were still a few hundred feet below Rock Bottom when the first hard raindrops pinged us.

I suppose they're called "raindrops" on account of they drop out of the sky. But these ones didn't feel like they were dropped. They felt like pellets fired out of a peashooter. Call them rainshots, instead. Each bullet of rain hit so hard, it raised a welt. I fished out my umbrella hat, but a sudden blast of wind filled it like a sail and ripped it out of my hands. "Cruddy trash!" I screamed as it flew away. "Good riddance!"

The barefoot stranger never slowed down. We pushed on, with no shelter in sight. Lightning bolts struck at the ground like electrified rattlesnakes. The thunder cracked so loud, I thought the sky broke. I wanted to turn back, but Vern, he just kept going. I reckoned he'd gone crazy. But I followed him anyway, on the suspicion that lightning is more likely to strike a person who's running away.

The storm intensified. The rainshots exploded on impact. I held my hand up to shield my eyes. The stranger topped the ridge and stood there for a moment — the tallest point on the landscape. *Suicide,* I thought. The rain was pelting my face — I may have shut my eyes for a moment. When I looked again, he was gone.

Vern stood agape. I yelled in his ear. "We gotta get low!"

A blinding flash hit the top of the ridge. The thunder shock nearly knocked us off our feet. Vern looked around. "There!"

He pointed to a pool of shadow in the crook of the eastern spur — either a cave or an abandoned mine. We staggered toward it, faltering under the weight of the storm. The air smelled like ozone. The sky crackled. We threw ourselves to the ground, just as a bolt of lightning ripped through our general vicinity. Vern's hair stuck out like porcupine quills. We crawled on hands and knees the rest of the way.

It was a mine. The entrance was half collapsed, there being no support timbers. But we rolled a couple of stones out of the way and crawled inside.

The tunnel was fairly spacious, with four-foot-high ceilings and room enough for both of us to squat side by side. An inch of water flooded the shaft, with more pouring in all the time. The only thing to do was to stick near the entrance and wait to see if the water got any deeper.

The floor of the tunnel was littered with chunks of rock. The ceiling was pocked with matching chunk-sized concavities. The mine obviously hadn't been worked in some time. I cogitated for a moment on just how driven — or desperate — or crazy you'd have to be to commence mining operations this high up in the mountains of Dett. I reckoned there was a story to be told. Or a heartbreaking ballad to be sung. But here and now, I was grateful for the shelter.

We built ourselves a little bench out of stone and sat there with our feet in the water. Vern stared out into the rain, while I regarded the ceiling with a certain lack of absolute confidence.

Another close strike. The earth trembled all around us. I threw my arms over my head. Vern barely flinched. I said "think it'll hold?"

"It wasn't him."

I looked at Vern. He stared straight ahead. "It wasn't Pedestrio," he said.

"How do you reckon?"

"Did you see him up there on the ridge?"

"Yeah. Risky move, tempting Big T like that."[46]

"Did you see what he did just before he disappeared?"

"Let me guess. Did he stoop down and arrange a few pebbles into a silhouette of himself?"

Vern didn't even blink. He stared at the rain, but his eyes were on the scene replaying itself in his mind. "No."

"Oh."

"He turned around and tipped his hat."

"You mean my hat."

"Whatever."

"I didn't see that. You sure you didn't imagine it?"

Finally, he looked down and shifted his feet. "I didn't imagine it. He looked right at us."

---

46 Big T is short for Big Thunderhead, a name sometimes given to the oft-misunderstood Sky spirit in charge of thunder and lightning. Contrary to popular legend, Big Thunderhead is not particularly bad-tempered. Most violent storms do not serve any vengeful purpose. Big T spins 'em out on account of He thinks lightning is pretty, that's all.

"Maybe he recognized you," I said. "I mean, you've spent your whole life on his turf. He's been your spirit guide since even before you knew he was real. Don't you think he knows who his followers are?"

"It wasn't Pedestrio," Vern insisted.

"Well, okay then." I pushed a wet shock of hair out of my eyes. "Whoever it was, I'd like to know how he got my hat away from the betchacant."

"What betchacant?"

"That night I lit out for Arcadia." I told him the tale, making it sound like I was only steps away from Youda Tank before the betchacant lured me away. "I'd be Town Side right now, if it weren't for her. Probly spinning yarns in a nice, dry café down on Easy Street. Hat full of coins, more'n likely. What do you think, Vern? That sound about right? Vern?"

Vern took his time answering. The violent edge of the storm moved on, but the deluge continued unabated. The rainwater continued to pour into the mine, and I worried we might get flooded out. But the water level didn't rise — must be a shaft somewhere further back. I didn't care to investigate. Finally, Vern offered up his thoughts.

"Mischief," he said.

"Mischief," I echoed.

At that particular moment, the word had no meaning to me — and being too wet and worn to cipher it out, I sat there like a hoodoo and waited for him to explain.

"The Trickster," he said. "She's another one of the Earth spirits — the spirit of games and puckishness."

"I know who She is," I said. "Any spinner of yarns knows who The Cozener is. But…"

I couldn't allow myself to finish that thought. My mind jumped to another thought, instead: Vern, who told himself Pedestrio stories his whole life, but never believed his own tales… until that day in the swaddle, when he stumbled across an impossible track and followed it to a pattern of pebbles on the ground. *So this is what it felt like when the truth began to dawn on him... when the story became real.*

I don't mind saying, my head was spinning like a fast eddy. I reached for a line, a tree branch — anything to pull me back into the current. "But... why would She steal my hat? And why would She keep showing Herself?"

"I don't know," said Vern. "But it doesn't bode well."

I nodded. Mischief is a fun-loving Earth spirit. She doesn't have a destructive aspect, like the Eater of Worlds — but her sense of humor can occasionally be deadly. "You think She's ever taken the form of a hornswoggle?"

"All the time. Mischief and hornswoggles have a lot in common."

"So it could have been Her all along."

Vern grunted. I could tell he was running out of words, but I had more questions.

"What about Pedestrio? Is he real, or was it Her?"

Vern thought about that. "I don't believe it was Mischief in the swaddle. I don't think it's been Her leaving all these rock patterns everywhere."

He was probably right. Mischief plays around the edges. She doesn't drive the narrative. She's more likely to slink around foiling everybody else's plans. I couldn't imagine Her wearing the role of a wandering barefoot stranger for a million years. That would be too much like work.

"Is Pedestrio an Earth spirit?"

Vern shifted on the stone bench. "No. He's just a man, like us."

"Only a lot older."

"Yes."

"If he's just a man, how did he get to be immortal?"

"I don't think he's immortal — just fantastically long-lived."

"I stand corrected," I said, rolling my eyes. "You ever cross paths with an Earth spirit before?"

"Not so's I've noticed."

"Me neither. So why now? Why us?"

"I don't know."

We sat quietly for a while, watching the rain. Finally, I couldn't stand it any longer. I just had to know. "Do you think there's a chance I'm ever going to get my hat back?"

CHAPTER 35:
Deep Hole

Violent thunderstorms generally don't last all that long. This one abated after an hour or so. The clouds scattered. The sun reached out, and we debated whether to push on or take the rest of the evening off to dry our togs.

I hate walking in wet clothes. I get chafed all the way up one side and down the other, till it feels like I'm wearing pants made out of sandpaper. On t'other hand, I didn't want to spend the night on a windswept ridge, either — especially on a cloudless night after a soaking rain. Probly freeze to death before morning.

We decided to push on. But before we struck out, Vern said "hang on a second," and ducked back into the mine.

I said "what are you doing?"

He didn't answer. I stuck my head in. Couldn't see a thing, but I heard him splashing around, heading further back into the mine. The ceiling wasn't high enough to walk upright; he'd have to crawl, or duckwalk. The rock debris littering the floor wouldn't make it any easier.

I said "I think there are bats back there! Big ones. Vampire bats!"

A handful of dirt and a rock the size of an apple dislodged itself from the lintel above the mine entrance. The rock clipped me on the back of the neck. I withdrew my head again.

"Vern? You still in there?"

No answer.

Time passed. I stood guard at the mine entrance, imagining all sorts of things. He'd fallen down a mine shaft. Whacked his head on a rock. The cave bears found him and dragged him back to their lair. He'd come out another entrance on the other side of the mountain. Big T snuck in the back way and ran him through with a lightning bolt.

I did think about going in after him. But seeing as how neither one of us had a flashlight, that seemed like a fool's errand. Besides, if I went back in there, my clothes would never get dry.

It's spooky, hanging around outside an abandoned mine. It seems unnaturally quiet. Not that it's any less noisy than any other place in the Wild — but mines are symbols of vigorous, cacophonous human activity. Take away the activity, and the first thing you notice is the absence of sound. It's the silence you hear when the band stops playing, and nobody gives a clap.

Vern shook me awake. I said "was I asleep?"

"A little bit."

"You were gone a long time," I said. "I was worried."

"Yeah, I could tell."

"Well, sometimes I get a little drowsy after a good rain."

Vern checked the shadows. "Let's get going," he said. "Should be more vegetation on the north-facing slopes. Maybe we can scare up some dry firewood."

I brushed the mud off my backside and took off after Vern, who walked like he was two steps behind the sun and one step ahead of the wind. I said "what were you doing back there?"

"Prospecting."

"Prospecting?"

"You never know."

"You find anything?"

He pulled a rock out of his pocket and showed it to me. It was about the size of a small acorn. It sparkled like a diamond on one side and glowed like a ruby on the other.

"What is it?"

"It's a strata gem," he said. "They're pretty rare. But you can find them occasionally, if you know where to look."

"What's a strata gem?"

"It's a gemstone that forms between two different layers of rock. Because the top and bottom sides are in different strata, they form separately into completely different gems. Then the two halves are fused together metamorphically to make one rock."

I pretended to know what he was talking about. "Yeah, that makes sense. But if it's a raw gemstone, then why is it so polished?"

"Strata gems form along fault lines. Whenever there's an earthquake or a tremor, the strata rub against each other, polishing the gems."

"Getting the Earth to do your work for you, in other words."

Vern showed me that ghost of a smile again. "Be kind to the planet, and it will be kind to you."

"But how did you find it? I mean, you don't have a flashlight, or even a torch."

Vern's eyes kept scanning the ground, but the trail of the barefoot stranger had been washed clean by the rain. "That's what took so long. I had to wait till my eyes got used to the dark. But even before that, I saw the telltales."

"What telltales?"

"The strata and the fault lines. You could see them from the mine entrance. But I knew the light would be better once the rain stopped, so I waited."

"Bad luck for the miners who dug this tunnel," I said. "How do you reckon they missed a find like that?"

Vern shrugged. "Tunnel vision. Sometimes you don't see what you're not looking for."

"You think there are more?"

"Probably. But we'll leave them where they are for now. If we need any more, we can always come back."

Turned out Rock Bottom wasn't the highest point in all of Dett, after all. We crested the ridge and started down the other side, only to find ourselves an hour later somehow looking down on Rock Bottom from an even higher peak. Vern looked confused. He knows Wild Side from Bottle Neck to Fargone, but I expect he doesn't spend a lot of time in Dett.

He was right about the vegetation, though. The northern slopes were a lot greener than the side we'd come up. None of the trees were very tall. They stood with hunched trunks and drooping limbs, as if they were ashamed of their situation. But they were a welcome sight, all the same. We camped in a grove of gopher broaks and talked about how we'd be swimming in Rattlin Creek by noon tomorrow.

Only noon came and went — twice — and we never did find a way out of the mountains. We knew the direction, right enough, but every path seemed to go in circles. When we tried to travel cross-country, we inevitably found ourselves looking down at a thousand-foot drop. Finally, along about dusk on the third day, we smelled a cookfire and traced it to a camp.

Two crooked lean-tos and the half-hearted beginnings of a tiny log cabin stood around a clearing. In the middle of the clearing, four dusty miners huddled around the source of the aromas: a flame-blackened pot suspended over a smoldering fire.

"Hello, the camp!" said Vern. He beat me to it — ordinarily, he hangs back and lets me handle the introductions.

The miners looked up. There were two men and two women, though I could only tell that when they showed their faces — they all wore the same sort of denim work shirts and patchy overalls. Their cheeks were smudged, their necks dirty, and their close-cropped hair showed evidence of being trapped inside a helmet all day.

"Hello, travelers!" said a woman kneeling over the pot, ladle in hand. "Welcome to Deep Hole."

"Might we join you?"

"Not much in the pot, but you're welcome to whatever we've got," said a red-haired man. "Name's Gray. This here's Kurt and

Gabby. That's my wife, Rusty, over there. She's on cook duty tonight."

"I'm Vern," said Vern. "He's Abner."

"Rusty?" I said, feeling thick. "But she's got black hair."

"Didn't used to be," said Rusty. "Used to be blue."

"Then how'd you get a name like Rusty?"

She grinned and gave the pot a saucy little tap with the ladle. A reddish-black flake fell into the fire. "It's my pot."

I couldn't think of a single thing to say to that. Me, a banter-tested veteran of countless mornings at Elmer's Café. Rusty stared at me as if the entire interview depended on what I'd say next. I just stood there like a stump. Rusty returned to stirring the pot. "Y'all want some borrower's broth?"[47]

Vern said "yes, please." Rusty ladled a watery concoction into a bowl and passed it to him. Vern sniffed the bowl and handed it back. "Smells delicious!"

Rusty offered me the bowl. "You want some?"

My stomach growled. I was hoping for something more permanent than borrower's broth. "No, thanks. Not that hungry, I guess."

"What are you boys doing this high up in Dett?" said Kurt. "Prospecting?"

"Just passing through," said Vern. "We'll be on our way come the morn."

"Assuming we can find a way out of here," I added.

Gray said "oh, that's easy. Just follow the paybacks."

"The what?"

"The paybacks. The trail zigs and zags all the way up and down the mountain. Makes the climb easier."

---

47 Borrower's broth is like stone soup, only you have to give it back when you're done with it. Local rules apply: most communities will serve up a single bowl of broth, and everybody gets a sniff before passing it on. Some let you taste it, as long as you spit it back out again. For obvious reasons, borrower's broth is not very filling. On the other hand, there is usually enough left over that everybody can have a second helping.

You mean switchbacks, I thought. But I didn't argue the point, on account of another thought was beginning to creep through my mind.

I said "speaking of just passing through, I don't suppose you've seen a barefoot man wearing a bush hat, have you?"

Rusty said "what else has he got on?"

Something about the way she said it got stuck in my head and sort of jammed everything to a halt. I looked at the ground and tried to think. "He's… uh… ahh…"

Vern said "tan shirt, soft leather. Light brown britches, cut off below the knee. Sort of blends into the landscape."

"Can't say we've seen him," said Gray. "Friend of yours?"

"Never met him," said Vern. "Hoping to, soon."

Kurt said "not many strangers roam these peaks. Those who get this far generally stay a while."

"He's got my hat," I explained — only the words came out a shade too loud and a tick too fast. The pause in the conversation dragged on a beat too long, and not even Vern could bring himself to look in my direction. *Dang it! I used to be good at this.*

"That's good broth," said Vern, sniffing the bowl a second time. "You folks been mining long?"

"Not long enough," said Gray.

"We opened our first mine out in the Kitchen Range," said Kurt. "That was back during the Year of the Whist. Everybody wanted woolstones back then. Gabby and I got caught up in the rush — we sold everything we owned and then some to pay for mining equipment. But one day the mountain shook, and everybody thought the Burners were about to blow."

"We were there, too," said Gray. "It was like a dog shaking off fleas, only we were the fleas."

"The miners all scattered. We four teamed up and decided to try our luck elsewhere. But the Whist petered out, and nobody wanted woolstones anymore. We've been in Dett ever since."

"We lost everything," Rusty said cheerfully. "Everything but this here pot."

Vern said "I'm sorry to hear that."

Gray said "oh, things are bound to turn 'round. Got to. The Deep Hole Mine'll pay off any day now, you mark my words."

"So marked," said Rusty with a jaunty thunk of the ladle against the pot.

"Demand for woolstones is on the rise," Kurt said. "So I heard. We'll be writing our own tickets before you know it."

Vern said "you're still set on pulling out woolstones?"

"You betcha."

Vern grimaced and sucked a small but audible quantity of air through his teeth. "I don't think you'll find any. Geology's not right."

"We'll settle for greenstone."

Vern shook his head.

"Brownstone?"

Vern said "was that your tunnel we saw the other side of Rock Bottom Ridge?"

Kurt said "yep. We called that one the Yorziz Mine. Didn't pan out, though. We abandoned it a few years back."

Vern took the strata gem from his pocket and handed it to Gabby, who hadn't said a word. "Might want to give a thought to reopening it."

INTERLOGUE:
The Year of the Whist

You probably remember the Year of the Whist — or the Great Dream Shortage, as some folks like to call it. That was the year there just weren't enough dreams to go 'round.

It happened gradually; lots of folks didn't notice at first. For some — meaning those who struggled to make it through another long day — a peaceful night's sleep was a dream come true. Even those who made a point of recording all their dreams in a dream journal weren't terribly bothered by an occasional blank page. After all, who could imagine the river of dreams running dry?

But then it started happening more often. Not all at once, but over the course of weeks, and then months… well, the dreams, they just stopped coming.

By the flower moon, the Whist might catch a body twice before Saturday waltzed 'round the corner. That's when the more sensitive types caught on, and things began to get squirrelly. Nobody knew how it began, though a lot of folks had theories. Some blamed it on a rare kind of ionic disturbance in the phantasmosphere. Others openly speculated the Whist could be the work of an evil sorcerer, or possibly some crazed, quota-wielding bureaucrat.

All anybody knew for sure was that there weren't enough dreams to go 'round.

Come the full buck moon, the average had sunk down to three dreams a week. That's when the general hue and cry commenced. Not that it did any good — before the rise of the green corn moon, it was two dreams a week. Then one. Then maybe none at all.

Doctors tried writing more prescriptions, but of course that didn't help. So they wrote fewer prescriptions, and of course that didn't help either. So they published a heap of papers in all the best medical journals — which didn't do a lick of good, but it kept the doctors busy and out of trouble, and that's all anyone could ask.

By the time of the harvest moon, it was catch-as-can. You see, there just weren't enough dreams to go 'round. And you know this as well as I do: when supplies grow scarce, folks have a way of putting their faith in some mighty unsound business practices.

Some of them took to hoarding their nocturnal fantasies. Others tried rationing: anyone lucky enough to be favored with a dream was expected to stay awake the next few nights — give somebody else a chance. Prospectors flocked to the hills. Woolstone mines sprang up everywhere, on account of it being rumored that a dream magnet with a woolstone at the center, tucked under one's pillow, could attract visions in the darkest part of night.

The biggest nightmare anybody ever had was that their dreams would never come back.

But if you remember the Year of the Whist, you know it didn't last. As the harvest moon began to wane, so did the Great Dream Shortage. Very few people noticed at first. But gradually, as the days got shorter and the nights got longer, the dream journals began to fill up again. Come the frost, the average had clawed its way back up to three dreams a week. Then it was four. Then five.

By the rise of the cold moon, it was all but over. The doctors and the scientists and the woolstone miners never did figure out what the Great Dream Shortage was all about. For a long time, they tried. A thousand books were written about the Whist. But as the years went by, fewer and fewer people bought them. Scientists moved on to pursue other Great Unknowns. Doctors went back to prescribing too many pills.

Like a mysterious ailment, the Whist ran its course and was gone. Nobody knows where.

And nobody knows if it will ever come back.

CHAPTER 36:
The Sea of Green

By the time we reached Rattlin Creek, Vern had his bearings again. Even I knew the way, generally speaking: you follow the creek downstream to Fathom River. You cross the river at Canta Ford, and from there you take two steps north and a shuffle to the west, all the way to Greenhaven. Be there in a month, easy.

We took more than two.

Truth is, we dawdled a bit. I insisted. I told Vern, I said "we just survived a month in the desert. What's your hurry?"

I scootched down into the water and splashed myself under the arms. Rattlin Creek isn't deep enough for swimming, but it didn't take us long to find a sandy-bottomed pool to soak in.

He said "I thought you wanted to get back to town."

"No, I wanted to get back to a comfortable climate where the sun doesn't feel so angry all the time and there's plenty of food and water enough for bathing. And here we are."

Vern scrubbed his face with a handful of sand. "We can take a few days off, if you need time to recuperate."

"Yes. And so do you. And you need to slow down. A lot. Because you're gonna walk right by a whole lot of clues if we keep pushing twenty-five miles a day."

Vern dipped his head under and came up shaking his mane. Water flew everywhere.

I pitched him my closing argument. "You think Pedestrio doesn't spend a good part of his day communing with Nature?"

And folks, I tell you, those magic words were all it took to cure Vern's Undivided Attention Syndrome. Not altogether — I mean to say, we still kept moving. Every day brought us a few miles closer to our destination. We still kept our eyes peeled for signs of Pedestrio, and found two more symbols that would have remained hidden if we hadn't slowed down. But we took time to appreciate our surroundings, as well. We explored every pool and backwater on Rattlin Creek. We named every cloud in the sky, and wrote their names in bits of dandelion fluff, and blew the fluff skyward like aerial name tags. We invented seven languages and tried each of them out on every species of tree we met, but none of them seemed to understand. We decided the trees weren't too bright.

In short, we did everything you normally do on a summer day out in the Wild. Meanwhile, the strawberry moon came and went. So did the solstice. We crossed Fathom River as the new buck moon showed a thumbnail of light, and that evening, we lay on a fern-covered hillside and watched the buckskin deer cavorting in the gloaming with their fringes flying. I fell asleep and dreamed one of the stags had dropped my old bush hat on the ground and was prancing around it in a very complicated four-legged dance, the whole time daring me to come and get it. I think it was a dream. But I woke up with a powerful urge to get on with the journey.

We dawdled less. We hiked more. Still, it took us another month to reach Greenhaven.

The Sea of Green isn't the oldest patch of woods on the planet (that would be the Great Forest of Middle Nerth). Nor is it the most treacherous (compare, for example, the Pine Barrens of Vannish Gonaway). But I reckon the Sea of Green covers the most territory. It's the wildwood most likely to wear holes in your shoes and make you forget what direct, undappled sunlight feels like.

"Where's Blue?" I muttered for the umpteenth day in a row.

Vern didn't bother to look up. "Feels cloudy out. Won't rain today, though. Maybe tonight."

"Is it still the buck moon?" It's easy to lose track of time when you can't see the sky.

"Not by my count."

"Green corn?"

"New moon was yesterday, I think."

I frowned at the dense canopy high above our heads. "I bet Pedestrio never even sets foot in these parts. If he can't see the stars, how can he find his way home?"

"Oh, I expect he knows the way by now."

It's called the Sea of Green on account of when you're inside it, you feel like you're drowning — not because you can't breathe, but because you can't ever seem to break the surface. And it goes on and on for miles and miles and miles. There are no roads, except along the outer edges. Once in a while, somebody tries to build a thruway from one end to the other. But sooner or later, the road crews always succumb to the endlessness of it all and turn back.

This is not to say that the Sea of Green is unpopulated. Settlements crop up here and there like shipwrecks, providing homes and communities for stranded adventurers. Then there are the Wodewosen — indigenous woodlanders who mostly keep to themselves. They are rarely seen, and even Vern — who can track a spider across a spiderweb — even Vern swears they leave no trace.

I said to Vern, I said "maybe Pedestrio is a Wodewose."

"I don't think so. The Wodewosen almost never leave the forest."

"How do you know?"

"Well, because they're part of it. And it's a part of them."

I looked around. Nothing but moss-covered tree trunks in every direction. "Maybe one of them got sick of seeing the same old scenery and decided to roam the world instead."

"You could be right. Tell you what: we'll ask the next Wode-wose we see."

"Good plan," I said with a straight face. Vern doesn't have a sense of humor, but sometimes he tries to hide that fact by saying something funny. Actual Wodewose sightings are about as rare as nocturnal rainbows.

Of course, I think Vern could track one down, if he really wanted to. But as they say in East Tealeaf, you cannot gather air in a basket if you haven't got a basket.[48]

Sure enough, a cold rain blew in overnight. By morning, we were soggy and miserable. We spent the next two days tramping through a steady downpour that seemed intent on dowsing the fiery heart of summer. Then the storm broke. The days warmed up again. Summer tried to reassert its seasonal rights and privileges, but it wasn't the same — the dog days had lost their bite.

"How far is it to Cleanshaven?" I said.

"*Green*haven. We should be there sometime tomorrow, if we can find it."

If we can find it. Well, that's definitive. "What if we can't?"

"Then we'll sit down and wait for it to appear."

"Terrific. Good plan. I like that plan. Did I ever tell you about the time I threw a pinch of salt into a puddle and waited for an ocean to grow?"

---

48 The actual saying is: "you cannot gather air in a basket made of holes." But the renowned linguist and ruiner of dinner parties, Dr. Sema Phorre, has famously pointed out that a basket *made* of holes is nothing but a basket-shaped hole. "What you should be saying," advised Dr. Phorre, "is 'you cannot gather air in a basket *full* of holes.'" To which the East Tealeafians replied, "we know you mean well, but in point of fact, our entire cultural identity is predicated upon the basket being *made* of holes. To question this axiom is to question the very heart of our existence." Alas, Dr. Phorre persisted. Lawsuits were filed, and the highly disciplined forces of logic fought a swarming, chaotic horde of cultural anthropologists and idiomologists to a standstill. The courts, in their infinite wisdom, ruled that no one but an East Tealeafian may gather air in a basket *made* of holes, and any persons attempting to use a basket *full* of holes for the purpose of air-gathering may have their air confiscated and their baskets taken away for a period of not less than three (3) years.

CHAPTER 37:
Greenhaven

OKAY, fine. Technically, Vern is right: Holly Green calls her little cottage Green's Haven, or Greenhaven. But sometimes I can't resist calling it Cleanshaven, even though the shadows seem to grow larger and loom overhead like deadfalls every time I say it.

You see, her cottage is nestled deep within the wooliest part of the forest. The trees are draped in so much green and brown and bluish gray moss, you can't hardly tell them from a passel of long-haired, great-bearded, very tall, tatterdemalion wizards, all curiously frozen in place. The Wodewosen seem to prefer this patch of forest. I suppose they find in the profusion of moss and ferns and dangling epiphytes a reflection of their own hirsute features.

Precious few outlanders have ever caught a glimpse of the wild folk of the woods, yet somehow everybody knows they're the hairiest creatures on the planet. My friend Stretch says he once heard of a Wodewose who turned over in his sleep and fell into his own beard. Took him a week to climb out of it. I've heard tales of Wodewosen who nearly starved to death, on account of they couldn't fight their way past the bristles to load a few crumbs into their own gullets. Some folks say the Wodewosen are ten feet tall, but only half that size if you take away the hair.

I supposed we could ask Holly if any of those tales are true. After all, she would know. But the same rules that govern polite discourse in the Great Empty Desert apply out here in the Sea of Green: one doesn't pry. And anyway, a tale is a tale — trying to measure the truth of it is like trying to tie a rope around a cloud.

Holly lives in one of those cozy little stone-walled, sod-roofed, ivy-clad cottages — the sort you don't even know are there until you're practically stepping through the front door. It blends into the forest so well, even Vern sometimes has trouble locating it. In fact, Vern believes the building itself can disappear and reappear at will.

I don't know how that's possible, being made of stone and all. But I spose even stones occasionally sink back into the ground from whence they came.

We started hallooing from as far as a mile out. Vern swears if you don't do that, the house won't make an appearance. That seems a mite superstitious to me — not to mention, Holly probly knew we were coming the minute we set foot in the Sea of Green. She's got connections, Holly does.

Still, when folks live this far out from town, it's best to give them plenty of warning before showing up on their doorstep. That way, they've got time to decide whether to put the kettle on, or lock the door.

If it had been me alone, Holly might have chosen the latter course. I don't think she likes me very much. Howsoever, she met us both at the open door with two earthen mugs of hot wintergreen tea.

"Howdy, Vern!" she said. "It's been too long since your last visit. Come inside!"

Holly favored Vern with a warm smile that was already fading by the time she turned my way. "Hello, Abner."

"Hi Holly!" I said. "It's good to see you again! You're looking well. How are you doing? You're looking great."

She looked old, is what she looked like.

Okay, not that old. It just always catches me by surprise, is all. She looked like she'd put on thirty years since I'd seen her last. Her brown hair showed touches of gray, and she'd gained an extra crease or two around the eyes. Her face had more gravity to it. Her skin didn't look new anymore. Her hands were rough, like a pair of gloves that somebody forgot about, then found in the backyard a month later.

It hadn't been much more than a year since I'd been out this way. But of course, that was early in the spring. Holly always looks younger in the spring.

Vern says he's seen her before the thaw, when she runs around like a little girl, singing happy little songs to warm the ground and make the ice go away. And he's seen her in the dead of winter, sitting hunched by the fire, looking like an old crag peeking out from under a snowy peak, patiently waiting for the sun to regain its loftiest arch. That's just the way of things. I understand that. Still, it's hard to get used to.

Anyway, Vern said to Holly, he said "you'll have to excuse Abner. He's a long way from home, and his manners are wearing thin."

I glared at Vern.

Holly said "well, you are both welcome at Greenhaven." She put just enough emphasis on *Greenhaven* to give me the idea that anybody who referred to her home as *Cleanshaven* would get a somewhat less enthusiastic welcome.

Most parts of the year, Holly's cottage serves as more of a hearth than a home. And so it was today: bunches of dried tautstrife and loosestrife and a dozen other herbs hung from the ceiling. Earthen bowls and jars lined the mantel. One wall held a rack for stretching animal hides, empty at the moment — though Holly's buckskin culottes attested to past use. An oak table, a bench, and a woven leather chair by the fireplace provided the only other furniture. There wasn't a cot, nor a bedroll, nor any sign of nocturnal occupancy.

Holly doesn't spend a lot of time indoors. I reckon she only uses the cottage to entertain guests, to cook the occasional hot meal, and to prepare for winter.

Vern and I sat at the table while Holly puttered around the cookfire. Vern and Holly had a lot to talk about. You know, the usual neighborhood gossip: Chuck Raven is in trouble again, got caught stealing an egg from Auntie Robin.[49] Old Man Hickory looks like he might drop his nuts a few weeks early this year. Could be a long winter. Did you catch that whiff of woodsmoke yesterday morning? Yes, but it tasted like pine. Ah, then it's on the other side of Deep Gorge. Nothing to worry about.

The room smelled like ginger. Having nothing much to contribute to the conversation, I amused myself by concocting a fanciful and staggeringly preposterous story about an old woman who lived alone in the woods, in a house made entirely out of gingerbread. She —

"Abner, wake up."

"Hmm?"

"Dinner. Hickory cakes and ginger syrup."

Now, as much as I favor Elmer's Café whenever I'm in town, there is nothing on Elmer's entire menu that can beat a dense, buttery hickory cake baked in a wood-fired oven until the top is golden brown and the bottom is dusted white with ashes, then taken out while it's still warm and smothered in a boiled ginger syrup.

I said to Holly, I said "Holly, these cakes are delicious! I don't believe I've ever had a tastier meal. I don't suppose you'd care to share the recipe?"

Maybe I could get Elmer to add hickory cakes to the menu. But Vern frowned at me and shook his head. Holly simply ignored the question.

Just as well. Wild Side victuals never taste quite as good in town, anyway.

Holly said "so what brings you boys out this way? Come for the colors?"

---

49 Not their actual names. But bird names are difficult to pronounce, and even harder to write down, so I like to give them little nicknames.

She gave Vern a little wink. Holly doesn't believe there are folks back in town who sometimes travel millions of miles just to see the leaves turn color. Not that she's immune to the majestic splendor of walking through a deciduous forest in autumn — in fact, I doubt many people appreciate peak foliage more than she does — but she doesn't get why anybody would make a special trip for it. Anyway, the leaves hadn't begun turning yet.

Reminds me of the time I traveled all the way to Gigantalopolis and walked around all day long, staring up at all the tall buildings. The locals laughed at me. One guy said "what's the matter, ain't you got skyscratchers where you come from?"

Sure we do. We call them mountains.

Vern said "we're chasing down a legend, Holly." He grabbed a handful of hickory nuts from an earthen pot and arranged them on the tabletop in the sign of Pedestrio.

Holly stared at the symbol, then turned her gaze on Vern. She said "that's the Mark."

I said "yeah, that's the mark. We've seen it all over the place."

"I'm not talking about the symbol," she said. "I'm talking about the man it represents. We call him the Mark."

I said "you call him Mark? That's an odd name — I mean, for a guy like Pedestrio."

She said "the Mark isn't a name. It's a fate. And it's an awful one."

Vern leaned forward. "Do tell."

"First, tell me what you know of the Elementals."

"Spirits of the Earth and Sky," said Vern. "Sometimes called the Old Ones. They are Beings of unimaginable power, said to have made the world and everything in it."

"Yes," Holly agreed. "The Elementals are the creative forces that govern all of Nature — but They can also destroy."

I said "yeah, no kidding. One of Them tried to destroy *us* not too long ago."

Holly finally paid me a modicum of notice. I felt proud to contribute.

"Great big ravenous worm-like Thing," I said. "Attacked us one night. Back in the desert."

Holly looked at Vern for confirmation. He nodded slightly. "It was the Eater of Worlds — known locally as the Great Empty."

"I call it The Worm," I said. "It chased us for a while, but we got away."

Holly's eyebrows shot up. "It chased you? And you got away?"

"It wasn't very fast," I said.

Vern explained. "It wasn't really after us, I don't think. But It did follow us a ways through the desert before diving back underground."

"Do you know how lucky you are to be sitting here right now?"

"Yep," I said. "Incredibly lucky. Is there any more hickory cake?"

Holly crossed her arms. "The Elementals don't have to catch you to destroy you. They can end your life with a mere thought. You should take steps in the future to stay out of Their way."

Vern said "believe me, we weren't looking to get in Its way."

"But you did," said Holly. "You went looking for the Mark. It's only common sense that the Chewer of Roots would take an interest in you."

"Hang on," I said. "What's the Chewer of Roots?"

"That's what the forest folk call the Elemental who accosted you. Chewer of Roots — because It travels underground, churning up the soil and disturbing the life below the surface."

"Catchy name," said Vern.

"Better than Eater of Worlds."

"Matter of debate."

"Not at all," said Holly. "Chewer of Roots is far more descriptive."

"Eater of Worlds better captures the sheer magnitude of Its destructive capabilities."

"Perhaps. But it sounds dumb."

Vern said "on that point, we'll just have to agree to disagree."

"The Worm works for me," I said — but all I got for my trouble were a matching pair of scornful looks.

Served me right. Only a fool brings a monosyllabic name to a scientific nomenclature fight.

"So," said Vern. "Are you saying the Mark is one of the Old Ones?"

"No," said Holly. "Although he is nearly as old as They are. The Mark is so called because he is a marked man: an outcast, and a thief. The Chewer of Roots has pursued him for countless millennia. One of these days, It will catch him, and when that happens, the fury unleashed upon the world will be beyond catastrophic."

"Yeah, so said the desert rats. They think the Great Empty Desert used to be some sort of paradise."

"It could have been," said Holly.

"Well, let's hope Pedestrio doesn't get caught any time soon."

"Yes. Let's hope."

Holly wasn't telling us everything. But then, why would she? If she really is married to a Wodewose, I reckon she's learned to keep a secret or two.

"Your quest is an admirable one," Holly said to Vern. "But beware the Elementals. You may, indeed, cross paths with Them again."

"We already have," I said. "One of Them stole my hat."

Holly's eyebrows moved like waves crashing against her brow. She looked to Vern for an explanation. "Mischief appears to be playing a game on us," he said. "Not sure what the game is. She came to us in the guise of Pedestrio, and we gave chase — but a lightning storm forced us to take cover."

"This is bad," said Holly. "You should reconsider your mission. It is not wise to court the attention of a single Elemental, much less a brace of Them."

I held my tongue. But I knew Vern: he'd climb a mountain of tinder to get a better look at a fire-breathing dragonfly. He'd crawl into a pit full of spring-loaded wriggle-ticks just to see what they're like when they're not launching themselves at unsuspecting warm-blooded prey.[50]

If Vern spotted an Earth spirit from ten miles away, he'd break seven bones to get himself a closer look.

"We were fooled by Her disguise," said Vern. "Next time, we'll be more careful."

"The Trickster's involvement will make the coming showdown all the more unpredictable."

Suddenly, I felt lightheaded — as if a thousand irrelevant thoughts had packed up and left the premises, all at once. I said "what showdown?"

Holly ignored my question — choosing to address Vern, instead. "You came to ask if the forest folk know the Mark's whereabouts."

"Do they?"

"Generally, no. The Mark is rarely seen in the same vicinity on successive days. He does, however, favor certain places — and he returns to those places frequently."

"Are there any close by?"

"He is often seen in the vicinity of the Kitchen Range."

I flicked a hazel nut shell at Vern. "Told you." The Kitchen Range is one of the few places in the Sea of Green where you can see the stars.

Holly aimed a frown in my direction. I felt a headache coming on. I rolled my head from side to side.

"What about the Eater of Worlds?" said Vern. "I assume the trees would know if It were anywhere close by."

---

50 Actually, wriggle-ticks (imagine a cross between a tick and a very small viper) enjoy a quite peaceful and satisfying home life. Out in the Wild, of course, they spend their days coiled up like unsprung springs, biting their own tails to keep from prematurely boinging. When a victim gets within range, they let go and fly through the air, hoping to sink their teeth into a nice, tasty blood vessel. If they miss, well then they have to wriggle themselves back into position for another try. It's a tense way to make a living — which is why they have such nice homes. Everybody needs a comfortable place to unwind.

"They would, indeed." Holly took a deep breath. "Perhaps it is The Trickster's doing: at this moment, the Chewer of Roots is hastening in the direction of the Kitchen Range."

"What are the odds?" I said, rubbing the back of my neck.

"So, that must be the showdown you talked about."

Holly nodded. "The Chewer could not have chosen a more dangerous location for a confrontation. The only reasonable conclusion is that It does not know."

"Doesn't know what?" I said.

"I understand," said Vern. "Thanks for the warning."

"Wait a minute. What doesn't It know?"

Vern said "I'll tell you later."

Saying it like I was a child amongst adults — a child who kept interrupting their conversation.

Well, I don't mind telling you, that riled me up by more than half. I'm *not* a child. I *do* know a thing or two about... well... about whatever it was they were talking about. And anyway, there's nothing wrong with asking questions. That's how people learn. In fact, I bet Vern was secretly glad I kept asking questions, on account of it saved him the embarrassment of having to ask for himself.

Vern said to Holly, he said "we surely do appreciate your hospitality — "

I said "wait a minute! You can't just talk in riddles and be done with it. Not when every riddle leads to a dozen more questions."

Vern said "if we stay much longer, we might wear out our welcome."

I growled at Vern. "Don't you want to know everything the Wodewosen know about Pedestrio?"

"That's not how it works," said Vern. "Answers never come all at once."

"She said Pedestrio was a thief! Don't you want to defend him? Don't you even want to know what he stole?"

"I'm sure we'll find out when the time is right."

I turned to Holly, I said "you can't just throw down a charge like that and walk away. What did he steal?"

Holly stared at me while the silence crept in.

She let it get comfortable. She let it spread out until it filled every corner of the room. It wasn't a dead silence — it was the silence you hear when an echo fades away, but you keep listening, thinking maybe it'll come back.

Finally, she broke the silence with a single word.

"Immortality."

That fly wouldn't land, though I could hear it buzzing. It buzzed around and around the room till my head felt dizzy, but I still couldn't make any sense of it.

"You mean the Wodewosen are immortal?"

The fire winked out.

That's all I remember. That, and the way Holly's face changed just before the fire went out. It was like when you're walking down a country lane, and you think you see a face peeking out of a hedgerow, only when you turn around to get a better look, the face fades back into the greenery and all you see is a couple of shady spots where the eyes used to be, and a thorn that vaguely resembles a nose. Then…

I don't know what happened after that. I must have lost consciousness. Seemed like all I did was blink, and there we were, Vern and I: sitting on a moss-covered log, staring at the base of an uprooted blow-me-down tree. The roots of the tree looked a lot like Holly's fireplace.

Vern blinked. Then he blinked again. Then he turned and gave me a very deliberate look.

It was a look I've seen before. I had no trouble deciphering it.

It simply said *nice going*.

INTERLOGUE:
Running Amok in the Garden

"Meeting *will come to order,"* said The Spider.

"About, face! Forward, march!" said Mischief.

"Knock it off," said The Spider. *"We are here to discuss… big surprise… your favorite ungovernable species."*

"Define 'ungovernable'."

"No. Enough time has been wasted. Your people are running amok in the Garden. Did We not warn You what would happen if You let them out of the Valley of Misfits?"

"You did warn Me," said Mischief. *"Yes, indeed: consequences most dire, You said. Banishment and loss of privileges, including the right to attend Council meetings — though it seems unfair to punish the other Council members, who will no doubt mourn My absence."*

"We will suffer through as best We can. Are You prepared to begin Your epoch of exile?"

"Hmm? No. Why?"

"You know why. It is for Your part in releasing a relegated species of Your own creation back into the Garden."

"Oh, that. Well, You see, the thing is, I didn't release them."

"You deny helping the… people… to leave the valley?"

"Yep. I deny that. Had nothing to do with it, actually."

"Then they found their own way out, and they will be unmade. It is so ord —"

"Excuse me! Umm… technically, they didn't."

"They are loose in the Garden."

"That I don't deny."

The Falcon, who always keeps a close watch on Council proceedings, was first to spot the implication. "*Do You mean to say that another Council Member set them free?*"

"*I mean to say that another Council Member showed them the way out, yes.*"

A general uproar ensued. The Wishing Star caught Mischief's eye and winked. Mischief stared back, apparently mystified. An enraged Old One currently taking the form of an angry bantam rooster clucked "a*ll right, You lot! Which of You did it?*"

Mischief made a calming motion (figuratively speaking, of course). "*I regret to inform the Council that the culprit is not currently in attendance.*"

"*Criminy!*" said an Old One currently taking the form of a frightened salmon. "*It wasn't The Bear, was it?*"

"*No.*"

"*Then…*" All of the gathered Old Ones looked around (figuratively speaking) as They took a mental inventory of the Earth and Sky spirits who were present and accounted for. The identity of the missing (and therefore guilty) party dawned on Them more or less all at once.

CHAPTER 38:

Spider Ropes and the Bushmen of Little Biting

VERN didn't talk to me for the rest of the night and half the next day.

I told him he was overreacting. I said "look, I'm sorry! I shouldn't have asked a direct question about the Wodewosen. But it's not like I demanded an answer. I mean, she could have just ignored me. That's what she usually does, right Vern? If she doesn't want to talk about something, she just ignores the question."

Vern didn't answer. He gets quiet sometimes. We all do, those of us who spend a lot of our time out on Wild Side. But I knew he was mad at me, on account of the way he kept ducking around and under the spiderwebs.

When two or more hikers are following a game trail through the woods, it's customary to walk single file. That way, only the lead hiker gets a face full of nigh on invisible spider silk every twenty or thirty paces. But Vern kept on sliding by them somehow. I tried to catch him at it, but he can be uncommonly crafty when he wants to be.

"Anyway, it was an ambiguous statement, so I didn't see any harm in asking for clarification."

They're a bold, ambitious lot, these woodland spiders — the way they spin a web between two trees, directly across a well-traveled path, as if they have designs on catching far bigger prey than mere flies — perhaps an unsuspecting fawn, or even a full-grown stag. I've never yet seen it work, but still, you've gotta admire their audacity.

"And not only ambiguous, but unreachable. How can immortality be stolen? You either have it, or you don't. It's not like a hat. You don't just wake up one morning and find out somebody's walked off with it."

Vern didn't answer. Probly a bit winded on account of the expeditious pace he'd been setting.

I stopped talking, too — but not because I was out of breath or anything. It's just that I had so many spiderwebs plastered across my face, I could barely get my mouth open.

That's when I understood: the spiders were playing the long game. They weren't trying to catch me all at once. But a strand here and a strand there… a little wrap-around knot, with a cross weave to connect the strands…

By the end of the day, they'd have me all sewn up like a caterpillow.[51]

Another web appeared out of nowhere. *Why do they always spin them at face level?* I clawed a hole in the webbing and said "Vern, help me get these spider ropes off me!"

Vern stopped and looked back. He seemed genuinely puzzled. "What spider ropes?"

"You know very well what spider ropes! You've been ducking them all day!"

"No I haven't."

"Well, it's certain you're not missing them all by accident. You're not that short."

"I'm almost as tall as you are, and believe me, I haven't seen a spiderweb since the other side of Greenhaven."

I pointed out the mass of sticky fibers still clinging to my face and beard. "What do you think this is? A cargo net?"

---

51 The interior of most caterpillar cocoons is rather spartan. Not much furniture is needed when all one plans to do is lie dormant for a month or two. That said, there isn't a caterpillar in the world who doesn't try to sneak a pillow into their cocoon before sewing it shut.

Vern leaned in close and examined the strands with interest. Then his eyes got wide. He whipped off his vest, threw it on the ground, and began stomping on it.

Seemed a mite foolish to wear that vest all summer long, only to abandon it now, with cooler weather approaching. But I try not to judge.

I said "hey, when you're done celebrating the end of winter over there, can you give me a hand?" I couldn't even run my fingers through my hair, the webs were that thick.

Vern said "hang on, I think I've got a cowboy."

"Oh," I said. "Right. Yeah, that would explain it."

A cowboy spider is one of those rare species of itinerant arachnids who don't wait for prey to come to them. Instead, they weave themselves a saddle. Then they lower themselves, saddle and all, onto the back of a suitable mount and ride around the countryside, trying to rope everything in sight.

Just my luck to be the only other thing in sight.

Vern finally flushed the critter out. It had been hiding in one of the vest's back pockets. Big hairy feller, the color of sunburnt skin, with a tuft of hair on the top of its head that stuck up like the world's tiniest ten-gallon hat.

It tried to rope Vern around the ankles, but Vern picked up a stick and managed to get the spider rope all tangled up in it. Then he twirled the stick between his palms, winding the rope tighter and tighter, slowly reeling the critter in.

The cowboy sensed early on that it wasn't going to win this tug-of-war. It let go of the rope and lit out on foot, still lugging its saddle. It headed for the nearest tree.

Vern and I watched it go. The tree had some nice, low-hanging branches extending out over the trail. Wouldn't be long before the cowboy was back in the saddle again.

I said "I've never seen a spider walk bowlegged before."

"Is that a joke?"

"No."

Vern shook out his vest and put it back on. "They walk that way all the time. That's the only way spiders *can* walk."

"I know. But that one acted like it was saddle sore."

"Yeah, well, that's your fault. Why didn't you tell me earlier about the webs?"

"You weren't talking to me, remember?"

"For good reason." Vern got his bearings and marched off in the direction of the Kitchen Range. "You've got a lot to learn about people, Abner."

Maybe he's got a sense of humor after all. Coming from him, that's downright hilarious. I hustled to keep up. "The Wodewosen aren't immortal, are they?"

"No."

"Then whose immortality got stolen?"

"My guess is, the Old Ones."

"So, does that mean They're no longer immortal?"

"Doesn't work like that. It's more like Pedestrio took a drink from a well he had no right to drink from."

"Ah," I said. "The Well of Eternal Wandering. I've heard of that."

Vern shook his head. "The well is just a metaphor. Don't take it too literally."

"So Pedestrio really is immortal, after all."

He took his time answering. "The Eater of Worlds is after him for a reason."

"Yeah, that's another thing. Holly said The Worm could have thought us dead, and we'd be dead. So, if It can kill with Its mind, then why doesn't It just think Pedestrio dead? Unless he can't be killed?"

"Bear with me for a second."

Uh oh.

When Vern says "bear with me," that means he's about to try out a new theory. The last time he said it, he very nearly had me convinced that clouds take certain recognizable shapes on account of the existence of natural depressions in the sky. These natural depressions aren't stationary. Instead, they float through the air like anti-bubbles, and the clouds tend to fall into them and take their shape. But seeing as how the depressions are very shallow, it's only a short while before some breeze comes along and blows the cloud out of the hole.

It's not a bad theory, actually. But that doesn't make it true.

The truth is much more simple: clouds that look like whales or eagles or galloping horses are really balloon animals in disguise.

Anyway, I said "bear away."

"Pedestrio can be killed. He just can't be unmade."

"What's the difference?"

Vern said "the bushmen of Little Biting believe the world and everything in it is a dream. You and I are dreams. These ash trees are all dreams. That boulder over there is a dream. The bushmen believe in a supernatural Being called the Great Dreamer, who is even now dreaming all the different dreams that make up the world as we know it. But each dream is like a bubble, and it can be popped at any moment. Or the entire dreamscape could be wiped out, if the Great Dreamer decides it was all a mistake, and the only way to fix it is to pop all the bubbles and start over."

I reached out and poked Vern with my finger. He didn't pop. "Just checking," I said.

"Okay, bad analogy. Forget the bubbles. The point is, you and I can kill each other, but we can't *unmake* each other. We can't cause each other to cease to exist, just by thinking about it. Much as I'd like to, sometimes."

I said "what about the bushmen of Little Biting?"

"What about them?"

"You're the one who brought them up."

"They've got nothing to do with this. I'm just using them to illustrate the point."

"Well, I hate to tell you this, Vern, but you'd make a lousy sketch artist."

Vern was beginning to lose patience. He took a deep breath, considered his options, and concluded to tie a bow around the discussion. "The Great Dreamer is akin to the Earth spirits. For all I know, the Dreamer might even be one of Them. So, let's say Pedestrio started out as a dream, but somehow, the dream woke up and found himself in the same world as the Dreamer. That explains why the Eater of Worlds can't just wish him away — It has to find him, and catch him, in order to put an end to him. In other words, he can't be killed with a thought — there has to be physical contact."

I tried to get my brain around what Vern was saying. Tried so hard, I believe I bent my skull. Still, I couldn't reconcile the columns. "So what you're telling me is, Pedestrio is safe as long as he doesn't cut a trail through Little Biting."

It was long about three days before Vern would talk to me again. 'Course, by that time, I'd forgotten all my other questions. Even the one about the Kitchen Range being a dangerous location for a confrontation.

In retrospect, I probly should have asked about that first.

CHAPTER 39:
Whiskerland

FOUR days past Dunfer Castle,[52] we took a half-turn east through Whiskerland. Witches'-brooms swept the forest floor — as usual, making a royal mess of everything. They swept the leaves into piles, then chased after the piles the way a yapping dog chases seagulls on the beach. The leaves reluctantly threw themselves into the air, swirled around a bit, then settled back down again somewhere just out of reach. I said to Vern, I said "I bet it's impossible to track anything with all these witches'-brooms flailing around."

"They do make it a challenge," he said. "But you might as well complain about the wind, or the rain, or the rising tide."

I watched a venerable oak tree attempt in vain to drop a leaf at its roots, like laying down the first square of a nice, cozy winter quilt. Before the leaf even hit the ground, a witches'-broom whisked it away. "If I were that tree, I'd drop a widowmaker on that pesky whisker."

Vern absentmindedly touched the top of his head. "Sometimes you have to take the macro view."

"What's that mean?"

---

52 Dunfer Castle is about a week's journey beyond Greenhaven. It's not really a castle. What it is, it's the remains of a stockade built a million years ago, back in the days of the angry caribou. Nobody ever did figure out what set the caribou off on such a rampage. Maybe they ate something that didn't agree with them. Anyway, the entire herd turned super aggressive overnight, and tore through the province with small, furry woodland creatures dangling from their racks. All the people living in the area panicked. A lot of them couldn't bring themselves to do much more than run around in circles screaming "we're done fer! We're done fer!" But a few steady hands kept it together long enough to build Dunfer Castle and herd everybody inside. It was a good, sturdy fortress back in the day, and it would have kept everybody safe as houses — if the caribou hadn't figured out how to pick the locks.

"You see any squirrels?"

I looked around. "No."

Vern nodded. "You see, the brooms might be annoying, but they're filling an important ecological niche. They're doing the job the squirrels usually do."

Well, now, I agree that squirrels can be mighty obnoxious from time to time. But I didn't realize there was an ecological niche for that. I said as much to Vern.

He said "I mean, they're helping to scatter the acorns. Soon as one drops, they sweep it away. They've probably scattered acorns from here to the Kitchen Range."

"Maybe the Kitchen Range is just a big pile of acorns."

"Oh, I doubt that. Witches'-brooms are brisk, but they're not very efficient. Plenty of nuts will get swept to the side and forgotten about."

"I druther give all my acorns to a squirrel than lose all my leaves to a broom."

"That's not how the trees see it."

It was an old argument. Vern is always trying to get me to think like a tree. He says trees don't like squirrels, on account of they're always running around, digging their claws in, ripping off bits of bark and showboating all the time. I say, if they don't like squirrels, why don't they dodge out of the way when a squirrel jumps from one tree to the next? But Vern says that would be like ducking whenever somebody sneezes: you can't avoid the sneeze, and you look silly trying. To which I say, on the other hand… if, by some wild chance… *if* the dodging worked… well, the tree wouldn't look half as silly as the squirrel, would it?

But since it was an old argument, I figured just this once, we could take the rest as read.

"Speaking of thinking like a tree, I mean… we're spending all this time chasing after a man who could be anywhere in the world on any given day, all because you think he can teach you something you don't already know. You ever thought about asking the Wodewosen to teach you how to talk tree-talk?"

Vern shook his head. "The Wodewosen are halfway to being trees themselves. Be like asking a pine how to talk to a birch. Anyhow, it's not about me. It's about preserving a million years' worth of Wild Side lore before the Eater of Worlds buries it forever."

"Plus, you know, the secret of immortality."

"There is no secret. Nothing that can be passed on, anyway."

"How do you know?"

"Because I pay attention." Vern sounded just a tiny bit exasperated.

"So do I, believe it or not. You know what it gets me? More questions. For example, where are the squirrels?" This neck of the woods seemed a lot quieter than it should have been, given the predominance of oak and beech trees.

"Gone."

"Where?"

He shrugged. "Eaten. Or driven off."

"Eaten by what?"

He kicked a clump of leaves lying at the base of an okheed oak. Something had ripped a squirrel's nest to shreds and tossed it to the ground. "Hippopotamouth, by the look of it."

"Uh oh."

Hippopotamouths are airborne creatures with leathery wings and mouths so big, they can swallow themselves. They're like miniature flying sharks. Usually, they don't get much bigger than fruit bats, but when their jaws are fully extended, they look like jagged tunnels in the air, flying straight at your head, promising to chew you up and swallow the bits.

Vern said "relax. They almost never go after humans. Just try not to repeat anything."

"Try not to repeat anything," I echoed.

Honestly, I didn't do it on purpose. The words just slipped out. It's like when somebody tells you "don't even think about whistling!" and then all you can think about is whistling — even if you don't know how to whistle, you can't help trying.

And no sooner did the words cross my lips than a hole full of teeth appeared in midair, right in front of my nose.

I ducked. The hippopotamouth just missed taking a chunk out of my forehead.

Trouble was, I ducked my head so fast, my hair swished through the air like a fisherman's net. The hippopotamouth flew right into it.

The impact came near to yanking me off my feet.

The more the hippopotamouth tried to escape, the more entangled it got. My head jerked from side to side as the little gnasher struggled to tear itself free.

I panicked, a little bit. It's bad enough when sparrows build nests in your hair. That only happened to me once, but I can tell you, those sparrows are not shy about rearranging your coif to suit their domestic needs.

Anyway, as bad as sparrows are, getting a hippopotamouth stuck in your hair is a million times worse. It made terrible screeching noises, and my scalp felt like I'd accidentally stuck my head in a fire anthill.

"Ow!" I said.

"Quiet!" said Vern.

"Ow!" I said. "Ow! Ow!"

Big mistake. Hippopotamouths seek out their prey by echo-location. That's why they feed so often on squirrels, whose chatter is both repetitive and reverberative. Their echoey voices make them the perfect target.

Half a dozen fanged monsters came roiling out of a hollow beech tree and darted in my direction.

Vern lost his head. He ran over to that poor tree and started yelling at it.

"Hello!" he hollered into the hollow.

The hippopotamouths veered and took a wide turn around the tree. Then they flitted back and forth in a standard search pattern, as if trying to pick up a weak and intermittent signal.

Vern's mania grew steadily worse. He dashed over to a nearby paper birch and began slashing at it with his knife. In no time at all, he'd cut off a strip of bark as long as his arm. He rolled it up into a tube, then ran back and pointed the tube into the hollow.

"Hello!" he hollered into it.

Vern's voice echoed back: "hello! hello! hello!"

The hippopotamouths went berserk. They dove at the hollow, flying at suicide speed. Even the one tangled up in my hair managed to chew itself free in time to join the chase.

From inside the tree, we heard a series of dull thumps.

"What happened?" I said.

Vern allowed himself the ghost of a smile. "I think they bit off more than they could chew."

I risked a peek into the cavity.

All seven hippopotamouths were tacked inside — their pointy little fangs buried in the wood all the way up to the gums. They hung there like weird leathery ornaments.

"Thanks," I said.

"Don't mention it," he said. "Not again, anyway."

INTERLOGUE:
Just Get Me Through This Night

T HE first day was pure terror. Pedestrio ran, and when he could run no more, he crawled. His only thought was to remain out of reach of the Nightmare that pursued him.

The miles flew by. The empty black Void fell further behind, but Its terrible, booming thought-blasts still ripped through Pedestrio's mind. *Trespasser!* It howled, and the force of the accusation shattered several nearby rocks. *Foul misfit! I will unmake you!*

Pedestrio ran blindly. He fell into a stream and accidentally swallowed some water. It didn't burn his throat. He swallowed some more. The Void surged ever closer. Pedestrio struggled to get his feet under him. He scrambled up the opposite bank and beat his way through the dags.[53] *Trespasser!* The Void roared. *Defiler!*

That first night, Pedestrio didn't sleep. Shadows stalked him. Unseen horrors hooted and howled from deep inside the darkness. The sky was awash in a million points of light — he couldn't locate his Wishing Star, but he said a quick prayer to Her, anyway: "just get me through this night," he said. "Please, just see me through this night."

---

53 Dags (usually plural) are tall, reed-like plants that grow in marshes and mud puddles. They sprout up so fast, they can go from seed to six feet tall in a couple of hours — pushing up through the mire at such a rapid rate that the heads don't have time to get clean. Hence, when the plants are fully grown, they look like a mop with its handle stuck in the muck and a head full of dirty, mud-caked yarn waving around in the air. When a breeze blows through, the dry heads clack against each other to make a rattling sound. Thus, when two or more travelers are passing through a marshy region and one of them falls behind, the others will encourage him by calling out "come on, rattle your dags!"

The next day, he ate something that made him sick. He didn't know what it was. He'd been famished; he'd eaten a lot of different things. He found another stream and drank some water. It soothed his insides. When he felt better, he tried eating only one thing: a green leaf that grew close to the ground and tasted like dew. He felt fine afterward. He would have to remember that plant.

At night, pure exhaustion drove him to lie down on a carpet of old leaves. He dreamed of Paradise — but it was different. It was peaceful. The usual nightmares failed to terrorize him. He dreamed all night — and woke to a searing thought-blast from close by.

There! Trespasser!

Pedestrio ran.

CHAPTER 40:
A Posterous Middle and a Postposterous End

THE Kitchen Range is an isolated set of volcanic mountains rising up from the forest floor to form a sky island about sixty miles long and ten or so miles wide. The four peaks don't have individual names — they're just collectively known as the Burners. It's been a million years since the last eruption, but they say the Burners are still active. Every once in a while, you can feel the mountains rumbling.

I said to Vern, I said "you're sure this is a good idea?"

Vern kept bobbing his head up and down, side to side, always looking for a better view through the trees. "It's our best lead yet."

"Won't be much help to us if we fall into a lake of boiling lava."

"The Burners are dormant, Abner."

"The folks back in Deep Hole didn't think so."

Vern's legs carried him four or five steps before his tongue could push an answer past his lips. It wasn't much of an answer. Vern's communication skills have got a long way to go, yet. "There's more to that story," is all he said.

"Great!" I said, clapping my hands together. "I love stories."

"Remember what Holly told us?"

"Yep. She said 'Eater of Worlds' is a dumb name for an Elemental."

"She also said the Kitchen Range is a dangerous place for a showdown."

"I bet it is — especially for a Being as slow as the Chewer of Roots. Do you think It's fast enough to outrun a river of lava?"

Vern sighed and shook his head. "There's no river of lava, Abner. I've been all over these mountains. I've been here a dozen times since the Whist, and I can tell you, there's no sign of an imminent eruption."

"Well, you haven't been here lately, have you? You've been off in the desert, and down there in the Wandering Hills. I know, because I've been with you the whole time. Who's to say the Burners aren't about to light up?"

Vern said "you can wait here, if you want. I should be back in a month or so."

I said "nope. I'm coming with you. You know why? Because somebody's got to be there to tell the story, that's why. And you're a rotten storyteller."

The first three thousand feet weren't so bad. Old Blue seemed genuinely interested in our progress. A light, westerly breeze kept us cool. The trail didn't meander too much. We hiked through groves of hackberry and chokecherry and ahemlock trees, climbing up slopes dotted with puce spruce and watt fir. I kept a sharp eye out for plumes of steam and geysers of molten rock and other signs of impending doom, but spotted nothing more dangerous than a long-eared maguffin. Vern kept his head on a swivel, as well — though if he saw the maguffin, he never said a word.

When he did speak, it came as such a surprise that I flinched. He'd been quiet so long, I figured he was mad at me on account of some of the things I'd gone on to say after calling him a rotten storyteller. I felt bad about saying that — but it hadn't bothered him a whit, and it bothered me that he couldn't be bothered. I mean, rotten storyteller is almost the worst thing I can think of to call somebody, besides liar. But Vern, he just took it in stride.

So I thought I'd dig a little deeper. I told him I reckoned Pedestrio was probly the worst storyteller in the world. I said the reason he's so bad is that he probly mucks up the ending all the time. That's the thing about living forever, I said: you forget about how endings are supposed to work. But Vern wouldn't bite. He just kept on walking, as if I'd never said anything a-tall.

I calculated he was doing it on purpose. So I got even by refusing to tell him about the long-eared maguffin — though, tell you true, he very likely saw the critter for his own self, and therefore my retaliatory silence was altogether wasted.

Anyway, after several hours of quiet tramping, Vern jarred me out of my reverie by saying "woolstones."

I gave him the side-eye. He was staring at a rock ledge off to our right. A jumble of rocks partially obscured the hole some miner had left behind. "What about them?"

"The Kitchen Range was always famous for its woolstones. But there wasn't much demand for them back before the Whist. Only one or two prospectors ever tried mining up here."

"Okay…"

"Just thinking out loud."

"Must you? I was in the middle of a very nice daydream about apple cider doughnuts. I hope they're still in season by the time we get back Town Side."

"Daydreams. That fits, too."

"Maybe Elmer will save me some. How long do you think apple cider doughnuts last?"

"Hmm? I don't know."

"Never mind. What were you thinking about, besides woolstones?"

"Thinking about how the Whist got started. Thinking maybe one of those old-time prospectors could have set it off. Accidentally, of course."

"How does one accidentally set off a dream shortage?"

"Don't know. Stick of dynamite, maybe."

I laughed so hard, I nearly blew the top of my own head off. "You think a stick of dynamite kicked off a dream shortage? What'd they do, blow up the factory?"

"Something like that."

I laughed again. "Might make a storyteller out of you yet, Vern. Okay, now down to business: you've got a preposterous beginning. That's the hard part. All you need now is a posterous middle and a postposterous end. You got any ideas where you're fixing to take this yarn? Vern?"

Vern didn't answer. I glanced at him. He was frozen in place — his undivided attention fixed on something he'd spotted the next ridge over.

I turned around. My eyes found the scar where a rockslide had wiped out the vegetation. Then they spotted movement: someone was casually making his way across the scar. I couldn't see his face — he was too far away. But judging by his outfit and his bearing, it had to be the same barefoot stranger we'd chased back in Dett. Only one thing was missing.

"Hey!" I bellowed. "Where's my hat!"

CHAPTER 41:
The Croon's Tale

T HE man stared back at us like a mountain goat assessing a possible threat. Vern grabbed my arm, same as saying *don't move. Don't make a sound.* We stared at each other so long, my legs turned to rubber. Then the stranger turned and continued on his way.

He didn't hurry. He didn't look back. We'd been studied and judged harmless. Boring, even. Seconds later, he disappeared into the forest.

Vern still didn't move. His feet must have grown roots. I knelt on the ground to keep my legs from trembling. "You think that was Mischief again?"

He shook his head.

"Pedestrio?"

He nodded.

"Are we going after him?"

Vern took a deep breath, like he just woke up. He looked at me, then back at the next ridge. Then he smiled. "Yeah. Let's see what he's up to."

The way Pedestrio had crossed that scar, with his back straight and his arms swinging, I half expected to find a sidewalk running through it. What we found instead was an ankle-turning bed of loose rock — almost impossible to cross without flailing your arms for balance or bracing yourself for the inevitable fall. But Vern picked up Pedestrio's trail easily enough. A few minutes later, we were out of the scree and back in the trees.

Vern set a brisk pace. He practically jogged. I huffed to keep up. Fortunately, the route was more lateral than vertical.

"You sure we're still on track?"

"More or less."

"Where's he going?"

"Don't know. Maybe nowhere."

"It's getting late. Shouldn't he be climbing higher?"

"He is. He's just taking the roundabout route."

Vern stopped in a small clearing studded with lichen-covered boulders. I couldn't see any sign of Pedestrio, but Vern was staring at a clump of feathery-leaved plants. I said "what's wrong?"

"He watered the rockfoils."

I leaned in for a closer look. Sure enough, the ground under the plants was still wet.

He said "they needed it, too. You see how the leaves are curled up? They're too exposed here. That clump over there in the shade is doing better."

I didn't bother looking. "Yeah, I see that. Listen, if he's taking the time to water plants, that means we've got a good chance of catching up to him."

But Vern wasn't listening. He sat on his heels and combed his fingers through the rockfoils as if grooming them. Then he looked around, his eyes reading the life stories of everything they landed on. Finally, he nodded to himself and stood up. Without a word, he found Pedestrio's trail again and set off through the trees.

"Do you think we'll catch him?" I said.

"Yeah."

"How far ahead is he?"

"Not far."

"Sorry I yelled, earlier."

"No harm done. He knows we're here, is all."

"I wonder if he knows Mischief is impersonating him."

Vern didn't answer. He was walking in the footsteps of his hero. His eyes darted everywhere — taking in every rock and root and chittering chickaree. He didn't seem to be looking for Pedestrio. He certainly wasn't in any great hurry to find him. I couldn't figure that out. The sun hung low in the west. Time was running out. But Vern, he drifted along like he meant to burn every detail of Pedestrio's route into his permanent memory. Like he didn't want to pass this way without seeing everything as Pedestrio himself might have seen it.

'Course, I can't tell a watt fir from a watt gnau, so I didn't offer to help. About all I could do is hang back and wait to see how the episode played out.

My mind wandered. I reimagined Pedestrio as some kind of extraterrestrial spaceman, coming down every morning to explore the Earth while his ship remained in orbit. The vision grew in my head: Pedestrio as an interstellar Johnny Exoseed, sowing new and strange and otherworldly species all over the planet. The Worm as an empty Void in a policeman's uniform, determined to apprehend the pangalactic trespasser and frog-march him off the planet while a hornswoggle, a catawampus, and a vicious wild chook danced a jig around my hat. It all seemed so real. I even heard the music.

Vern stopped short. "There he is."

"Hmm?"

Vern motioned with his chin. Pedestrio stood a stone's throw ahead of us. He had some sort of blowatune hidden in the cup of his hand, and he piped out a tune that sounded like birdsong.

"What's he doing?" I whispered.

"Talking to the birds."

A velvet-throated croon came out of hiding and alighted on a spruce branch. Pedestrio piped a welcome song on his blowatune. The croon answered with a flurry of notes. Pedestrio piped again, varying the inflection slightly. The bird again responded, but this time the song lasted a full five minutes. Pedestrio occasionally punctuated the croon's solo performance with a quick staccato burst that sounded like laughter. Then it was over. The bird flew away, and Pedestrio resumed his journey. Vern and I tagged along behind.

I said "it's uncommonly rare to see a croon out in the open, isn't it?"

Vern gave a slow, shallow nod. "They're notoriously shy."

"What kind of blowatune was that? I couldn't see it." I could almost believe he wasn't even using an instrument, only I didn't reckon a human voice could have made those sounds.

Vern didn't answer. All his attention was on Pedestrio.

"Maybe we should ask him where he got it — or how he made it. Seems pretty handy."

"Shh."

Pedestrio walked as if every step was a conversation. He reminded me of Buford Colic working his way through the crowd at his annual harvest party: giving this person a hearty hello, that person a nod and a grin, stopping to chat for a brief spell before moving on. When Pedestrio stepped on a root, his bare foot gripped it like a handshake. When he passed a moss-covered boulder almost as tall as he was, he caressed the moss with his fingertips, then laid the flat of his hand against the basalt — saying hello to both as if they were old friends.

Some species were open to the conversation. Others ignored it and went on about their business. Once in a while, some garrulous critter demanded a bit more of his attention and time than Pedestrio thought he could spare. In those cases, Pedestrio was polite but firm. I actually laughed out loud when Pedestrio scolded a chipmunk for chattering too much.

Vern said "keep your voice down, will you?"

"Why don't you go over and talk to him?"

He held up a hand as if telling me to stop.

"Why not? He seems friendly enough."

"I don't need to talk to him."

"Don't be shy."

"I'm not — I don't need to talk to him."

"Then what are we doing out here?" I snapped. "I thought that was the whole point of this little adventure."

Vern flashed me the same look he showed me back at Greenhaven — you know, after Holly switched out the lights and left us staring at a tree stump. Only this time he added a few choice words. "Abner, shut up! I don't need to talk to him! I can learn more by watching."

He turned away. In my head, I prepared a brief statement of contrition. But before I could get the words out, Vern kicked a fallen log. "Dang it!"

"What?"

"He's gone."

INTERLOGUE:
A Place Where Dreams Come to Life

S EVERAL moons had passed since Pedestrio's escape from Paradise. He had traveled many miles, and he had learned many things: what parts of which plants were safe to eat, and what parts were bad for you. Where to look for water to drink. How to avoid the charge of a certain lopsided, five-legged beast. Every new day brought a surfeit of wonders to behold: rainbows and snowflakes and pretty-colored birds and dazzling sunsets.

He especially enjoyed sunsets. He loved watching the stars come out. He could find the Wishing Star now. She was right where She had always been, only now She was surrounded by a million other stars. On clear nights, he loved lying on his back and staring up at the night sky — but clear or cloudy, he never failed to give thanks to the Wishing Star for another day of wonders and miracles. Sometimes he caught Her winking back at him.

In time, Pedestrio began to see other people in the Garden. He was glad for them. He remembered what it had been like to live in Paradise. It was good to know his old friends and neighbors had found a way out. Still, he avoided their company. After all, The Void was still after him. He had no desire to put anyone else in danger.

Years passed. Mountains rose and fell. Seas dried up and turned into deserts. Pedestrio never tired of being a daily witness to the grand earthly celebration — but he understood that he was not immortal. Just as he had a beginning, he knew that someday, he would have an end. He did not shy away from this fact — nor did he see any reason to court his own demise. He learned to seek shelter from cyclones and violent thunderstorms. He developed the good sense which told him to stay away from erupting volcanoes. He never tried to climb a tree in order to escape a forest fire. And he never stopped moving — not for long, anyway — because The Void never slept.

Constant wandering is hard on a body. Pedestrio often wished for a full night's sleep to give his tired muscles time to recover. He longed to lose himself in a sea of pleasant dreams. Instead, he taught himself to sleep light — his senses ever watchful, his subconscious mind ready to wake him instantly at The Void's approach. His dreams were weak, fitful, and frequently interrupted.

Then one day, while hiking along a particular mountain range, he closed his eyes for just a moment — and he dreamed a most vivid dream: he was walking in these very mountains, and they were awash in a flood of scent and sound and color. In the dream, he knew that each of these sensations carried meaning — that each conveyed a message of some sort. And in the dream, he understood these messages. Sometimes he could even answer them.

It was the most powerful dream he'd had since the night he left Paradise. He awoke feeling energized. Immediately, he began opening his senses to the messages all around him.

He also vowed to return to this mountain range as soon as possible. He knew he could not stay — The Void would surely catch him if he tried. But the mountains contained a power he could not ignore. It was a place where dreams were so real, they practically came to life. Pedestrio could not resist the attraction. He would be back — even if the journey took years.

CHAPTER 42:
Showdown

Vern couldn't find the trail. Not a single dislodged pebble or crushed blade of grass pointed to where Pedestrio might have gone. I thought he'd be angry about that. I braced for high dudgeon, followed by a month or so of cold shoulder and silent treatment. But Vern, he only smiled and shook his head — same as saying *how do you like that?* Then he set out in roughly the same direction Pedestrio had been heading before he disappeared.

I held my tongue. I still couldn't reconcile why Vern would be so skittish about meeting his idol, but it wasn't my place to play matchmaker. Anyway, I didn't like to think what might happen if Vern got fed up and left me to find my own way home. Probly fall into a lake of boiling lava before I got two steps.

We climbed into the saddle between the second and third Burner. The trees were getting shorter. I judged we must be approaching treeline. The sun drooped lower and lower. Still no sign of Pedestrio. Vern hesitated, then continued up the eastern slope of Burner Two.

A few minutes later, we cleared the treeline. The last remaining dwarf firs stood around, worn and haggard, like they'd attempted to storm the mountaintop — leading the charge with an army of scraggle trees close behind — only to be driven back by giant rolling boulders and punishing gusts of wind. You had to admire them. They were beaten, but they refused to give up.

I gazed up the steep, rocky incline. It would be a hard scramble up to the summit. The cone of the old volcano formed a sheer rock wall about thirty feet high and about as plumb as a fall from Grace.[54] I doubted even Pedestrio could make that climb without a rope.

We had the easy part in front of us — just a hundred yards or so of boulders, ledges, and tumbling rocks spread across a rugged, uneven ground. Vern led the way up the slope. Still no sign of Pedestrio. Behind us, the sun touched the horizon, and I had this crazy thought: *what if it bounces?*

The visions came so quickly, they made me stumble. I had to sit down for a second. A cascade of scenes played through my mind: *the sun, bouncing from the western horizon to the east and back again. Giants wielding paddles hitting it back and forth. Oops! It hit Old Blue! Now Blue is mad. He slams the sun down on a pointy-topped mountain — and it bursts like an egg. Gooey rivers of sun slide down the mountainside...*

Vern said "you okay?"

"Just had the weirdest daydream."

Vern looked around. "Lot of woolstones in these Burners."

"You think they really do attract dreams?"

He shrugged. "Looks like a cave over there. Probably an old lava tube." He started for it. I dragged myself back up to vertical.

"Wait!" I said — but Vern didn't stop. "You don't want to go in there! What if it fills up with lava?"

"For the last time, these volcanoes have been dormant for a million years. They're not about to blow their tops just because *you're* here."

The cave was off to our right, almost directly across the notch from Burner Three. I couldn't see into it, but I fancied I could almost hear it breathing. *Do volcanoes breathe all the time, or only as they're waking up?* I looked around for signs of an imminent

---

54 Grace is the name of a very tall, very straight tree that lives out in Rosario province. She has no limbs — just a crown of leaves that sits like a big fuzzy hat on top of a pole, 120 feet off the ground. Her bark is slicker than nine coats of elbow grease, but that doesn't stop folks from betting they can climb all the way to the top. Needless to say, when they fall, they fall straight down.

eruption. By chance, I glanced over at Burner Three — and that's when I saw Pedestrio.

He'd pulled a zag on us — made us go up the wrong Burner. Even then, we might have spotted him earlier if he hadn't been sitting so completely still.

I threw a pebble at Vern to get his attention. When he turned around, I jerked my thumb urgently at the outcrop where Pedestrio sat cross-legged, back straight, hands on his thighs, eyes closed. The stories were true: he sort of blended into the background.

Vern's eyes popped. He stared at Pedestrio, then whipped his head around and gawked at the mouth of the cave — and I understood: Pedestrio had chosen a seat a respectable distance from the cave, but facing it.

Why? What did he want, a front-row seat for the eruption? If so, we didn't have a chance — the cave was only a dozen feet away. I considered running. But Vern dragged me down behind a slab of basalt, out of sight of the cave entrance. I looked a question at him — instinct, for once, told me to hold my tongue. But Vern didn't answer. His attention remained fixed on Pedestrio, who remained in plain view. I watched Vern struggle to breathe deeply — to relax his trembling hands — to get ahold of his fear. Or excitement — not sure which. Cautiously, he poked his head up to sneak a peek at the cave. A marmot barked. Vern jumped. So did I.

The sun didn't bounce. It had a schedule to keep, and important business on the other side of the world. Pedestrio opened his eyes and watched as it sank below the horizon. He sat there a long time, gazing out at the fiery colors lighting up the cloud bellies. Whatever danger lurked in the cave, it didn't fret Pedestrio a-tall.

The colors drained away. Old Blue faded back into the shadows. Pedestrio leaned forward and picked something off the ground — a pebble, my guess. Lazily, he set the pebble where he wanted it, then reached for another.

The ground beneath him shifted. Pedestrio somersaulted backward. The outcrop imploded — and I felt a touch — a mental touch running over and through me. It prickled and shivered both at once, like hot and cold water coursing through my bones. It was a sleepy touch — a vaguely annoyed touch — like when you wake up in a fog, and all your senses reach out in a drowsy attempt to discover the cause of your wakening.

Pedestrio rolled to his feet as a plume of Darkness billowed out of the crater where he'd been sitting. The plume reached for Pedestrio — and I caught on.

The Burners weren't erupting. It was the Eater of Worlds.

Pedestrio darted away. A psychic thought-blast ripped through me like a jolt of electricity. It was different from the earlier touch. This one had a menacing edge. I'd felt that edge before.

Trespasser! It shrieked. *Now I have you!*

The Worm surged ahead — but Pedestrio skipped away. Before I could catch my breath, he'd put a dozen paces between himself and the perilous Void. Then he turned and looked around.

I swear, he looked right at Vern and me before his gaze settled on The Worm.

The Worm howled. It lunged. A thin tendril of absolute desolation stretched out, aiming to touch Pedestrio — to send him, at last, to oblivion. But It was too late.

Turning and facing north, Pedestrio stepped up into the sky and disappeared.

CHAPTER 43:
A Mountain of Potentially Violent Endings

THERE'S a moment before the lightning strikes.

There's a moment when you know it's coming, and there ain't a thing you can do about it. They say your whole life can flash before your eyes in that moment.

Mine didn't. Not my whole life, anyway.

Mind you, I'd have welcomed reliving most of it. I'd have gladly taken a moment to recall all those mornings down at Elmer's Café, or all those lovely summer days out roaming Wild Side in search of a new tale to tell. I'm not unreasonable. I understand the Eater of Worlds is a very busy malevolent supernatural Being, with places to go and people to unmake. I didn't expect It to conjure up a couple of thumbs to twiddle while I sorted through an entire lifetime's worth of memories and experiences. Still and all, I'd have been grateful for the opportunity to choose a handful of scenes to fade out on.

Sadly, that's not how it happened.

What happened was this: Pedestrio vanished, and there was that moment — the one just before the lightning strikes. And all I could think about in that moment…

…was young Sputter and his gruesome dioramas.

It just didn't seem fair, having to face the end of the world with those horrible images in my head. I wondered if, a million years from now, some desert rat living in the middle of the Great Kitchen Desert will put my bones on display. I wondered if there'd be any bones left a-tall.

Then The Worm cut loose. The mountains trembled. Shad-ows cowered in dark corners. Boulders the size of houses looked around for something bigger to hide behind.

Somehow, my mind found a gap in time long enough to flash through one final scene: the miners back at Deep Hole, sitting around the cookfire, recalling the day they quit this place. *One day the mountain shook,* they said. *Like a dog shaking off fleas...*

That's when our Burner roared to life. The ground tilted. I got thrown sideways as another mighty thought-blast exploded somewhere beneath our feet. There were no words to it — just a bellow of intense rage — a blast so powerful as to make even The Worm recoil.

As I scrambled back into the shadow of our slab, something huge and furious came barreling out of the cave entrance. It did not stop, but sailed across the notch, covering a thousand feet in a single bound. I caught a blur of red fur — then The Worm disappeared in a blizzard of teeth and claws.

The air felt broken — like breathing it would cut my lungs to shreds. A whiff of ozone drifted past my nose, and somewhere in the back of my head, an epiphany flared to life: there was more going on than we could see. The battle was being fought on multiple dimensions.

And just like that, it was all over. The Worm was gone — noth-ing left but a wisp of battered emptiness wafting through the air. Standing on the remains of Pedestrio's outcrop was a gigantic red Bear — twice the size of the biggest grizzly I've ever seen. Unlike The Worm, The Bear appeared solid. She had bulk, and muscle, and claws like battle rakes. She was a mountain of potentially violent endings, and She stood up on Her hind legs and howled into the gathering darkness. It was a don't-mess-with-Me howl. A can't-you-see-I'm-sleeping howl. A wake-Me-again-and-I-will-destroy-the-world howl.

It wasn't us, I thought. *It wasn't us, it wasn't us, it wasn't us.*

The Bear growled a more ambiguous growl. It was softer than the don't-mess-with-Me howl. Less belligerent. More introspective. I hoped it wasn't a now-I'm-hungry growl.

Then, slowly, Her massive head bobbing from side to side, The Bear plodded down the rocky slope of Burner Three and back up to where Vern and I were crouching in plain sight.

Plain sight? Sickly pickles! Why didn't we move when we had the chance? I waited for The Bear's bobbing head to swing away from us, then I nudged Vern. I doubt he even felt it, though.

Worst flare-up of Undivided Attention Syndrome I think I've ever seen. A ram on the rampage couldn't have driven Vern from that spot. A circus-load of cancan-dancing centipigs couldn't have turned his head. He crouched and stared at the lumbering Behemoth like She was a visiting dignitary from the Land of Awe. His eyes sparkled. His lips were parted, the corners upturned in a mindless, gawping grin. Vern wouldn't have missed The Bear's promenade if you'd promised him the world in a walnut.

The Bear moseyed up the hill. Closer and closer. Shrinking a bit as the battle rage wore off—but losing none of Her might and majesty.

Silently, I gave thanks to Old Blue for better days… and cursed Pedestrio.

I didn't ask for immortality. I didn't need to know how to speak to the trees. All I wanted was a tale to tell. Well, the tale was almost complete, but it looked as though Pedestrio would be the only one left to tell it. And he was already mucking up the ending.

You can't kill off your hero before the final scene. What kind of story is that?

Yes sir, Pedestrio is the world's worst storyteller. Can't trust him. He doesn't know how stories are supposed to end. So imagine my surprise when The Bear passed us by. Never even looked in our direction. But She came so close, I could feel the heat of Her breath.

Felt like the east wind, if you're looking for the full account. Smelled like clover. You asked, I told you. You think I'd make that up?

She must have known we were there—but She paid us no mind. Up the slope She plodded, till She disappeared behind our chunk of basalt.

Vern poked his head up over the slab.

"Is She going back into the cave?" I whispered.

"Yeah, but… huh."

Huh? What does that mean? I peeked over the rock—and caught a flicker of movement on the ledge overhanging the cave entrance.

The Bear didn't notice. The Bear had done all the noticing She cared to do at this juncture. She had taken stock of Her surroundings. She had identified the Entity who had disturbed Her slumber, and that Entity had felt Her wrath. There was nothing left to do. Nothing in this world could hurt Her—just as nothing in this world would ever dare to come between Her and the resumption of Her nap.

As She lumbered up to the mouth of the cave, a Hornswoggle leaned over the ledge and dropped my old bush hat on the crown of Her head.

The Bear whirled about. I felt another touch—not sleepy at all, this time. This one felt more like someone nine times my size grabbing me by the scruff of the neck and hoisting me up for some intense, eyeball-to-eyeball scrutiny. I am certain The Bear's touch was not for me alone. Everything for miles around must have felt it. Even the basalt slab cowered and trembled—but the culprit was nowhere to be found.

The Bear stood on Her hind legs and sent a what-did-I-tell-you-about-not-messing-with-Me thought-blast. It was powerful enough to reach all the way to Hinterland. I reckon it should have killed Vern and me both. I can't rightly say what saved us.

Maybe it was Mischief. Maybe, for reasons of Her own, She placed us temporarily under Her protection. Or maybe the sight of such a powerful Being — such a mighty Earth spirit — such an unbeatable Force of Nature — throwing down the gauntlet while sporting a battered, weather-stained, droopy old bush hat… maybe that spectacle was just incongruous enough that it turned our minds sideways, allowing the brunt of Her thought-blast to sail on by.

Anyhow, we stayed alive and conscious enough to watch The Bear drop down on all fours and stomp into Her lava cave — my hat still comfortably nestled on Her size 29XL head.

The moon was late coming up. Probly waited somewhere below the horizon till it knew the coast was clear. When it finally rose, Vern let out a breath he'd been holding for at least an hour. Then he turned and gave me the fish-eye.

"How 'bout it, Abner?" he said. "Still want your hat back?"

CHAPTER 44:
I Can't Believe You Mucked Up the Ending

WE dropped back down to the saddle and stumbled around in the dark till we found a relatively flat campsite. I'd have preferred to put a couple hundred miles between us and The Bear, but Vern, he reckoned it was better to hunker down.

"We keep wandering around blind, we're bound to attract attention," he said. "Just try not to snore too loud — and for Blue's sake, don't go screaming and thrashing about in your sleep."

"Do I do that?"

"You thought a giant squid was attacking us."

"Was it not?"

"No. You used your shirt as a pillow, and one of the sleeves got wrapped around your neck."

"Honest mistake."

"Happened twice last night."

"Fine!" I said, stuffing my shirt back into my pack. "There! No pillow. Are you happy?"

"Shh! Keep your voice down."

The sky was clear. The night air was cooling down rapidly. It was still summer down below, but at this elevation, we might see frost by morning.

I wondered how long it would take to get back to my old stomping grounds. A month, at least. Maybe two. I thought of apple cider doughnuts. Elmer only makes them while the leaves are falling. When the trees are bare, no more doughnuts.

Not asking for much. Just save me an apple cider doughnut or two.

Sadly, I let the thought go on account of there being no profit in it. All it did was make my stomach growl and my mouth water. I said to Vern, I said "Holly was right about the Kitchen Range, wasn't she? Bad place for The Worm to get tetchy."

"Yep."

"Did you know about The Bear?"

"Not specifically. But I knew something must be there. Holly's warned me before about traveling through the Kitchen Range. I really should have put it all together — the Whist, the warnings from Holly, even the powerful daydreams we were both having."

He lay there with his arms folded behind his head, staring up at the stars poking through the trees. Then: "the Wodewosen consider these mountains taboo, but they still come here from time to time on vision quests. Now we know why."

"You're saying The Bear made the Whist?"

"The Bear makes dreams. If you disturb The Bear's slumber, the dreams go away. I reckon it'll be a while before any of us dream again, after this evening's ruckus."

"Fine by me," I said. "Be a long while before I dream anything but nightmares."

But Vern wasn't listening. His mind was still back in the Land of Awe. His voice had that dazed, detached, wow-I-can't-believe-that-just-happened floatiness to it. "All my life, I've never seen a single Earth spirit. Today we saw three. There's your story, Abner."

"No, it ain't."

"Hmm?"

"Oh, don't get me wrong. The Worm, The Bear, and The Cozener all have Their parts. But They're not the story. The story is you — and I can't believe you mucked up the ending."

Vern smiled a lazy smile. No words of mine could take the shine off his jubilation. Still and all, he decided to go along and humor me. "All right, how did I muck up the ending?"

"You were so close. You could have walked right up to Pedestrio and said howdy — but in the end, you chooked out."

"You reckon he speaks our language?"

My jaw flapped, but no words came out. Finally, I said "why not? He speaks every other language on the planet."

"Human language is different. It changes too fast, and I expect he's out of practice. Anyway, it took me till now to work it all out."

"Do tell."

"I did want to meet him, at first. I thought he could teach me things. Then, when we found out The Worm was after him, I was afraid all his accumulated knowledge would be lost. But then I *saw* him. I saw what he was doing, how he moved, how he was part of it all, and I realized it *can't* be lost. Everything he knows is still out there, waiting to be rediscovered. All you have to do is open your senses."

"I spose. Though it would have been nice if he could have taught us a few words in treeish."

"I don't think he understands humans," said Vern. "It's his one blind spot. Mine too, I reckon. I mean, he *saw* us. He just didn't seem to know what to do with us."

I flashed back to Rusty, back in Deep Hole, asking all innocent-like, *what else has he got on?* Maybe I don't understand humans, either. What did it matter what he was wearing? But now I thought about it… "I wonder how he gets his clothes?"

"Makes 'em, I spose."

"Out of what?"

"Whatever he finds. Whatever's in season. That tunic was deerskin — I bet he found one that didn't make it through the winter."

"But when does he ever sit long enough to sew a tunic together? And why doesn't he make himself a pair of moccasins?"

"Don't know. Maybe he feels more connected when there's nothing between his feet and the ground."

Nothing but an inch of calluses. It's a wonder he can feel anything at all through that roughage. But there wasn't any profit in that thought, either, so I tried another one. "You reckon that's the end of The Worm?"

"No. But It'll be a long time nursing Its wounds." Vern thought for a while before musing out loud. "I wonder if that was Mischief's plan all along."

"What's that?"

"Play a trick on the Great Empty. Maybe even get It to stop chasing Pedestrio. And at the same time, have some fun poking The Bear while making sure somebody else is there to take the blame."

"So that's why She wanted my hat."

"Just guessing. You know you're never gonna get it back, right?"

"Yeah," I sighed. "I know."

"Maybe that was part of Her plan, too. Put it beyond your reach, once and for all."

Of all the dirty tricks… With great effort, I coaxed my brain to chase a different lure.

"Did you see him disappear? It was like he stepped up into thin air."

"Yep. Gone to the stars."

"How does he do that?"

Vern shrugged.

"What's it like up there?"

"No idea."

"I hate loose ends."

"It's all loose ends, Abner. Even if you live forever, you'll never know everything."

"I think I'll start practicing. It's a pretty handy trick, don't you think? I mean, if a malevolent supernatural Being ever got after me, all I'd have to do is take a step into the sky…" I yawned a great, lionesque yawn and settled myself in for the night. "Yeah… I think I'll start practicing that. Tomorrow…"

EPILOGUE:
The Wishing Star

T HERE is a constellation of stars, way up high in the northern sky, that closely resembles a figure caught in midstride. Some folks call that constellation Pedestrio. Each night, through every season of the year, Pedestrio perambulates endlessly around the heavens, never far from the Guide Star — the Wishing Star — the star at the very top of the sky.

The constellation is a marker, of sorts. It is a signal that the man called Pedestrio has taken up residence for the night.

Life among the stars is not unlike an evening spent dozing by the fire. Up there, Pedestrio can rest and relax, well out of reach of his Pursuer. He can tease out a roll of fleece, or scrape a hide, or sew a patch on the seat of the britches he's finally worn out after one too many willy-nilly slides down an icy slope. Or he can spend a pleasant interval chatting with his host and patron — the Entity whose astral presence is marked by the Wishing Star.

It was that Entity to whom Pedestrio had made his appeal that fateful evening, long ago, when all hope seemed lost — when he could walk no more, and his Pursuer was closing in…

The chase had lasted many years. But his Pursuer never stopped, and on that day, Pedestrio could go no further. His body ached. His mind felt fuzzy from lack of sleep. He had made errors. A fortnight ago, he had allowed himself to be cornered on a gravel spit with no option but to swim for it. He learned that he could not swim faster than The Void could reach. He had barely escaped. Then, he had somehow walked in a great circle, and The Void had set a trap in his path. He had leapt clear — but landed awkwardly and injured his ankle. Now he desperately needed to rest it, but he could feel his Nemesis pulling ever closer. Sure as night follows day, the chase would end before the stars could take their places.

Slowly, wearily, painfully, Pedestrio crawled up the tallest mountain he could find. When he reached the summit, he gathered a handful of pebbles. He had walked this Earth for more than a natural lifetime. If the journey were to end here, on this spot, then perhaps he could leave a symbol behind to mark his passing:

Having placed the pebbles just so, he sat back to watch his last sunset and wait for his patron star to pierce through the gloaming.

Darkness grew. The Void inched closer. The Wishing Star found an opening in the blanket of black and peeped at Pedestrio through the hole.

"Just give me this night," Pedestrio said. "Just give me shelter through the hours of darkness, and I will continue my journey at first light."

All his life, Pedestrio had sent his prayers and grateful thanks to the Wishing Star. The Star never answered with anything more than a wink. But this time, to his surprise, an answer formed in his mind: *I have no dominion over the world below,* She said. *But stand, and step into the celestial sphere. Join Me at the top of the sky, and I will grant you safe haven till morning.*

The Void loomed in front of him. It extended a tendril. *Now I have you!*

Pedestrio stood. The Void lunged. Pedestrio stepped up into the sky and disappeared.

The Void's displeasure was felt for a thousand miles. Mountains were reduced to rubble. Fields and forests were incinerated. Oceans dried up and turned to deserts. Hills that had been comfortably situated for a million years pulled themselves up by the roots and rolled out of range of the devastation.

From the safety of the heavens, Pedestrio watched the destruction. It seemed to go on forever. Pedestrio turned to his patron, who twinkled back at him. "Might need to stay with you tomorrow night, too."

You are always welcome, the Wishing Star replied.

ABOUT THE AUTHOR

ABNER SERD is an itinerant storyteller and self-proclaimed supervisor of sunrises. You can find more tales about Abner and his friends at www.abnerserd.com.